For Erin Underwood,
who keeps me from screaming.
Most of the time.

THE SCREAMING SEASON

NANCY HOLDER

An Imprint of Penguin Group (USA) Inc.

The Screaming Season

RAZORBILL

Published by the Penguin Group
Penguin Young Readers Group
345 Hudson Street, New York, New York 10014, U.S.A.
Penguin Group (USA) Inc., 375 Hudson Street, New York, New York 10014, U.S.A.
Penguin Group (Canada), 90 Eglinton Avenue East, Suite 700, Toronto,
Ontario, Canada M4P 2Y3 (a division of Pearson Penguin Canada Inc.)
Penguin Books Ltd, 80 Strand, London WC2R 0RL, England
Penguin Ireland, 25 St Stephen's Green, Dublin 2, Ireland (a division of Penguin Books Ltd)
Penguin Group (Australia), 250 Camberwell Road, Camberwell, Victoria 3124, Australia
(a division of Pearson Australia Group Pty Ltd)
Penguin Books India Pvt Ltd, 11 Community Centre,
Panchsheel Park, New Delhi – 110 017, India
Penguin Group (NZ), 67 Apollo Drive, Mairangi Bay, Auckland 1311, New Zealand
(a division of Pearson New Zealand Ltd)
Penguin Books (South Africa) (Pty) Ltd, 24 Sturdee Avenue, Rosebank,
Johannesburg 2196, South Africa

Penguin Books Ltd, Registered Offices: 80 Strand, London WC2R 0RL, England

10 9 8 7 6 5 4 3 2 1

Library of Congress Cataloging-in-Publication Data is available

ISBN 978-1-59514-333-4

Printed in the United States of America

Silence is the most powerful scream.
—Anonymous

BOOK ONE: CRIES AND WHISPERS

Insanity is relative. It depends on who has who locked in what cage.

—Ray Bradbury

Reality is merely an illusion, albeit a very persistent one.

—Albert Einstein

ONE

February 20
possessions: me

my sanity? they think I've lost it. at least my loyal dormies keep reminding everyone about my fever. who knows how long I was wandering in that snowstorm?

pneumonia.

all my stuff back in my dorm room:

my textbooks, mummy-wrapped in Marlwood book covers.

six filled regulation Marlwood Academy notebooks (my first semester's work).

six 1/3-filled notebooks (my second semester).

the vast Marlwood logo-land of my school supplies: highlighters, pens, pencils, etc., etc.—they must make a fortune off all this stuff.

my clothes, including Memmy's UCSD sweatshirt & the socks I knitted my dad.

my ash-caked Cons. PROOF.

here with me in the loony bin:

the borrowed clothes I wore to the Valentine's Day dance, ruined.

my St. Christopher's medal, which they will not let me have (do they think I'll try to strangle myself with it?).

my Tibetan prayer beads—wearing them down, but no prayers have been answered.

the red string Miles Winters wrapped around my wrist when he came to . . . to do what? did he come to see how I was? or to make sure no one would listen to me?

Panda, Julie's little corgi stuffed animal—proof that I'm not alone.

with me always:

the ghost of Celia Reaves.

haunted by: a hundred years of fury.

listening to: the screams of dead girls, dying over and over again.

mood: is "possessed" a mood?

possessions: them

couture clothes, shoes, purses, all designed for them and featured in *Vogue* and *W* and shown at Fashion Week. but it's not enough. it's never enough. it's like they have a *having* disorder.

family jewels: the wristwatch Picasso gave Great-grandmama, in lieu of marrying her. blood diamonds.

techie gear so advanced their fathers have to sign nondisclosure agreements to get them. bringing sexting and character assassination to new lows.

everything they want, on demand, without a single moment's doubt that they're entitled.

has Mandy ever told them that ghosts are living inside them? do they shed them as carelessly as their other possessions?

haunted by: have hauntings become déclassé? have they moved on to something more interesting . . . like serial murder?

listening to: they don't listen. they don't have to.

mood: they don't have to feel anything they don't want to. *Do I envy that? Or is that what insanity is?*

———

"HEY, SWEETIE," JULIE said, squeezing my hand. "Welcome back."

I want to go home, I thought, wobbling and weepy. *If I make a wish and tap my heels three times, all this will have been a dream. Three, two, one . . .*

I opened my eyes.

And I saw . . .

"Oh, my God!" Julie shouted, jumping to her feet and leaping away from my hospital bed. Her chair slammed on its side and she tripped over one of the legs, slamming hard against the wall. "Lindsay, stop! Stop, it's all right!"

Tongues of orange flames whooshed up around the bed. Ebony smoke billowed toward the ceiling, fanning out and rolling across the light blue surface like rushing water. Searing heat slapped my face.

Flashes:

Dead blackbirds in the snow.

Splatters of blood.

Claw marks in the trees.

Shadows in the forest.

The lake house.

The Ouija board.

The white head.

The fog rising from Searle Lake, where the dead drifted, waiting for one of us to look into the water and see . . .

That horrible, horrible face, laughing at me, pushing me back against the bed, showing me the ice pick and the rubber mallet and whispering, *"Do as I say, and it'll be all over."* His words were a whisper that echoed around the burning room, ricocheting and bouncing off Julie's sobbing and my screams. His *ssss*'s were hisses of steam, and everything I saw morphed into his bloodshot eyes and the gleaming tip of the ice pick. One jab, one thrust.

"Get him away!" I shrieked.

I wailed and shouted. I could hear myself, but I could also hear *him*, and I heard Julie whimpering. My focus snapped back and I saw her hugging herself as she pushed against the wall with her back, as if she couldn't get far enough away from me.

"Calm now, Lindsay, calm down *now*," Ms. Simonet ordered me. The middle-aged nurse sounded angry, scared, impatient. But of course I wasn't going to calm down when *he* was going to shove an ice pick into my eye socket, twitch it back and forth like a cat's tail, and split my brain apart. What sane person would?

He's not there, he's not, I told myself—but he *was*. Just because they couldn't see him didn't mean that he existed only in my imagination.

I knew better.

At Marlwood, the enraged dead possessed the living and made them do horrible, unspeakable things. Made them torment, and torture, and kill. Spirits, ghosts, whatever you wanted to call them, *could* hurt you. He was really there, in the blazing infirmary; he wanted to shut me up. I knew the terrible secrets of Marlwood. I knew that dead girls roamed the halls and spied on us, and sent bothersome, nosy girls to drown in Lake Searle, or pushed them over the edge into insanity so no one would believe them, no one would—

"He's here!" I shrieked, trying to push the nurse away. And that was when I realized they had tied me down. There were leather cuffs lined with felt around my wrists, attached to my bed.

They think I'm crazy.

They know I'm crazy.

"Lindsay, I'm here too," said the ghost of Celia Reaves, the dead girl who had possessed me on my first day at Marlwood. I could hear her inside my head. Celia, who had died in the fire she had started in 1889. Celia was evil, and mad, and *oh, God,* had *I* hurt those birds and that cat? Had *I* pushed Kiyoko Yamato into the lake and watched her drown?

"Let me calm you. Let me help you," said the madman no one else could see. He was Dr. Abernathy, the handsome young doctor who promised to take Celia away from all this and meant it, but not in the way she had believed. *"You will never suffer again."*

So much fear, so helpless. I jerked my head; then I kicked my legs, realizing they hadn't tied them down. I tried to raise my knees to my chest to push him away with the soles of my feet, but all he did was laugh.

And then he became the nurse, jabbing something into my arm. I felt Celia thrashing inside me. I couldn't tell if she was fighting the drug or fighting me. Did she want to burrow in deeper, or did she want to escape?

"No, please," I whispered as the nurse studied my face. My eyelids were drooping. She was taking my pulse. "Please, don't do this."

"There. Now you'll calm down." Her face was tight. I was pissing her off.

Julie was standing behind Ms. Simonet. With her cute new haircut, wheat-colored hair all chopped, my roommate looked like the a slightly more grown-up version of the sweet, shy girl who had glommed onto me when I showed up, roommates and instant best friends. Her hazel eyes were smudged with smoky makeup that was running down her face. She looked so worried, not at all like the Julie who had become possessed, her eyes completely black, shouting to the others to come and get me . . .

She didn't remember any of the horrible things that had happened. She had no idea that she'd been possessed . . . and had been set free.

I wasn't free.

Not yet.

The nurse said to Julie, "You'll have to leave."

"Please, let me stay for a few minutes," Julie murmured. She slipped her hand into mine.

I could barely keep my eyes open. I could see a blur of

shadow as the nurse bent over me and opened each of my eyelids.

"She has pneumonia," Ms. Simonet said. "She needs her rest."

Maybe they're going to kick me out, I thought. Ironically, even though Marlwood was a death trap, getting booted would be the worst thing that could happen to me. Celia had made it very clear that she had unfinished business here, and I would never be free of her until she had gotten what she wanted.

But what she wanted was Mandy Winters dead.

"You have two minutes," Ms. Simonet told Julie. I wondered why she couldn't stay longer. It *was* the middle of the night, but so what?

My roomie gave my hand a squeeze. I tried so hard to keep my eyes open, but everything was going very blurry. I wondered if Celia would be drugged too. Or if she walked when I was asleep; if that was when she made me do things that I couldn't remember when I woke up. If that was the case, I should be glad for getting tied down. Except, if the specter of Dr. Abernathy returned, I would be defenseless.

Julie cleared her throat and gently slid her hand away from mine. It was a little awkward; we hugged each other on occasion, but we weren't hand-holders, that was for sure.

"Are you, um, *okay*?" she asked. "Bad dream, huh?"

"Yeah. It's the fever," I managed, but my tongue was too large for my mouth. My chest was too heavy to catch a breath. I felt as if someone were sitting on my chest, and I could hear deep breathing and a low, sadistic chuckle.

"You were out in that snowstorm for *hours*," she said. "They were really worried about you."

They still are, I wanted to tell her, but I couldn't make sound come out of my mouth. My hospital bed was spinning. The inside of my body was a cold block of ice—the sensation that came over me whenever Celia took charge.

"Maybe you'll get to go home," she said in falsely cheerful voice. "You know, your friend back home, Heather? She's been texting you. I hope you don't mind that I looked at your phone. It kept vibrating and I thought maybe it was Troy."

Drifting, drowsy, I wasn't sure I'd heard her right. Heather Martinez used to be my best friend back in San Diego. But that was before I proved my loyalty to the cool clique by publicly dissing her every chance I got. When I had gone home for Christmas, we tried to reconnect by going to a movie together. The hugeness of that blunder could not be overestimated.

Riley, my hot, sexy, lying creep jerk ex-crush, had shown up at the theater too, and there we were, the three of us, watching a Christmas horror movie like back in the old days—except that Heather had never been present at any function when Riley and I had been a couple. That night was like two different versions of my past colliding, none of it working because I was already on the verge of losing it and being there was stressful in the extreme.

"Linz?" Julie said. I tried to open my eyes. "She just texted again. She said she has to talk to you about Riley. Not in so many words, of course. Because it's texting."

"Lemme see," I whispered, but I wasn't even sure I said the words aloud. My heartbeat was slowing because of the drugs, but in reality, it wanted to pump into overdrive. It was like being artificially possessed, aware that I wasn't all there and something else was taking me over. Not ghosts, in this case, but "modern" medicine. At least it was temporary; lobotomies were forever.

"Here. Look."

More shadows shifted; I was pretty sure Julie was holding the cell phone close to my face. Her head was a white blob, and behind it, darker shapes floated through the room. Something crept along the wall, sneaking a look at me now and then. Light glinted.

The ice pick.

"She left you a voice message. Do you want me to play it?"

I couldn't speak, couldn't utter a sound.

Don't leave me, I wanted to beg her. *I'm so afraid I won't wake up.*

"I'll put it in your hand," Julie said. "And maybe I can loosen these things." She began to fumble with my restraints.

If she untied me, I could fight *him* off. But if Celia wanted to roam, I wouldn't be able to stop her.

I felt the coldness moving inside me, almost as if Celia were waking up too. I hated the feeling. Hated her. She was evil, insane, and she was using me.

"You have to go now, Julie," Ms. Simonet said.

Julie's hand jerked, and the phone slipped from my rubbery grasp. I groaned. Something soft and fuzzy moved against my forearm.

"Here's Panda," Julie said. "Remember that I brought him for you?"

Julie had gotten the stuffed animal for Christmas. It was so sweetly sad to me that she was still excited about little toy dogs.

Christmas. Christmas was when Celia's white face had appeared in my swimming pool, and she had told me I had to come back here, to Marlwood, or I would never be free of her. That if I stayed safely in San Diego, my friends would die, one by one—as payback, revenge. It seemed so long ago.

It seemed like it had happened to someone else.

I was so drugged up and freaked out that I didn't feel like anyone at all. I was floating in an endless sea of identities or souls or loose, unbound emotions, and none of them were mine.

"Julie, it's time." The nurse's voice was gentler. She *liked* Julie. My roommate was like the baby of the Marlwood family, agreeable and cute. I'd always thought nice girls got stomped on, but Julie's charm . . . *charmed* people. That was a kind of power that sarcastic chicks with wild hair and bad clothes were denied.

"Okay, sorry. Sweet dreams, Linz." I smelled Juicy Couture as she leaned over me, maybe debating about kissing me good night. I was going so numb that I didn't think I'd be able to feel it if she did.

I heard footsteps. Julie murmured, "Does she have to sleep tied up like that?"

Ms. Simonet replied, but I didn't hear what she said. I assumed the answer must have been yes, because no one came to free me.

Then the door to the clinic opened and I heard the wind. I didn't want Julie to go out in the cold. I wanted her safe, always.

But who could ever be safe, here at Marlwood?

I continued drifting on icy currents, wondering if I would ever be warm again. There was truth to the saying, *Cold as the grave.* Ironic, that someone who had burned to death could chill me to the bone.

Something vibrated against my side, and I started. I was so out of it that at first I couldn't figure out what it was. Then I realized it was my new phone. My old one was rusting at the bottom of Searle Lake, where I myself had nearly wound up. I had a new number, and not that many people had it. I could count them on one hand.

Was it Heather? Why was she calling me all of a sudden? Had something happened to her or my family? *No more,* I begged the universe.

"Yes, Dr. Ehrlenbach, she's been sedated," Ms. Simonet was saying, and I grunted, startled by the sound of another human voice. Had my scary headmistress arrived to check on me? "Yes, have a good trip." *She's leaving? Abandoning us?*

The room went silent again. Ms. Simonet must have been talking on the phone to Dr. "Ehrlenfreak," as we called her. I envied my headmistress; she could get out of here. Then I thought of everything hanging on her shoulders—Kiyoko's death and the school's reputation. The wealthy parents *had* to be asking if Marlwood Academy was safe enough for their blue-blooded children. For them, Marlwood had been one choice among many when it came to posh boarding schools that cost around fifty thousand dollars a year. For me, a scholarship student given late entry from the wait list, it had been my only escape.

I screwed up again, I thought, tears sliding across my temples. *I had a breakdown in San Diego, sure, but here, away from civilization . . . I tried to kill my boyfriend with a hammer.*

Only, Troy wasn't my boyfriend. And when I had tried to kill him, I had thought he'd been possessed . . .

. . . by the ghost who, at that very moment, might be creeping around my room in the infirmary. Out of body, not in someone's else, like Celia was in mine. I sensed frosty shadows moving against the wall, then dripping down onto the floor and sliding toward my bed. I had dreams of someone crawling over me, pinning me where I lay. Dreams both waking and sleeping.

"*Count backward from ten to one,*" whispered the ghost of Dr. Abernathy, "*and I'll make it all better. You will never, ever be afraid again.*"

I shook with fear as he floated closer. I was alone in the bed, unable to call for help.

"*I'll make it all better,*" he said again. "*I'll make it stop.*"

And in my hazy desperation, I was tempted to obey.

"*Ten,*" he prompted.

Nine, I thought.

And then I heard Celia screaming.

TWO

"Wrong."

"You are so wrong, and so stupid," Celia hissed as I shifted and twisted in my bed. I was sinking into the mattress. Something was wrapped around my neck. I couldn't call out to Ms. Simonet; I couldn't push the little button attached to the bed.

"You have no idea what's been going on out there while you hide."

She was *pissed.*

"You know what you have to do. You know how to set me free. And instead, you lie in here . . . " Darkness engulfed me. I was frozen to the bone; I could see nothing but blackness. I couldn't touch anything. Smell anything. There was dirt in my mouth, and mixed in with it was something burnt.

"This is where I lie. This is my soft bed and my pillow. And these are my visitors."

Razor-sharp pinpricks sliced my face as furry paws ran over my cheek and across my nose, down the center of my forehead to bite my cheek. Rats. I fought to move my arms or shake my head, but I could do nothing to protect myself. They kept biting and scurrying.

My hair was coated with mud, and I couldn't breathe. I had been buried alive.

"It's not even as good as a grave," she said spitefully. *"It's a garbage heap, in the forest, on the road. It's where I am. And it's where you'll be if you don't help me. I swear it, Lindsay. You will end up here. For the rest of eternity. Awake. Aware. And suffering."*

"Like me."

I finally managed to gasp, opening my mouth. My nostrils were clogged with dirt. Something wriggled against the roof of my mouth. I wanted to kick and scream, but I couldn't move.

Then she yanked me out of the dirt and down a lane. Smoke surrounded me. The black trees to my right bobbed as I passed, as thunder rumbled. Branches encrusted with jet-colored ice began to pump up and down as if heavy objects were tied to them.

The forest is trying to grab me, I thought. I glazed over . . .

. . . and saw phantoms sitting in the boughs of the trees: glowing blurs of girls in linen shifts, with skulls for faces and bones for arms, shrieking. They leaned toward me as I ran past, extending their arms, wailing and sobbing. From a tree on my left, a figure dangled from a noose around her neck, rocking back and forth, back and forth, like a bell. Her bony fingers grabbed at the rope. A crack shot through the darkness, and her neck broke.

She screamed. Everyone was screaming.

I was screaming.

The trees began to thin, and the figures dropped from the trees like rotten fruit. The hanged girl vanished. Other girls appeared on either side of the road, standing in rows and banging on walls I couldn't see. They were screaming; all around me; the world was nothing but one giant scream.

The wind mixed up all the shrieks and I heard the desperation, the terror and fury. I heard them dying. White shapes, white figures; the mountain was alive with the ghosts of dead girls, enraged by their fate.

The screams stretched into echoes. Clouds crossed the moon, throwing me into darkness as the girls glowed and winked out, reappeared, sizzled with white light. Their shifts disintegrated into tatters; their skull faces shattered; something of them became nothing more than a weak, shining mist in the darkness.

But I kept screaming.

"Stop it, Lindsay!" Ms. Simonet yelled. The lights flared on. *Dream. Oh, God.*

"I'm sorry, sorry," I managed, weeping. "Please, please."

She did something to my arm. It hurt.

I slid down deeper.

The screams came back.

THREE

"FEELING BETTER?" MS. Simonet asked me, trying to sound like she cared. She was checking on me in the shower room, where she had brought me to clean up.

Maybe she knew I was fragmenting beneath the warm spigot of water. I was pressing against the shiny white tile, back flat, head lowered, eyes shut so I wouldn't see what I was imagining there . . . a pair of hands, pushing me under the water, in one of the huge bathtubs in the bathroom that was in my dorm. I knew it wasn't happening; I knew it was one more of Celia's horrible memories, but I couldn't stop my panic.

It was the drugs, I told myself. The drugs that had thrown me into one nightmare after another the night before, torturing me with flashes of images like this one and worse—the girls in the forest; eyeless faces laughing; the ice pick; the mallet; and what the girls looked like after Dr. Abernathy finished with them—the living dead. Zombies. The phantoms of Marlwood.

And all their rage lived on.

"Lindsay?" Ms. Simonet said, in the curt tone I was

beginning to recognize as her *What do I do with this girl?* voice. Other students at Marlwood had gone bonkers, but they were rich. That was understandable: being able to have what you wanted whenever you wanted it created a lot of pressure. It was less cool for me, a poor girl, to be a problem. I was on scholarship; all I did for the school was use up resources.

"I'm fine," I managed to say, clearing my throat. My throat hurt. My lungs hurt. I was tired. I raised my chin and opened my eyes. Just white tile and a spigot. No hands, no drowning.

"This will keep happening until you stop it," Celia promised me.

"Go away," I whispered fiercely. "I hate you."

"I can't stop it," she replied. *"It's up to you."*

Gritting my teeth, I pushed back the shower curtain and grabbed the freshly laundered hunter green towel, burying my face in it as I shook. There would be more drugs if I lost it again, and they might send me home. That was all I wanted to do, but it was the one thing I couldn't do. It had to end here.

There was a little cherrywood dressing room off the shower room, and I found my favorite raggedy jeans, my mom's UCSD sweater, and a black turtleneck sweater neatly folded. I smiled weakly, realizing that Julie had brought me a care package from our room.

There was also one of my preferred black sports bras and a pair of black boyshort underpants. The boyshorts were a Christmas present from my stepmother, CJ. Freckly, young, strawberry-blonde CJ was more fashion aware than I was. Back when I was in Jane's superclique, I had been totally fashion conscious. But it was a good thing I had quit the style race before I'd arrived at Marlwood. There was absolutely no way I could compete with the other girls, who truly thought nothing of dropping a grand on a pair of jeans.

"Now *that's* nuts," I said aloud, feeling a little like my old self.

I dressed, swallowed down the cold dose of bright pink antibiotic Ms. Simonet left for me, and brushed my teeth. As always, my hairbrush hated my OOC curly black hair. There were matching black smudges around my eyes that gave me a cool, smoky look. For free. Eat your heart out, Urban Decay.

I went back to my holding cell, aka my room in the infirmary, and found all my dorm mates sitting in a quasi-semicircle on plastic chairs: Marica, Claire, Ida, Julie, and Elvis (whose real name was Haley). It was either a party or an intervention.

"Good morning!" Julie cried.

Julie jumped up and crushed me in a hug. She was five-seven to my five-two, with another two or so inches added by her heeled boots. Heeled anything was new for her; she used to hunch over to compress her height. Now she was in love, and that made her feel both powerful and pretty.

On the gray-metal-and-Formica roll-around table by my hospital bed sat a green plastic tray with covered dishes and a large Marlwood coffee carrier with a lid. Next to it they had positioned the only normal chair in the room, an overstuffed burgundy leather chair.

"We brought you breakfast," Julie said, stating the obvious.

"And homework," Claire drawled, her Maui tan from the holidays finally beginning to fade. "You'd better get your butt back to classes or you're going to flunk out of here."

"Oh, my God, don't stress her out," Ida snapped, smacking Claire on the arm. Ida was Iranian, very exotic-looking in a sleek black trench coat and messy Kate Moss I-don't-give-a-damn hair.

Elvis was equally beautifully dressed in a bronze cashmere sweater, black leather pants, and expensive boots. Marica, from Venezuela, played off her flamenco-dancer looks with scarlet and black, plus her enormous emerald earrings, which had been her grandmother's. Everyone's makeup and hair were in place. At an exclusive all-girls school like ours, the stakes were incredibly high when it came to parading your family's ability to make you look as good as possible. We had professional models and actresses in our midst, but even the amateurs were *Teen Vogue* worthy.

"Seriously, Linz, it's not that bad," Ida added.

"Maybe your parents could hire one of the faculty to tutor you," Elvis suggested, then blanched as she obviously remembered that my parents had no money. My dad was still trying to pay off the stacks of bills our insurance hadn't covered when medical science had failed to save my mom.

"Um, or *we* could help you," Julie said, as everyone started nodding like bobble heads and smiling brightly. Too brightly, with eyes a bit too wide to be genuine. They didn't know what to make of me. I had gone completely crazy in the operating theater, but the cracks had been appearing way before then. At least, that was how it would appear to someone who didn't believe in ghosts.

"Rose too, of course. She wanted to come with us," Julie

said, which seemed a bit random. Poor Julie was nervous. "But she had to cram for a test."

"Oh, that's okay," I said.

I felt Celia shift anxiously inside me. It wasn't okay with her. She had begged me to kill Rose when Rose had become possessed. If Rose hadn't been so drunk at the time, she would have posed a greater threat, and I might have had to hurt her—at least -to defend myself. For some girls, the possessions came and went. The spirit that had possessed Rose seemed to have moved on. Same thing with Julie. I didn't know why.

Mandy Winters, whom I had detested on sight, was possessed by the spirit of Belle. Allowing herself to become possessed was a deal Mandy had made—a pact with the devil—in some twisted bargain to protect Miles, her twin brother, or be his girlfriend, or both, at least as far as I could tell.

Miles. My skin crawled. My face tingled. Ruled by his own demons, Miles had been the one to carry me out of the operating theater when I had raged at them all, shrieking that I would kill them. At the time, I had been fully possessed by Celia, who was even more insane than he was.

Cold flooded me as if she were protesting my opinion of her. Denying her my attention, I sat down in the leather chair, and everyone else sat back, as if they could relax now that my academic fate was being seen to.

Celia's grip faded. Not for the first time, I realized she had a greater hold on me when I was under stress. Even after all that had happened, I still had moments when I wondered if she was real. I had suffered a nervous breakdown back in San

Diego. But I hadn't imagined things, hadn't seen things that weren't there. And I wasn't imagining them now. Marlwood *was* haunted.

It was.

I was.

I lifted the lids to the breakfast selections—they had brought me everything from a veggie-and-cheese omelet to a bowl of Froot Loops—and my stomach lurched. I was hungry, but I didn't know if I could eat anything. I wanted to sit my dorm mates in rows like elementary school students and give them a lecture on the real history of Marlwood. To tell them about Celia, and Belle, and the man the two girls had loved— the doctor, David Abernathy. The man who had betrayed them, leaving them and five other girls to die an excruciating death. But who would believe me?

"Okay, so here's the dealio," Elvis said, and everyone scooted a little closer, getting down to business. "Ehrlenfreak left. They're saying it's a fund-raising tour, but we all know it's damage control."

"Oh, my God, don't say that around Lindsay," Claire said. "Jeez."

Ida huffed. "Oh, please, hardly anyone saw Lindsay go bonkers. No offense, Linz, I know it was a high fever. I think they paid off Troy with a starting position on the basketball team over at Lakewood, and Miles and Mandy are *here*. So what damage is there to control?" Claire looked unconvinced. "Word gets around. You know how connected our parents are. Look at Rose's parents' divorce. It's in all the tabloids." She wrinkled her nose. "They don't want *us* in the tabloids."

"Yeah," Ida said, "but the Hyde-Smiths are way juicy. Rose's dad owned half the world before the collapse and her mom's, like, thirty."

"Forty-five. She's had a lot of work done," Marica said. "She has to get out now, or she'll be too old to find another billionaire. Poor Rose. No money, and her mother's nothing but an aging trophy wife."

Marica took the lid off my coffee and offered it to me. I shook my head. She took a little sip, perfectly lined and colored lips blotting on the cardboard, and sighed with pleasure.

"But Claire is right," Elvis said. "Marlwood has a board of directors and trustees. Ehrlenbach probably needs to convince them that she's still in charge."

There was a brief moment of silence, and then they all burst into laughter. The corners of my mouth twitched, but I couldn't let myself go, not like them.

"In charge. Right," Ida said, guffawing.

I started picking at the food, watching them as they laughed harder and harder, thinking about all the ways our headmistress was *not* in charge around here, until they were almost screaming. They shrieked like wild birds. Marlwood had been a pressure cooker from day one. Even for them, it appeared. Maybe we were all one scream away from losing it.

"So is Mandy talking about what happened?" I asked. It would be so like her to take advantage of my breakdown and use it to focus attention on herself.

"Strangely, no," Claire said, shrugging and giving her head a little shake. "Everyone at Jessel has actually been pretty quiet. Withdrawn."

"They're recharging. So they can drive someone else crazy. And I don't mean you. I mean Shayna." Maricia pointed to the omelet on my plate. "Speaking of recharging, that's protein."

"Have you heard from Shayna?" Ida asked me, and I was startled, because no one had brought her up since we'd come back from the winter break. Marlwood had beaten Shayna down.

"I called her once," I began, not sure how much I should reveal. I would definitely not tell them that Shayna and I had discussed various methods of exorcising dybbuks, which was the Jewish term for restless, disembodied spirits that possessed the living. Dybbuks had unfinished business.

After she had left school, I had found her phone number and called. She was crying. Everyone thought she'd gone crazy, but I had reassured her that I completely believed that she had seen a ghost. We'd gotten disconnected and I had called back, but her number was suddenly no longer in service. I figured her father the rabbi had had it disconnected to prevent anyone from shattering whatever hold on reality Shayna had regained since she'd left Marlwood. I hadn't heard from her since and I didn't know any other way to reach her. I had thought that in this day of texting and the net, no one could lose track of anyone. But I wasn't even sure I could keep track of myself.

"How is Shayna?" Julie asked. "Do you think she'll come back?"

"Sure, that'll happen." Claire snickered.

"What really happened to her?" Julie looked at me. "No one's ever said. She was so scared that night."

I did say. I tried to talk to you about what was going on, I thought, looking at Julie. *But you didn't want to hear it. You thought I was jealous of your friendship with Mandy. While I was afraid that Mandy might try to kill you.*

That was what I couldn't tell them—we weren't talking about the politics of normal high school life, as abnormal as they were. This wasn't about mean girls and cheating boyfriends. This was about life and death. And the ironic thing was, a mean girl and a cheating boyfriend had pushed me over the edge in the first place, back in San Diego. But the life-and-death evil at Marlwood had pulled me back up.

But my dorm mates didn't want to hear about it. I'd tried before. And now . . . no one would believe me about anything.

"Linz?" Julie asked. "Are you okay?"

Her question focused attention on me, which I did not need. I needed someone to tell me I was okay. I was so tired of being questioned about the state of my sanity.

"I just get tired," I said. "Pneumonia and all."

"Mandy says she had pneumonia two years ago, in Gstaad. She nearly died from it," Elvis declared. "Of course, you know that her case was worse than yours."

Everyone smirked. They were no bigger fans of Mandy than I was.

The wind whistled hard as the main door to the infirmary slammed open. We all jumped, and Julie let out a little cry.

"It's just the nurse," Marica said, not naming her, as if Ms. Simonet was one of the anonymous army of staff that catered to our every whim.

The door opened, and we all turned expectantly. A very

tall figure with straight, square shoulders stood framed in the doorway, obscuring the hall light, so that all I saw was a silhouette. Then he stepped into the room. He was wearing a black wool overcoat and white muffler. Tendrils of gray hair framed his face like a fluffy halo. He had a small nose and full lips and very blue eyes, nearly as deeply blue as Troy's. For an older man, he was kind of hot.

Ms. Simonet came in behind him. She looked around the room, her attention landing on me, and she made a little gesture—*That's the one.*

"Ladies, this is Dr. Anthony Morehouse," she announced in a chipper tone I had never heard her use before. "He's joining our staff."

Julie stood. "Hello," she said politely.

No one else got up. Everyone just looked at him.

"What about Dr. Steinberg?" I asked. He had been in to see me every day since I'd collapsed. He had discovered that in addition to having pneumonia, I was anemic.

"Oh, he's still on the staff," Dr. Morehouse said. He had a funny accent, almost Scandinavian.

Then I got it. By my friends' looks of polite confusion, I was the only one who did get it.

"Dr. *Melton* is gone," I murmured. My other doctor. The school shrink. I had liked him. Very much.

"Dr. Melton was offered a wonderful opportunity he felt he couldn't pass up," Dr. Morehouse said smoothly. "He wanted very much to tell you all goodbye personally, but he had to leave on short notice."

Canned. Possibly because of me. Had he had time to dismantle his pretty fish tank?

No one else looked particularly distressed. Some of the girls had been to see him when they found the dead birds and the cat, but no one else had had a standing weekly appointment, as I had.

"It's time for all of you to go, or you'll be late for first period," Ms. Simonet informed my visitors. In other words, I was supposed to see Dr. Morehouse alone.

As they got ready to leave, I could sense their embarrassment for me, their possessive unease. The new shrink had braved the elements to come see their girl. A therapeutic house call for the current school psycho.

"We'll come at lunch to start catching you up," Julie said. This time, she did kiss my cheek. She smiled at everyone. "We'll each take a subject."

"Rose will do math," Ida announced, and Dr. Morehouse chuckled. High school high jinks. We were cute.

Dr. Morehouse smiled pleasantly at the group at large. I didn't want them to leave me alone with him. I was afraid I would slip and tell him the truth.

But they did go. He said, "I think Trina said she had some coffee," and excused himself from the room. It took me a second to connect "Trina" to Ms. Simonet. Maybe they had a thing. Maybe she knew him from some other job.

You have to get rid of him, Celia told me. I was afraid that she was speaking through me, that I was speaking aloud. That happened sometimes. I still didn't fully understand how the possession worked. I didn't know if Celia was inside me all the time, or if she somehow slid in from time to time. All I knew was that sometimes I would feel very cold, and then I would sense that she was there. And then I would hear her speaking.

But there were times, I knew, when I blanked out and she took over. I had found myself waking up in places I had no memory of going.

The operating theater, for one.

"Make him go away," she demanded just as Dr. Morehouse came back in the room with a white cup stamped with the Marlwood crest in hunter green. The steam was rising from the cup, and he blew on it as he sat in one of the plastic chairs the girls had left scattered all over the room.

"Well, you've certainly been through the wringer," he began. "The death of your mom, your breakdown, coming here . . . "

"Breaking down again," I filled in. I was already weary, and we hadn't even gotten started. As far as I was concerned, when you'd been to one therapist, you'd been to them all. They all said the same things. Asked the same questions, looked for the same answers. And I was fighting overtime to ignore Celia's thrashing, like a bird in a chimney.

"Is that how you see it?" he asked me. "You had another breakdown?"

"Hallucinating and hitting a guy with a hammer; that's pretty much the standard definition." I heard the petulance in my voice.

He took out a pack of tissues from his pocket, extracted one, and genteelly brought it to his mouth, depositing some gum into it. Sipping his coffee, he shifted in his chair, moving his shoulders as if he had an itch he couldn't reach. I wondered how much he'd gotten paid to take over Dr. Melton's job on such short notice.

Jane used to say that people became psychologists because they had issues of their own to work out. After my mom died, the hospital had suggested that my dad and I join a grief support network. The social worker running the group had asked my dad, in front of me, "Are you angry with your wife for leaving you with a child to raise by yourself?" We left at the break and never went back.

"Tell me about the Marlwood Stalker," Dr. Morehouse requested.

I jerked, caught off guard. But of course he would have heard about it. Dr. Ehrlenbach would have told him.

"We were scared." I picked up a purple Froot Loop and popped it into my mouth. "Someone was killing birds. And leaving slash marks on trees."

"That would be scary," he agreed.

"Dr. Ehrlenbach told us that mountain lions were spotted during the break. Someone's dog at Lakeshore Prep got taken. That's the boys' school," I added.

"So the night of the Valentine's dance, you were scared, and you were upset." The steam from his coffee reached up, as if to tickle his chin. "I gather there was a fight about a boy you liked. And you left the dance in search of him in a snowstorm, without dressing warmly enough."

I nodded. That didn't sound so crazy. That sounded like good solid teen drama.

"And you were out there for quite some time."

"So you're going with the exposure scenario." I made a show of picking out more purple Froot Loops, then wondered why I was doing it. As if to prove I didn't care. But that was dumb. I needed the brand-new shrink of Marlwood to recommend that I stay. I needed him to think I was going to work at getting better. So I dropped the Froot Loop back into the bowl and put my hands in my lap.

"Actually, it works for me," he replied. He peered at me. "But you're not convinced."

He set down the coffee cup on the chair to his right and fished in his pants pocket. He pulled out what looked like a thick gold pen; then he flicked it on and I realized it was a thin flashlight.

"Let's go back over what's been happening to you. Together."

"Don't say anything," Celia hissed.

He raised a brow. "Sorry, what was that?"

"Nothing." I raised my brows too, trying to look innocent and approachable. I was grateful there was nothing close at hand that I could use to hurt him. Correction: that *Celia* could use to hurt him.

And then I spotted the hot cup of coffee, an arm's length away, as the beam of light wove an arc across the floor. The steam rose.

It would burn.

FOUR

DR. MOREHOUSE CROSSED back to the light switch, unknowingly removing himself from the trajectory the hot coffee would make should Celia force me to fling it at him. He flicked off the room lights. The thin beam of his flashlight sliced the blackness. Then he experimented with the switches until the lights were dim, and I could see everything except the colors of my cereal. I licked my lips. My hand was shaking. Celia was still trying to make me pick up the coffee. Wasn't she thinking this through? If I hurt him, they might expel me. Expel me, and she was stuck with her unfinished business.

And I would wind up screaming in an unmarked grave.

Stop. That's just drama.

"I know you've been to a lot of therapists," he began.

"Only three, unless you count the hospital social worker. Then it would be four." Instead of the coffee, I lifted a glass to my lips. It was grapefruit juice. Julie knew I preferred it to orange. I had a friend. I had lots of friends. I wasn't alone.

But I was never alone.

"Three's a lot."

"Not if you live in Southern California."

He chuckled. "I'm from Fargo, North Dakota."

That explained the accent.

"Have you seen the movie?" he asked me. *"Fargo?"*

"Before my time," I replied. "Are you going to hypnotize me?"

Celia thrashed. *"No. Refuse. Get him out of here."*

He inclined his head as if to say, *I sure can't get anything past you.* "I thought I'd give it a shot. During all this therapy you've had, has anyone discussed the notion of the committee?"

I shook my head. "Is it like the Spanish Inquisition?"

"Maybe." He raised the light and pointed it at the wall. It flattened onto the wall like a yellow hole. Sipping my grapefruit juice, I tried to ignore Celia's movements. My brain felt like an iceberg. The bridge of my nose ached. She really didn't want me to do this. If ever there was a reason to give something a shot, that was it.

"Some people think our personalities are really a number of *layers* of individuality, established at different times of our lives and molded by various situations."

I fought as Celia tried to make me put the grapefruit juice down. My foot moved forward; she wanted me to stand up.

"When we talk about being 'of two minds,' some of us mean that literally."

He sounded kind of pompous, and I tried not to laugh. If only he knew.

"And those people are mentally ill," I ventured.

"Not at all," he replied. "We all have a committee. We talk to ourselves, rehearse scenarios, write ourselves notes and 'to do' lists."

Kill people, I filled in.

"So what is schizophrenia?"

"We all have an 'I,'" he said. "The committee leader. If you have more than one leader . . . "

"You get bickering. In public." An understatement.

"Exactly. Bickering. Lack of functionality."

"You don't get anything done," I said.

"Right. Now, if I suggest to you that we walk along a path . . . " He glanced over at the bloom of light on the wall. Drinking more coffee, he cocked his head, appraising the view. "Let's walk along that path and meet some of your committee members on the way. Are you comfortable in that chair?"

I wasn't particularly, but the only piece of furniture more comfortable was my bed, and there was no way I was doing that. I had never been to a therapist's office where I had to lie down. I wasn't about to start now.

I could feel Celia struggling, and I coughed to hide it. The grapefruit juice sloshed on my index finger. He noticed.

"I'm making you nervous."

Why hide it? Therapists valued honesty. Crazy people told themselves lies. Sane people faced trouble head-on. Or so I had been informed. Over and over again.

"Maybe I'll tell you how the exercise works, and you can do it on your own later."

Said the spider to the fly. I smiled politely, pretending to buy it. I knew full well that he was going to try his mojo out on me.

"So, are you ready?" he asked.

"I'm taking a vote," I said, and when he grinned, I honestly thought there might be hope for the relationship.

"You're walking along a path," he said, looking not at me, but at the circle of light on the wall. "You make the path as real to yourself as possible. It's bordered with palm trees, or ice plants, or geraniums . . . "

Southern California borders, then. We had geraniums in our front yard. I could smell them now, their pungent, earthy-lemon odor. I could see the glint of light on my mother's wedding ring as she weeded the beds of shocking pink and orange blossoms. The wheels of my trike, squeaking as I rode up and down the driveway, up and down, watching her weed, impatient for her to finish because I wanted a grilled cheese sandwich.

When she got sick, we let the geraniums go and our front yard became a weedy mess. We had never had a sprinkler system because my mom liked to water the yard herself. Someone put an anonymous note in our mailbox and called us white trash because parts of our yard were so overgrown, while others were dry as dust. When CJ started dating my father, she hired a service to install sprinklers and we weeded together. She called them our "dirt dates," and pretty soon I relaxed around her. In no time at all, I could smell the geraniums again, even from the backyard.

The backyard . . . where Celia had appeared in the pool and told me I had to come back here . . .

The little girl in me resented CJ for taking my mom's place.

But the young woman that I was becoming was grateful to her for the weeding, the home-cooked meals, the snacks for sleepovers. And the two goofy little boys who became my stepbrothers.

"And as you walk along the path, bordered by geraniums..." He paused. "What's on the path? Gravel? Dirt?"

Ashes, I thought. *Open graves.* But I said, "Sand. From the beach. We're barefoot."

"The warm sand squishes between your toes and above you, the ... seagulls? ... are circling."

Vultures. Ravens. But now I was just fighting him in my private, childish way.

"You discover you've been moving up an incline. And as you look down over the crest, it looks ... "

"Like Marlwood," I said, surprising myself.

"Which looks like ... "

"Something out of Charles Dickens, mostly," I said. "The old buildings, anyway."

I pictured Founder's Hall, with the bell tower, very creepy. Always cold. When we sat in there for assemblies, we took turns seeing who could make the most clouds of breath. And my dorm, Grose. The brick walls covered with bad art, the dark wood floors, so shiny that when I walked down them, I could see ...

I felt Celia's icy presence. She was joining the party. Mad tea party.

"You can see your reflection in the wood," I told him.

"Go on."

"And there are five huge bathtubs in the bathroom, and you can see where they used to have lids on them. They put the bad girls in them and locked the lids on. Only their necks and heads stuck out.

Celia moved inside me. *Stop it, Lindsay. He's going to know.*

"Hydrotherapy. They don't do that sort of thing now."

"No. The lids are gone. But before, when we . . . when they were bad . . . " I heard what I was saying and tried to turn it around. "The faucets in the tubs don't work. We take showers."

"What else do you see when you look at Marlwood, walking down the path?"

"Jessel. The other old building in Academy Quad. It has four turrets and a lake view. It's supposed to be haunted," I blurted, before I realized what I was saying.

"Do you think it's haunted?"

"Of course not." *I don't think it's haunted. I know it's haunted.* "Mandy Winters lives there, with her friends."

"I've met her brother, Miles."

"They're twins," I said. I heard the tremor in my voice. I was sure he could hear it too.

"Go on," he prompted again. I relaxed a little. He wasn't going to ask questions about the Winterses. He wouldn't pry. Not yet, anyway. First he had to gain my trust. That was how it worked in therapy.

"Past Academy Quad, there's the commons, where we eat. There are around a hundred of us. Then the gym. And the library." *And the statue garden.* I didn't mention it. Someone had stalked me there. And it's where I found Celia's locket, given to her by David Abernathy a hundred years ago as a token of his love.

Of course, he had given Belle an identical one ...

"There are some abandoned buildings, but those are off-limits." Except for parties, and séances, and attempted murders. The lake house. The operating theater.

"Don't, don't!" Celia protested.

"Excuse me, what did you say?" he asked softly.

I pressed my mouth shut. To distract myself, I gazed at the yellow circle of light on the wall, golden and warm as the sun. There were weeks at Marlwood when the sun hadn't shone even for an hour. Gray, scary days, when the fog boiled off the lake and the birds wouldn't land on the water. Where Mandy and her ally, Belle, tracked girls for the other ghosts to possess so they could try to kill Celia, through me.

I shifted in my chair, barely able to keep still. I couldn't tell him about any of that. I stared at the yellow circle.

And suddenly, I was remembering my ride back to school with Troy. Driving up the Pacific Coast Highway as surfers rode the waves and Troy grinned at me, tanned, his eyes an unearthly blue. Dimples. Freckles. And the best kisses, ever. Then he dropped the bomb two hours before we were scheduled to arrive on campus: he was still Mandy's boyfriend. Despite his promise to break up with her—a promise I had not asked him to make—he hadn't. Kiyoko had died, and Mandy was so torn up about it that he hadn't had the heart to add more agony to her life.

That was the reason he gave me, anyway.

"All men are lying bastards," Celia hissed.

"You were telling me about the sun," Dr. Morehouse said.

"On the water," I said drowsily. "Riley likes to surf." I couldn't remember telling him about Riley.

"Do you surf?"

"Body surf." I felt myself smile. A real smile. The warm ocean water enfolded me; salt water crusted my lips. "We eat dried mangoes from the Asian market. Diet cream soda."

Riley and I got busted by a lifeguard for making out. He told us there were too many young kids around for that kind of PDA. I couldn't believe I had gotten in trouble for kissing the hottest guy at school. It was quite a coup. The sun had beat down so bright and yellow and I dribbled mango juice on my lips. Riley licked it off and it was so fun and so amazing that my school's first-string quarterback was kissing me that I started laughing.

I chuckled now, low in my throat. Warmth seeped through me. I felt safe. San Diego. Home. I heard the breakers. I smelled my suntan lotion.

Home.

———

LATER, WHEN I woke up, the dimmer lights were still on, but shadows from the windows threw stripes on the walls. I was curled up in the oversized chair with a goose down pillow under my head and a soft green blanket wrapped around me. I was alone. I had fallen asleep during our ramble and Dr. Morehouse had gone.

I had slept well. No nightmares had shaken me; there was no sense of being spied, crept in upon. If Celia was still with me, I couldn't tell.

That didn't mean she was gone. But it was the first decent

rest I had had in weeks—every night had been a succession of nightmares. To actually sleep, and to wake up normally, not because I was screaming inside . . . it felt as good as body surfing. And sunshine.

But had I *said* anything?

I rode the wave of peacefulness as it began to ebb. It had been mine, for a time.

A sandwich had been left for me. Turkey and Havarti cheese on a croissant, my favorite lunch item on the Marlwood menu. And two chocolate chip cookies. Had I given Dr. Morehouse my food order, under hypnosis?

Wind rattled the windows. Ms. Simonet cracked the door open and smiled—genuinely—when she saw that I was awake and eating my meal.

"You've slept for hours," she told me. "The girls came at noon to help you study. Then they came after classes. But I thought it would be better if you caught up on your sleep." Before I could ask, she said, "It's nine-thirty at night."

I'd been out for almost twelve hours.

"I have to go to the bathroom," I told her, and she came forward to help me up—which was good, because my left leg had fallen asleep. I stood and let the blood flow back into it, then wobbled into the bathroom and shut the door. I had to cross in front of the mirror over the sink basin to get to the toilet, and my first impulse was to avoid it.

But tonight, I stopped and looked. And instead of a crazy, possessed lunatic, I saw a fairly good-looking high school sophomore. And that was *it*.

I blew that girl a kiss.

———

THE NEXT DAY was Sunday, and Troy came to visit me. He had driven over in his '68 T-bird with Spider, Julie's boyfriend. Boys weren't allowed on campus, but Troy the charmer had permission to drop by whenever he wanted. A bribe, I supposed, so his parents wouldn't sue the school. Or me.

He was wearing a white T-shirt and over that a thick dark-gray hoodie. He had on jeans and hiking boots—normal person clothes—but somehow he retained his rich-guy air. Maybe it was his perfect hair, or his teeth. His arm was still in a sling; I spun a microfantasy of Troy ten years in the future, overseeing his father's vast business empire, explaining to people that his hoped-for professional basketball career had ended through a "fluke accident." Although, thus far, he hadn't told me about any plans to become a pro ballplayer.

He must have read the expression on my face. Color crept up his neck and spread across his cheeks.

"I told Mandy not to say anything. About what happened in the operating theater." His voice was low.

Some of the coolness left the moment, like air out of a deflating balloon. Mandy. Of course he had been talking to her. She was his girlfriend, wasn't she? And I had attacked them both in the operating theater.

Sitting in one of the plastic chairs, he surveyed the stacks of textbooks and notebooks. Julie had brought my laptop, too. And most of my clothes.

"Why don't they just let you out?"

"They're going to," I said defensively. "I have pneumonia."

I couldn't stop looking at the sling. He had sat by my bedside after they had brought me in, me raving that he was going to kill me, kill all of us. But after they drugged me, I heard him whispering to me that he loved me. I had clung to that. Now here we were face-to-face. I wondered if he would say it, when I was awake.

"It, um, doesn't hurt." He touched it, as if to prove it. "I didn't really even notice when you hit . . . " Trailing away, he cleared his throat. "It was stupid of me to set up the operation like that. I knew how upset you were about the lobotomies and all. I've got this gore factor streak . . . "

"I appreciated the gesture," I said, although he was right: the idea was pretty bizarre. My big Valentine's surprise was that he and Marica had lovingly re-created Dr. Abernathy's lobotomy surgery in the operating theater, down to a hospital bed, an ice pick, and a hammer. "And the dinner was nice." I was lying. Our dinner at the posh spa marked the moment I had become convinced that Troy had become possessed by the ghost of David Abernathy. Then things had spiraled out of control at the dance, when Spider had accused him of attacking Julie.

But he hadn't. And we still didn't know who had. We called our scary, unidentified bad guy the Marlwood Stalker.

Maybe it was something that lives in the woods, waiting for us, to hurt us and kill us. Maybe it was one of us, possessed. Maybe me. I was there when she was attacked. I was the one who found her with her skirt torn off, and she was half out of her mind.

I knew someone else who was half out of her mind—Celia. There were hours I couldn't account for, when I found myself in places I had no memory of going: the operating theater, the haunted library, the lake. I didn't know what I had done—or what Celia had made me do—had I killed the birds, and the cat? Had I made slash marks in the trees and followed people in the fog? Had I attacked Julie?

Did I—no, Celia—have *anything* to do with Kiyoko's death? Had I told Dr. Morehouse any of that?

My chest tightened and I couldn't breathe. I couldn't, wouldn't lose it in front of Troy again. But I could feel myself pulling apart, like a dropped stitch in a knitting project, not noticed, unraveling.

I began panicking about panicking—that was how anxiety attacks worked—and bitter cold spread through me. Celia. Oh, God, she was going to say something, do something . . .

"Hey, are you okay?" he asked me. "Sorry to bring up a sore subject."

It seemed like the most bizarre thing he could say. Hitting him with a hammer was "a sore subject." *Hitting* him. I wanted to laugh, but I was afraid I would cry.

Suddenly, the scent of geraniums wafted across my nose. Earthy, lemony. I inhaled it; my lungs were working again. I thought of my mom, and my panic weakened its death grip on me. *Memmy.* Was she here? Was she where Celia was? Maybe I was the unfinished business that kept her earthbound. Maybe she'd been waiting in case I needed her. And I did need her. Terribly.

"I'm okay," Troy said as he jerked and pulled his cell phone out of his jacket. He looked at the faceplate and blinked. I knew by his expression that it was Mandy.

How convenient; he could come over to Marlwood

whenever he wanted to, because of me. Then he could see Mandy too. Rich and gorgeous, Mandy was just mean. Poor and less than gorgeous, I was crazy.

He probably figured he'd stuck with the right girl.

"Hey, you know what? I'm really tired," I said, so he wouldn't tell me to my face that he had to go now. Firing him before he fired me.

"Oh." He sounded surprised. "I thought maybe we could go for a walk or something."

So you're weren't going to bail? I kept the question to myself. Confident girls didn't beg. Jane had taught me that.

"Maybe another time," I said. I basked in his disappointment and reveled in the knowledge that all was not lost when it came to matters of Troy's heart. And now that he'd mentioned going on a walk, claustrophobia welled inside me. In the past, when I was stressed, I had two modes—extreme burrowing or running it off. Exercise was good for panic. It burned off the adrenaline.

"Okay." He got to his feet. "So, um, take care." He turned to go, paused, turned back. My traitorous heart skipped a couple of beats as he looked hard at me and licked his just-as-sweet-as-mango lips.

"Hey," he said, "remember when I told you about seeing that, um, that burning girl on the road when we were driving up here?" That burning *ghost*? Yes, I did remember. It might have been Celia herself, or the memory of her, lost in the endless loop of failing to save her own life. Or it was just the flash of his headlight on a patch of fog.

Wordlessly, I nodded.

"Well, on the way over here, I thought I saw her again."

In daylight. That made it scarier. If things went bump in the darkness, at least you could turn the lights on to make them go away. I feigned mild interest, but I twisted my hands together in my lap.

"Did Spider see her too?" I asked.

"No. He was texting Julie. Or trying to. Reception around here sucks." He tried to smile. "I was so scared I nearly ran off the road."

"You've been to too many séances," I tossed off. Mandy was famous for them, pulling out all the stops with Ouija boards and candlelight. The irony was, she really could communicate with the dead.

"I haven't been to a séance in forever," he insisted, his expression solemn. Then he smiled tentatively at me. "Anyway, when you're up for it, I thought we could get back to researching Dr. Abernathy and the lobotomies. Unless you're done with that. Thanks to me."

"I am done, but only because we've solved the mystery. He performed them, and he died." I was sorry to lie to Troy, but the situation had gotten too strained. If I went off again—if *Celia* went off—he'd dump me for sure.

"Okay." He sounded disappointed. I had a moment of doubt; what would we have in common if we didn't keep looking into the buried history of Marlwood? *Mandy?*

"What did your parents say about . . . ?" I gestured to his arm.

"I didn't tell them. My mom's at a retreat," he said. "And my dad's in the middle of some big merger deal."

"What does your mom have to retreat from?" I asked, and he quirked the right side of his mouth.

"She's always got something. Anyway, I told everybody I fell. Coach says I'm a klutz. We all covered for you. Mandy and Miles, too."

"That was really nice of her," I managed to say, even though I thought I might strangle on the words. Either she was covering her own butt or trying to show Troy what a great little gal she was. But for sure she didn't have my best interests at heart. We had thrown down over Troy. Like he was a bone. Or a toy.

A possession.

He turned to go, and I was sorry that I'd pretty much told him to leave. But I knew I couldn't take it back. That would make me look too eager. Did we always have to play games with guys?

"I'll see you soon," he murmured. "I hope."

I gave him a genuine smile, remembering when I'd phoned him at the crack of dawn and begged him to meet me. And he had. He must have thought I was pathetic, weeping and whiny. After that, he kept promising to break up with Mandy, even though I had never asked him to in the first place. Kept promising, and kept not doing it.

I felt a little pissed off.

My cell phone rang. We both jumped a foot and laughed.

"I'll let you get that." His voice was a bit strained. Jealousy? That would be nice.

He turned on his heel and waved over his shoulder. I gave him a wave back, and then he left the room. I looked at the caller ID. Heather. I took a deep breath. Okay.

It was time.

FIVE

I HEARD TROY talking in the hall to Ms. Simonet—her voice was sugar sweet; everyone liked Troy—as I connected to the call and put my phone to my ear.

"Oh, my God, you're actually alive," Heather said, aiming for funny, but sounding nervous. We hadn't spoken since Christmas Eve. Which was, in part, why I had been avoiding calling her back.

"Lucky for you," I said.

"Yeah, well, maybe." After a beat, she said, "Hello, *fea*." *Fea* meant "ugly" in Spanish. While the whole world felt obligated to call me "Linz," she had remained an American original. I knew that by using it, she was trying very hard to relate to the me I had been before I joined Jane's posse of evil.

Back in the day; that is, freshman year, we had mocked girls like Jane. Rolled our eyes in pity at all the effort Jane appeared to expend to stay at the top of the social heap—the right clothes, the right music, the right places to hang out. Funny thing was, once I was in, I discovered that for Jane, being number one was fairly effortless. The clothes, music, and loitering spots were right because that was what *she* wore and where *she* went, and not vice versa. Coolness was her reality bubble; trendiness was hers for the having. It was enough to make me believe in karma, or fate, like she'd paid for her good fortune by suffering in another life, and she was set. She never, ever fell from grace.

Then there was me, having not only fallen, but plummeted, and splatted on grace's sidewalk. I was the one suffering in this life.

Still, I had acquired skills that had proven useful in keeping me alive at Marlwood . . . such as keeping a safe distance from Mandy. Never letting her get the upper hand when she dangled entrance to her clique as the price for my soul. *So* not interested.

But I was interested in having my best friend back.

"*Hola,* Martinez." I kept my tone light.

"So, how you been?"

"Fine." Lie, lie, lie. No, wait. That was true. Ever since my visit from Dr. Morehouse, I was verging on fine. Sporadic bursts of fritz out were nothing compared to what I used to be like.

"That was . . . terse," she said.

"Isn't that a nice change? Me, kind of quiet?"

"Huh." She grunted. "Well."

I waited. She'd been the one to call.

"I'm sorry about the movies," she said. "I shouldn't have just booted you out of the car. I should have talked to you. Listened—"

"It's okay." *It was too much to ask. I was too high maintenance. I still am.*

"The thing is," she went on, "I had a nightmare last night. It was *awful*. And I woke up everybody, and my mom just completely unloaded on me for my drama."

"Sweet."

"She's going through menopause. But anyway, I thought about you and how, you know, that can just happen. Screaming without warning."

"A nightmare," I said slowly, tensing. Were they catching?

"What was it about?" "I don't remember."

I wasn't sure I believed her.

"Listen, Riley talks about you all the time. And he's not hanging out with the Jane-bots much."

"Maybe he'll become a human being someday," I bit off. "But I'm not betting on it."

"Guys do wild stuff. She was all, *you* know, 'come and get it, baby.' When . . . it happened. He'd been drinking."

"Whatever." I didn't want to forgive him. Maybe I was being hard on him because I had almost forgotten that Troy still hadn't broken up with Mandy. I'd managed to back-burner Troy's semi-cheating because he had big blue eyes and he'd very gallantly excused my bad behavior.

"Are you supposed to report back to Riley what I say?" I asked her.

"Not officially." She took a deep breath. "I miss you too, Lindsay. I'm so sorry I wasted the break. We could have hung out. My mom made the most rockin' tamales."

I loved her mother's Christmas tamales.

"Why are you telling me this stuff about Riley?" I asked. "It's not like I can do much of anything about it."

"Text, yo."

"He has to start it. And I'm not into long distance. I'm fourteen hours away."

"Then come home."

I hadn't expected that. "It's the second semester. *Yo.*"

"So? They'll make you a study plan." She hesitated. "I've just got this funny feeling. . ." Her voice trailed off.

"So which is it?" I said. "Riley misses me, you miss me, you've got a funny feeling?"

"Is it okay if he calls?"

"Did he ask you to ask me that?" In spite of myself, my voice rose, excited. My coolness was evaporating.

Wait a sec. I'm over him.

"No. I'm taking some initiative."

"Why are you doing this, really?" I asked, and I couldn't help smiling. It was nice to be wanted.

"Gotta go," she said impishly. "Call when you can."

We disconnected. It was all so complicated. I had left San Diego so I could leave San Diego. But it wasn't like an old novel, where once you were gone, no one could find you. Nowadays, if Heathcliff had left Wuthering Heights, he and his great lost love Cathy would have texted.

Ms. Simonet came in with my iron supplement and commented on the change in me. She left me alone to do some of my mountains of homework. I flipped open my laptop to get to work, but I couldn't help surfing the net first. The cell and internet reception in the mountains was very spotty, but the infirmary had an excellent signal. There wasn't much online about the troubles at Marlwood. Kiyoko's death was old news. Rose had sent me an animated e-card set to the tunes of "Send in the Clowns," and the ruckus about her parents' divorce was splashed everywhere. My parents had checked in a lot; I called them and spun the situation, as I was sure it had been spun before me. I was alternately miffed and relieved that they didn't seem more worried about me.

Maybe they didn't need to be. Maybe somehow, Dr. Morehouse had exorcised Celia, and I was finally free.

So maybe . . . I could leave. I stifled a giggle of joy. Oh, to be done with this. To be a normal girl, interested in free verse poetry, the cello, knitting, and guys.

Troy, I thought, and then, *Riley.*

It was all so complicated.

A FEW HOURS later, while I was curled up in bed, there was a jaunty rap on my door. The door cracked open and a single eye peered in at me.

"Hail, eyeball of Miles," I said, tensing. I knew he'd been by to see me before. I just hadn't been fully conscious for the occasion.

"Hail, weirdness of you," he replied, strolling in.

He was swathed in a really beautiful black overcoat and beneath it, a jet-black European-looking sort of suit, very slouchy and cool. He was wearing black leather gloves and loafers. The clothes were amazing. He had styled his platinum blond hair into his signature retro ducktail, and there was stubble on his cheeks. I couldn't decide if he looked good or slagged, but that was my usual reaction to Miles. Just as I couldn't decide if he frightened or repulsed me more.

"You're not wearing your red thread. That way lies madness." He pulled off his left glove and pushed up his sleeve, revealing the Kabbalah thread or whatever it was called. I'd lost the one Shayna had given me. After I lost my mind, Miles had wound a replacement around my wrist. As if it would really protect me from something.

"I think they were afraid I might saw my head off with it." I shut my laptop and set it aside.

"You might have."

"Thanks."

He inclined his head. "I live to annoy you." Cocked it to the side. "I thought sickbeds were for sick people."

"I have pneumonia."

"Some people will do anything to get out of classes." He flopped down into the burgundy leather chair. I had on my mom's sweatshirt but no bra. I wondered if he could tell. Probably not. Still, I felt a little weirded out.

He put a cigarette in his mouth.

"You can't smoke in here," I said. "Plus, you can't smoke around me anywhere."

"Oh, you've grown a pair." He let the cigarette hang off his lip, but he didn't light it.

"You're just less scary than you used to be." My voice cracked, giving the lie to my statement, and he grimaced sympathetically.

"Well, Mandy's scarier, these days." He leaned forward on his elbows and searched my face. There were circles under his eyes, and he was gaunt. "And I think you know something about that, scary girl."

I swallowed. Hard. He was giving me a look that said, *You know exactly what I'm talking about.* Guilt and fear and maybe even a little bit of hope rose inside me. "Wh-what?" I croaked.

He smiled grimly. "Lindsay Anne, don't even try to fake me out. I'm really smart, and as a former addict, I have mad lying skills the likes of which you can't even begin to appreciate. No one lies better than me. So don't embarrass us both. I need to know what's wrong with my sister."

"She's a bitch," I blurted without thinking.

"I *know* that." He took off his other glove and flapped them back and forth, studying them. He traced the stitching with his fingertips. He had very long eyelashes, and he looked vulnerable. Younger. Not for the first time, I wondered if money delayed the growing-up portion of getting older.

"But . . . okay." He dropped the gloves on the floor and sank his face into his hands. The overhead fluorescent light cast a halo in his hair, which I would have found laughable if I hadn't been about to implode. Miles knew. How much, I didn't know.

But he knew something.

I waited for Celia's reaction. There was none. Had Dr. Morehouse fixed me? Was I done with her too? Could I just walk away? Maybe I didn't need an ally. Maybe I just needed to pack. "Look, I know Mandy is your frenemy," he said to the floor.

"Not even."

"Okay, then I'm your frenemy." He paused, still cradling his head. I said nothing. "You really aren't going to make this easy on me, are you?"

"Why should I? You got off on scaring me. You threatened me."

"Not in so many words." He lowered his hands and sat up straight. The cigarette still dangled from his mouth. "Okay, I did. I'm a creepy, stalkery jerk and I did get off on scaring you. But something is really wrong with Mandy. *Really* wrong."

"I'm not sure you can be a former addict," I said.

"If you can recover from a nervous breakdown, I can stop being an addict," he insisted.

We looked at each other, and I felt a weird electricity zap between us. Miles was the epitome of those "layers of individuality" that Dr. Morehouse had talked about. My committee wasn't fond of him. But as before, there was something about Miles that extended past pure loathing. I hadn't screamed for my life when he had cornered me in the shadows on the night of the Valentine's Day dance. Instead, we'd danced the tango. And I wasn't screaming now, even though I was alone with the guy who could be the Marlwood Stalker.

Unless I was.

"Here's a thought, Lindsay Lou," he said. "If you help me declaw my sister, she won't be able to scratch you."

"She's a hundred percent claws," I retorted.

"She didn't used to be," he said. He scratched his cheek. "I've kept an eye on you, L. You're scared, and you need help. From the way you tried to pound in Troy's head with that hammer, I'm guessing he's too dumb. I'm the smartest guy you know. And I . . . happen to believe that what is going on is more bizarre than anyone realizes."

That caught me off guard. *Way* off guard. He must have sensed it.

"If you won't tell me what's wrong with Mandy, maybe you'll tell me what's wrong with Marlwood. Because there's something really, really wrong here. Am I right?"

Still I remained silent. But I could feel myself daring to hope that he *did* know that something was wrong with Marlwood. That I wasn't alone in this. But joining forces with Miles Winters? Was that just too whacked?

"How about a twofer?" he pressed. "You help me with Mandy and I help you with Marlwood."

"What's in it for me?" I asked. "I'm on scholarship."

"Something's keeping you here," he said. "You're no dummy. Having Marlwood on your college app's will keep you from night classes at the community college while you work retail by day."

"What a jerky thing to say." I was stung.

He gave his head a little shake, extracted the cigarette, and tapped the filter on the arm of the chair. "We don't have time for this. You need my help. And I need yours. Let's table everything else. Now."

My lips parted. I was about to tell him no when I realized I was thinking about saying yes. I was actually considering joining forces with Miles Winters.

"Where are you staying?" I asked him, trying to stall so I could regain my sanity.

"Guest house here on the grounds. I think Dr. Ehrlenbach's

trying to conveniently forget that while she's gone. When your family's buying the school a sports complex, you get a few extra perks."

He didn't smirk. He just stared at me, willing me to agree to his demand. He pulled out a pack of matches from his pants pocket and looked at me. I shook my head. Sighing, he put the matches back in the pocket.

"No smoking, just for you," he said. "Now come on, baby. Gimme something in return. Or I can go."

A thrill of anxiety shot up my spine and I surrendered. I needed help. Even if it came from him.

"Okay."

He caught his breath.

"See? I *knew* you were smart." He nodded at me. "Go. Start."

I licked my lips. My stomach clenched, and I felt exactly the same way as I had trying to jump off the high dive last year in P.E.

"A few people know bits of what I'm going to tell you," I began. "But no one knows all of it, except me. And if I tell you, you're just going to have to believe me, all right? There's no way to convince you."

He took the cigarette out of his mouth and rolled it back and forth on his palm. Then he peered up at me through his eyelashes, and I realized he was giving my request serious thought before replying.

"Okay." He bobbed his head. "I will suspend my disbelief."

Where to start? First I wanted to burst into sobs. Or laughter. Of all the people to tell this to, I had never imagined it would be Miles Winters.

"C'mon, Lindsay," he said. "I'm listening."

"You already know about the fact that this was originally a home for wayward girls," I said. "People dumped their female relatives here because they were willful or disobedient. Or boring, or had no dowries. One girl got sent here for killing her uncle when he attacked her."

I held up my hand so that he wouldn't remind me he knew all this. Since the Winters had offered to bankroll the multi-million-dollar Winters Sports Complex to replace our outdated gym, Miles had done a lot of research on Marlwood. I was betting he knew more of its sordid history than even I did. But I had to get it out in one coherent fashion. It was like taking the walk down the path with the committee, one foot in front of the others.

"You also know that a doctor named David Abernathy performed lobotomies on a lot of the inmates. He would take an ice pick and wiggle it around to sever the connection between two parts of their brains 'to calm them.'" I didn't bother with air quotes.

He nodded. "And thank God that's out of fashion, because they would have done that to me."

I believed him. Gossip was that he'd been to so many rehabs and clinics that his parents had invested in a special portfolio of mental health care stocks.

"So far, you're rehashing," he reminded me. "Stalling."

"Here's the new part, then," I said. "Our glorious founder, Edwin Marlwood, would pick out the victims, and David Abernathy would cut open their brains for him. But Dr. David messed around with them, too."

His interest perked up. "The brains? Or the broads?"

"He'd play them off each other. Make them compete to be his special little playmates."

Miles smirked. "Rehab-boy says, 'Not surprised.'"

"Stop interrupting me." He made a show of sitting up straighter, putting his hands on his knees, and politely raising his chin.

"There were two specific girls I know about who were in love with him. He promised each of them that he was going to get her out of here. Without telling the other one, of course."

"Nice," Miles said.

"One of them started a fire, and it got out of control. It killed seven girls. I have a news clipping," I added.

He took that in. "No way. I never saw that, and I even used our research firm. Heads are gonna roll."

"She said she set it to stop the lobotomies, but really, I think she wanted to kill her rival." I heard what I was saying. "According to what I've read."

"That's pretty hot stuff. I have to see that."

I'd gone too far. None of that was written down in the news clipping. I knew it because I had experienced it, in terrifying dreams and visions . . . and by confronting Belle herself. Nearly killing the girl she possessed, which was what Celia wanted.

Revenge.

And as for the girl I'd nearly killed . . .

"You're *still* holding out," he accused me. "Your body language is screaming at me. Lying skills, remember?"

I had been trying to tell him just about Mandy. I didn't

know what Celia would do if I told about her. But I had to take that chance.

"The one who started the fire was a girl named Celia Reaves." I lowered my voice and braced for Celia to react. She was quiet.

And so was he. He was chewing his lower lip. I heard him sigh slowly. Saw him swallow, hard.

"Mandy mentioned . . . that name. In a southern accent."

And there it was. There it was, finally. My confirmation. From someone who was not me, and not MIA—missing in action— like Shayna. Someone who was here, now, and relatively sane. He had heard what I had heard, and I hadn't told him about it first. He'd come to me with the information on his own.

The southern accent would be the voice of Belle, coming through Mandy.

"Go on," I rasped, but I was thinking, *Thank you, Miles, thank you, thank you.*

"When we dropped her off after winter break, I found some stuff she'd forgotten in the limo, and I took it over to Jessel. I went in the front door, and I heard her laughing.

"I called out, but no one heard me. There was just more laughter. It was Mandy, Lara, and Alis DeChancey. I thought they were on something." He chewed his lip again.

"I didn't want their housemother to hear them, so I went on up the stairs. They were in one of those turret rooms. The one on the right, farther back. It looks out on the lake."

Despite my relief, my blood ran cold. I knew that room. Oh, did I know it.

"I stood in the hall and they were all talking in different

voices, with different accents. About 'number seven,' and making sure she got what was coming to her. Then Mandy came out into the hall and saw me. She stared straight at me and her eyes were black. She started flirting with me and she called me 'sweet bee.'"

I nodded, flooding with intense relief, and he frowned. I gestured, indicating for him to keep going. "She kind of . . . jerked." He imitated it, as if he were stepping on a live wire. Or getting electroshock therapy. "Then she lowered her head for a moment and looked back up at me. She looked surprised to see me."

"And her eyes weren't black anymore," I filled in.

He looked at me through half-closed eyes. "They weren't black. But I still thought . . . maybe not such a big deal."

"Yeah, well," I replied.

"Mandy and I . . . we've pushed the envelope. Maybe you've heard a few things."

"Yes, I have." Stories about them sleeping together in the Lincoln Bedroom, in the White House. *Together*, together. And I'd seen pictures of them, far too cuddly, in a box of pictures Mandy hid under her bed.

"When you're as rich as we are, you don't have a lot of boundaries."

He wasn't bragging. It was true.

"Ergo, designer drugs are easy to score," he concluded. "So Mandy's gotten hold of something?" He wasn't telling me. He was asking.

"I thought that for a while too. That it was drugs," I said. I took another deep breath. "But it's not drugs."

Pushing himself up, he got out of the chair. I pulled back a little, and he held out his hands to his sides, almost as if he were showing me that he carried no concealed weapons. But he did: his mind. He was brilliant.

He walked around the room, like someone who was admiring the pictures in an art gallery, only here, the only art was what my dormies called "hotel room art"—a forest landscape—and some posters about sexually transmitted diseases and the food pyramid.

He stopped at the poster about STD's and scanned it. "In the operating theater, when Troy faked that brain surgery, you lost it—but *Mandy* lost it too. You two were screaming at each other, and neither of you was making any sense." He turned his head toward me. "Or so I thought at the time. But you actually were."

"We were."

He didn't speak. He blinked rapidly at me, looked at the poster, scratched his cheek. "Okay, LA, what *exactly* are we talking about here?"

A beat. Two. As with Heather, the time had come. My impulsive decision to trust him was beginning to fade—or was I just chickening out?

"If I tell you, what are you going to do?" Go to Ehrlenbach? Hire the world's most expensive ghost busters?

"I'm going to help my sister. And I'm going to help . . . you."

"I'm not sure you can do both."

He raised his chin. "I am." He scratched his chin. "So, just say it, damn it. Did Mandy, what, buy herself some voodoo magic?"

A beat. Two. It was as if silence had a sound of its own. Or was that my heart pounding?

"Yes." My voice was steady. "She did."

He didn't speak for a long time.

"Voodoo to do . . . " he asked leadingly.

Believe me. Please.

"Okay, then, here it is. Mandy is possessed by the spirit of Belle Johnson. A dead girl."

His answer was silence as agitated as my own had been. He was holding his breath.

"And Belle wants revenge. Against Celia Reaves, the girl who started the fire and was the other girl, er, woman, in their triangle."

More silence.

"Number seven."

I could tell he was trying hard to absorb it, believe it. I didn't know how I felt, telling him. Telling anyone.

"Is this . . . bullshit?" he asked.

I shook my head slowly. Was Miles going to think I was crazy, too? Of all the people I had to confide in, Miles was not my first choice. He wouldn't have been a choice at all. But I reminded myself that he had *heard* Mandy speaking like Belle. Independent of me. And Shayna had known about the possessions. She *had*.

And then she had gone insane.

"Why are you an addict?" I asked. "I mean, what happened to you?"

"*What?*" He stared at me. "How did this become about *me*?"

I began to shake all over, feeling sick, tired, scared. I needed someone to trust.

Maybe I should stop talking to Miles. Maybe I could level with Dr. Morehouse, I thought. A shrink. Right.

"You can't stop now," Miles said, pursing his lips and crossing his arms. I jerked. Had he read my mind? "Absolutely no way. I will totally screw you over if you don't finish this."

I believed him.

"I was spying on Mandy my first day here," I said. "It was so foggy. I—I snuck to the hedge in front of Jessel because I heard her doing something—something interesting."

"Interesting."

"Umm . . ."

"Cavanaugh, don't wimp out," he snapped, as if using my last name would make me pay better attention.

I went for it.

"She and Lara were performing a ritual on Kiyoko to get her to become possessed. And Celia Reaves took advantage and possessed me." I said it in a rush and braced myself for Celia's anger.

He stared at me. *"You?"*

I looked down. Saw my reflection on one of the metal lids of my breakfast tray. No white face. No hollowed-out eye sockets.

"Me." My voice caught.

He stared at me, then narrowed his eyes, giving me a once-over. Abruptly, he stuck his cigarette back in his mouth and lit it, dropped back his head, and gazed at the ceiling.

"Well." He moved his head this way and that, scrutinizing the two square feet above himself.

I looked at the shiny metal. It was still just me. I couldn't help the tears that streamed down my cheeks.

"So, now you know." I sounded angry, but I was scared. I had never said this much to anyone.

"Hmm," he said. He puffed out smoke, blinking, quiet. "Okay, then. A question."

I watched the smoke come out of his mouth, imagining Celia leaving my body and my life in the same way. Praying it had happened. Wondering about the timing of this conversation.

"Ask," I said reluctantly.

"Shouldn't you two—or you four—be on *Oprah*? Because she'd pay a lot for this. And your family is destitute."

My mouth dropped open, and he grinned at me. We both started laughing. Big, rolling belly laughs. I gathered up handfuls of my hair and smoothed them away from my forehead as I kicked my feet and cracked up, not like the night of the lockdown, but for pretty much the same reason. Then I gestured him over and made him give me a cigarette too, and I coughed all over him after he lit it. I had never been a social smoker.

"I see things," I told him in a rush. "All the time. I see Celia's reflection in mirrors and in water. I have her nightmares. On Valentine's Day, I was convinced Troy had become possessed by David Abernathy. I thought he had lured me to the operating theater to perform a real, actual lobotomy on me."

He made a face. "Oh, my God. No wonder you've lost so much weight."

"Yeah. But I think she may have left me, and now I'm telling you all this stuff—" I stopped. "And I'm scared."

"No wonder." He flicked ash on my omelet plate. "Being possessed. Well, that's really something."

"Yeah."

"I'm so sorry." And he was. Big, evil, scary Miles was sorry for me. I was boggled.

We smoked together. I felt a rush from the nicotine and from finally telling someone. I kept bracing myself for Celia's reaction. But as far as I could tell, she had left the building.

"No wonder you're hiding out," he said. "Smoking while being treated for pneumonia."

I hadn't thought of that. "I think it's over for me. Not sure."

"But not Mandy." He knit his brows together. "I mean, look at how she's acting."

My eyes were watering from the cigarette smoke. It really was a filthy habit. "I hate to break this to you, Miles, but Mandy was evil before she became possessed. She's a mean girl."

"You can take it."

"Why should I have to? She's a bully. But you probably find that attractive."

"While you want us to use our powers only for good," he said, making a pouty face. "I need you to help me. I mean, why did she do it? Seek out getting possessed?"

I wasn't sure I could go there, even though he probably wouldn't be fazed. But it was a fair question.

"Curiosity?" I hedged. It was a lie. Mandy had made a pact with Belle so that she could take care of Miles, be with Miles. At least that was what I had heard her tell Belle. Why didn't I just tell him that?

Because maybe . . . that wasn't true, or was true no longer.

Mandy *had* been curious. And now she and Belle were the most powerful girls on campus.

"My sister." He shook his head.

"Go process it on your own time," I said, putting out my cigarette. My lungs were blazing. Smoking had been a stupid idea.

"Right." He got up, patted my cheek, hesitated, then bent over and kissed me. Lightly, but deliberately. He tasted like ashes.

"Yum," he whispered.

Then he left.

SIX

I WAITED FOR Celia to punish me for breaking silence. Miraculously, I did homework to keep myself from going crazy while I waited. I got an incredible amount done, when I had expected just the opposite.

That night, I had trouble looking in the mirror, afraid Celia would be glaring back at me. I fought falling asleep, terrified of what she might put me through. I just couldn't go back into her grave, out in the forest where the dead girls screamed.

There was no shot from Ms. Simonet, but she did give me two small blue pills. I wanted to hide them under my tongue the way they did in the movies, then spit them out when she wasn't looking, but she watched me like a hawk as I swallowed them down.

I had no nightmares. None. Except for the one where I went to my history class naked and had to star in a play but didn't know any of the lines. So maybe my dozens of nightmares had been a combination of the drugs and Celia. And if both were gone . . .

The next evening, Troy called me and we talked forever. Basketball, the weather, classes, the upcoming spring beak. He would try to talk his parents into going back to San Diego. He was pretty sure they'd go for it, because they were worried that he'd ask to go to St. Barts like last year, and "St. Barts got crazy."

We talked about Spider and Julie. They were so cute. It was working out so well.

But we didn't talk about:

Mandy.

The Marlwood Stalker.

Whoever had attacked Julie, if it wasn't the Marlwood Stalker.

The death of Kiyoko.

Other guys.

And while we were talking, Riley messaged me.

RiKballz: HI?

The whole thing was monumentally weird. I was debating what to do when a figure walked into my room wearing a black leather jacket and a ski mask. I was filling with my lungs with air to scream when Miles whipped off the mask.

"*God,*" I said, exhaling.

"What?" Troy asked.

"Nothing."

"*Nothing?*"

Miles rolled his eyes and jerked his head toward the door. "I'm busting you out. Come on," he whispered.

"Are you crazy?" I mouthed back.

"Someone's there," Troy said. "I should let you go."

"No, it's all good," I insisted. "He was just leaving."

"He. The doctor? Hey, Spider," he said away from the phone. "Yeah, man." Back into the phone with me. "Linz, I have to go anyway. When are you moving back to your dorm?"

"No clue."

"Okay, well, we should enjoy the cell phone reception as much as we can." His voice was warm and fuzzy. I wondered what Miles would do if he knew I was talking to Mandy's boyfriend. That had been a huge issue, before. That was what he had threatened me about, in fact. I had to remember that Miles was a Winters. Duplicitous. Not trustworthy.

"'Kay," Troy said. "Good night." His voice got syrupy. "Sleep well."

"All right, good night." I pressed disconnect and looked at Miles.

"Awkward much?" Miles drawled, putting back on his ski mask. "Let's go."

I ignored the fact that he seemed to know exactly who I'd been talking to. I looked down at Riley's text message. I couldn't help my little smile. I was so over Riley. I really was. Troy was the guy for me, even if he wouldn't break up with his girlfriend.

"Where are we going?" I asked Miles.

"Away from here, for starters. I found some stuff I want you to look over."

"Bring it here. To my room. Tomorrow."

He wrinkled his nose. "All this estrogen is making me wilt. If it had been up to me, I would *never* have sent Mandy to an all-girls school. All you guys can do is turn on each other like inbred poodles."

"And share grooming tips." I crossed my arms. "I'm not going anywhere with you tonight."

"You must be going stir-crazy. C'mon, there's a roadhouse a few miles down the road."

I was going stir-crazy. And I had never been to a roadhouse. "Ms. Simonet will probably do a bed check."

"Not tonight." He grinned evilly at me through the mask. It made me squirm.

"Oh, God, did you kill her?" He said nothing. "Poison her? Drug her?"

"Don't ask, don't tell. If you don't know, you won't ever have to lie about it." He walked to the side of the bed and made as if to lift my blankets. "Are you in your jammie bottoms?"

I grabbed the blankets and held them down. "Yes." Said bottoms were white and black plaid flannel, old and baggy. "What time is it?"

He wrenched the bedclothes out of my hands and tore the blankets away, exposing my shameful cheap some-designer knockoffs. He nodded as if to himself.

"You look great. Let's go." He huffed at my hesitation. "It's not a fashion show, Lindsay."

"You probably have your pajamas custom made."

"Commando, baby." He leered at me. "Listen, if it makes you feel better, I read your medical chart. Your pneumonia is a cover story. You really aren't that sick."

"What?" I was stunned.

"Yeah. They're keeping you here because as we know, you went cuckoo. They don't want to send you home. They want to keep you at Marlwood, so they're trying to make sure you won't try to kill someone else. Which I find fascinating."

"They don't want any more bad publicity," I said slowly. They were lying to me about my health? Or was Miles? How would he be able to see my chart?

"Then why not send home the bad apple? That's what I would do. That's what they always do to me."

He had me there.

"You want to be free of this," he said. "Right? And I want Mandy out of it." He had me there, too. And we Marlwoodians had a fine tradition of sneaking out. Plus Miles *was* my new ally.

"Okay. I'm in," I said.

I pondered the insanity of that even as I slid my jeans on over my pj bottoms, adding a sweater, my hat, mittens, and my Doc Martens—all brought down from my dorm during the week—and we crept into the hall. It was pitch black. I felt a little wobbly, and I almost turned back.

When Miles pushed open the door and I gazed out on the pines washed with moonlight and the dark sky twinkling with stars, my breath caught in my throat. It was so beautiful. The cold smelled fresh and clean after the sickroom smell, which, until that moment, I hadn't noticed.

"This better be good," I told him.

"It's already good." He fluttered his lashes at me.

"Please, take off the mask," I said. "You look like you should be carrying around a chain saw."

With a flourish, he ripped it back off. He was made for moonlight, all angles and hollows. He wasn't classically handsome, but he was very arresting; there was something about Miles that made you take a second look, maybe even a third. He had so much going for him. Why was he so screwed up?

Leading the way, he headed for a tree, disappeared behind it, and reemerged with a motor scooter. More specifically, a Vespa. He left it standing, disappeared again, and came back with two helmets and a burnished mahogany leather messenger bag.

"What about your Jag?"

"In the shop. Down in San Covino. I thought this would be kind of fun." He sat down. "You sit behind me, put your arms around me, and we're in business."

"What's in it for me?"

He patted the bag. "I snuck a bunch of stuff out of Mandy's room. I think it's got the ritual that started the possessions. What opened the door."

"I already know how she opened the door," I began, but he shook his head.

"If all one had to do to get possessed was close one's eyes and say 'Come to me' five times, I would stand before you a possessed man."

I noted the correct usage of the word *one*. "You did that?"

He set one of the helmets on a rock and put on the other one. "Nothing happened. Very disappointing."

"You might be possessed and not know it. We could be driving along and you get taken over and then you kill me."

He stopped working on the strap and looked at me. "My God, you're serious. You've been living like this for how long?" He reached down for the second helmet. "I'm not possessed."

I didn't move. He grunted with frustration.

"You *said* you'd help. You want this to end, yes? So work with me."

Crap. Still not completely on board, I put on the helmet and climbed behind him. I crossed my hands over his torso. For someone who looked as thin as he did, he had a lot of muscle. He turned on the engine, which was quieter than I would have expected, and we glided onto the blacktop path.

The way was bordered, as were all the paths in Marlwood, with white, blank-faced horse heads holding oversized chains in their mouths. On bad nights, I had imagined those horses recording my comings and goings. On worse nights, I could tip my imagination into believing that they turned to look as I passed each one by. Why not? This was Marlwood.

We zoomed past the infirmary, up the hill, and through Academy Quad, where Jessel hung over the lake and Grose stared down at Jessel. The light was on in Mandy's room and I pushed myself down against Miles's back, wanting to yell at him that a little more stealth would be appreciated.

We went past the new library, the commons, and the gym; then Miles drove straight when he should have hung a right. We were approaching the old library, with its treasure troves of ghosts and mildewing books, one of which had been Dr. Abernathy's notes on his lobotomy techniques. Troy had found it. David Abernathy killed a lot of girls and turned others into vegetables. His notes about his failures were cold and detached. He was like a Nazi, keeping lists and records. Both Celia and Belle were on the last list in the journal. After the fire, he left Marlwood forever and died of old age in Colorado.

I tensed. I hated that place. Celia had warned me away from Troy, appearing in the broken glass of one of the library's cabinets, saying I couldn't trust him, that he was dangerous. She'd been wrong about him. Being dead didn't make you infallible.

There was a light on in the upper story, in the exact location where I had seen the ghost of Mr. Truscott, the madhouse orderly weeping over Belle Johnson's impending lobotomy. She had seduced him into caring about her. I tapped Miles on the shoulder and extended my arm into his peripheral vision so he could follow my pointed finger. I wanted to see if he saw it too.

Just before he glanced up, the light disappeared. I tapped his helmet, indicating he should just move on, but he slowed, then stopped and put his foot down. I cringed.

"Sorry, it's nothing," I said. "Let's go."

He looked at the library, then craned his neck around and looked at me. My face prickled. "Are you okay?" he asked.

"Define your terms," I answered. I couldn't help looking back at the library. He followed my gaze, then studied the black mouth of the doorway.

"What's in there?"

"Nothing. Forward motion."

He gripped my arm, and a chill shot down my back. This was Miles Winters. No one knew we were here. What had I done?

He gave my forearm a squeeze. "C'mon, play fair. You're shaking like a leaf."

"Let go of me or I'll gouge your eyes out," I said coldly.

His reply was a cross between a laugh and a grunt, but he did let go. Without realizing what I was doing, I rubbed my arm.

"What have I ever done to you?" he asked me.

"It's not what you've done. It's who you are."

"You have no idea who I am," he retorted. "And *what* I am is the closest thing you have to backup." He patted the messenger bag. "I have information in here. And I want to go someplace and sit down and sort through it. With you."

He looked at the library, obviously intrigued. "I wanted to get away from Marlwood when we do it. Just in case. But if this place is haunted, then wouldn't it be perfect to do it here?"

"No."

"But—"

"No."

"Wow. Okay. Fine."

I put my hands around him again and we took off, the Vespa buzzing like an angry hornet. Headlight beams hit the trees . . . and farther up, more light reflected against the leaves: The light from the library had turned back on.

He pointed to the left at a cluster of Victorian-style bungalows and bellowed, "That's where I'm staying. Too many neighbors," he added, as if explaining to me why we didn't hold our pow-wow there.

Miles downshifted and I held on as the Vespa worked its way up the incline. Above us, on the hill, the Victorian-style mansion that was the admin building perched like a vampire on a rooftop, waiting to spring. We thrummed through the mostly empty parking lot, past the dark stained glass windows.

Then we forked left, down the bypass where Troy had seen the burning ghost, and I could feel my heartbeat picking up. Was she a manifestation of Celia? I was on a scooter, unprotected; what if we saw her? What if she was mad at me for getting rid of her and came after us?

"Ouch, you're hurting me!" Miles shouted above the whine of the engine.

"Sorry." I tried to unclench my hands. I couldn't. I was too scared.

Then I recognized the landscape of my dreams of the screaming ghosts. It was all around us; I had been here with Celia—maybe in my mind, maybe out of my mind. And I had a terrible thought: I had always assumed that all I had to do to end the possession was free myself from Celia. But what if the possession worked two ways—what if *my* spirit or soul, or whatever it was, could be taken from my body and sent somewhere else?

"Ouch!" Miles bellowed. He batted at my hands. "Stop it!"

SEVEN

"I DON'T LIKE motor scooters," I muttered as we were led to a dark table in the back. I was disappointed. "Roadhouse" was another word for dirty, grungy bar. I hadn't ever been inside one of those—I was sixteen, and a fake ID could only take you so far—but I remembered the fancy spa Troy had taken me to for dinner and wished we could have gone there instead.

I sat gingerly on cracked brown pleather upholstery. A varnished wood table separated Miles and me. A red glass candle surrounded by white plastic netting flickered and spit. The silent waiter in jeans and a black corduroy shirt set down two small, greasy laminated menus. We were far away from the other patrons, who were playing pool, drinking beer, and watching a basketball game on ESPN. Miles ordered two Diet Cokes and some nachos without asking me what I wanted.

After the waiter ambled away, Miles opened the messenger bag and pulled out a stack of rumpled papers, a notebook with a jeweled cover, and a joint, which rolled onto the table. I gaped at it.

"Whoops," he said, stuffing the joint back into the bag.

"You brought drugs on campus? Don't you know we have zero tolerance?"

"Oh, sweetie." He stuck out his lower lip, making a sad face. "You are adorable beyond the telling." He patted the bag, where the joint now rested. "I guess there's no sense in asking you if you want to light up after this."

"No." Drugs had always been out back home in San Diego. Jane decreed that they were off-limits. A point in her favor. There were some. No queen bee was without her positive qualities.

"So." He didn't really care what I thought about drugs. He unfolded a piece of paper and tapped his finger on it. It was a list, written in Mandy's bad handwriting. No queen bee is without her failings, either.

possessions:
full moon
mirror
candle
item belonging to dead person
part of dead person (hair, bone, etc.)
"Part of dead person?" I cried.

"Could you please yell louder?" He gave me a look.

"Where could she find . . . ?" I thought back to my night-mares. I had believed that the ashes of the girls who had died had been thrown into the lake. I had worried that some of those ashes had been left behind in the operating theater and that I had actually walked through them. But Celia had shown me a grave in a forest. Maybe this was why.

"I didn't have any of that stuff," I said. I looked at the list again. "Absolutely nothing. It was broad daylight, okay, except it was foggy. And I got . . . " I lowered my voice as he crossed his eyes at me. *"Possessed,"* I hissed.

"This must have been to get the ball rolling," he said, tapping the list. "Your girl—Celia—maybe she caught a ride on what Mandy had already started." It was too weird that he was almost bragging on Mandy's being first.

"Well, it was a total accident, at least on my part," I said. "She told me she did it to hide from Belle and the other five."

"Hide." He set the paper aside and opened up the notebook. "They're all dead. Why not, you know, let it go?"

"They're angry. Terrible things were done to them. Celia…" I stopped. It had become second nature to me to brace myself for repercussions when I started talking about Celia.

Miles leaned toward me, locking gazes with me. His eyes flared.

"Celia?" he whispered. "Celia, Celia . . . "

Come to me.

Come to me.

They said if you said it five times . . .

"Don't," I said. "If she's gone, I don't want her back."

Something flickered over his face. I was an idiot. He *wanted* Celia to show. He wanted to see how it worked, maybe even talk to her. Maybe he wasn't even interested in helping Mandy either.

No. He loved *her*. Me? I was just convenient. Help me? Only if it worked out that way.

I wanted to stomp off, show my outrage, but he had the

transportation *and* Mandy's notes. I had never fully trusted him, so it wasn't like I was getting any big surprise here.

"Let me see everything," I ordered him, grabbing the jeweled notebook before he could stop me. It really was beautiful, with purple and green stones set in embossed swirls decorated with gold. I had started a journal when I came to Marlwood. I'd fancied myself quite a writer. My killer personal essay was what had snagged me a place on the wait list, despite my precipitous drop in GPA. But I'd learned very quickly that some things were best not written down.

"I want to see your news clipping," he said, "when you move back in."

The waiter chose that exact time to return with our Diet Cokes and an oval red plastic container loaded with tortilla chips and pale orange cheese goo, a few sad little jalapeños scattered over the mound.

"Yum," Miles said appreciatively as he scooped up a chip and carried it to his mouth. A purple flush crept up my neck. I recalled the last time he'd used that word: kissing me. He bobbed his head, inviting me to partake.

"Not big on 'em," I said, mostly to make a point that he should have consulted me before ordering.

"Yeah-huh." He pushed the container toward me. "I won't, you know, dump you once we figure this stuff out. I said I'd help you, and I will."

I didn't believe him. "What if the only way Mandy can get free of Belle is by doing something to me?" I asked, and the purple flush continued its march across my face.

He froze with a chip halfway to this mouth. "You scamp.

Celia's already told you how to free yourself, hasn't she? *You are supposed to do something to Mandy.*"

"No." I turned the page, to another list.

possessions in basement:
portrait
group photos
china doll
mourning brooch (lock of hair?)

There was a sketch of a floor plan labeled *B*. For "basement," I supposed. I blinked as I visually traced the layout of Jessel's basement. It had the L shape that reminded me of a hunchback when I looked down on it from Grose. Running along the back, where Mandy had written *DOOR*, were two lines that led into the basement from a ninety-degree angle, then appeared to rise up out of the L shape at an incline. She had written *TUNNEL!* And continued the angle, connecting it to a trapezoid, she had marked *ATTIC*.

So Mandy had known there was a tunnel in the attic, which I had stumbled upon—literally—when I lost my balance trying to escape from the haunted wheelchair. I fell through the thin wall into the tunnel . . . and the wheelchair had followed me. *Followed* me. How had I stayed sane after that?

Maybe the wheelchair wasn't really haunted, I thought. *Maybe she rigged it up to move when I was up there.* She had had access to all kinds of high-tech spook-house equipment, which her dorm, Jessel, had used to make the most elaborate haunted house that I'd ever been to outside of a theme park. She had also souped up the old library for one of her legendary pranks, terrifying two Marlwood girls, Sangheeta and Megan, as a hazing initiation to get into her superclique—those girls not realizing, of course, that Mandy was setting them up to be possessed.

Did Miles know about that? That Mandy provided girls for Belle's ghost clique so they could possess them?

I looked at the tunnel again. The wheelchair had chased me down that tunnel, and I had eventually escaped through the door, right there. It was the first time I had seen Celia's ghost hanging in the air. I had felt her slide right into my body. I shivered at the memory.

It's over. I crossed my fingers.

"Hello?" Miles said, tapping the map. "Am I boring you?"

At different places around the basement there were *X*s. Four. For the four items on her list, I was guessing. She hadn't labeled them. I don't suppose she needed to, since these were her personal notes.

"I saw a couple of these things in Jessel," I said. "The group photos are on the mantel. And the portrait, if it's the same one . . . " I trailed off. The portrait of Belle (so I had assumed) was in Mandy's room, and it was creepy. A large daguerreotype framed in worm-eaten wood; half of Belle's face had been eaten away by mold.

I had seen the picture when I had snuck into Mandy's room with Rose. And that was when we had seen the kinky photographs of Mandy with Miles. It made perfect sense that I would have been in Mandy's room at some point in my life, but I was so uncomfortable about the photographs of her and Miles that I lost track of what I was saying.

"Look," I said.

At the bottom of the page, there was a large bubble outline in brown, with an arrow pointing to the words: ***body part!!!!***

"You are such a liar. She *did* tell you how to get unpossessed," he said. "Do you need one of Mandy's body parts to break the spell? Will any Winters body part do?" He leered at me. "C'mon, baby, I'm happy to give it up."

"Sorry, I'm not your type. I'm not related to you," I snapped, still thinking of the pictures, flipping the page. A plane ticket was taped in the center of the page, surrounding by swirls and exclamation points in neon shades of puffy gel. And across the bottom of the page, *YES!*

"You . . . *bitch*," Miles ground out. I glanced up. He was staring at me as if I'd slapped him. As I blinked, he grabbed the notebook away from me.

"What? Why are you so angry?"

He clenched his teeth. "You know why. You know exactly why."

"No." I shook my head. "I don't."

He rose out of his seat, pulled out his wallet, and dropped a twenty on the table. Then he gathered up all the papers and crammed them into his messenger bag.

"Don't mess them up!" I yelled at him. "What's wrong?" He didn't look at me as he stomped toward the front door. He was furious. Following him, I replayed the conversation. *Oh. God.* I had made a crack about his supposed incestuous relationship with Mandy. But so had he. Crossing boundaries. He'd said that, right? No?

He hadn't meant *that*?

"Miles," I called after him. Two guys in ball caps playing

pool looked at me and chuckled. Look at those crazy kids, having a lovers' quarrel. *Hyuk*. "Hey, I'm sorry."

He let the door slam in my face. I grabbed the knob and propelled myself toward him, discovering en route that it was raining. Hard. I hadn't heard rain on the roadhouse roof, but within seconds I was drenched. I hadn't brought an umbrella.

He was sitting on the Vespa with the messenger bag slung over his shoulder. The engine started humming, and he pushed up the kickstand and held out my helmet. As I took it, he sat staring straight ahead, as if he couldn't stand the idea of riding with me but knowing that he had to take me home.

I slid in behind him, wet body to wet body. I sneezed, hard. The Vespa rolled forward toward the road and I hastily put on the helmet, fastening the chin strap.

"I'm sorry," I said as lightning crashed and thunder rumbled. He didn't respond—I was sure he couldn't hear me—so I tapped him on the shoulder. He leaned to the left and turned his head in my direction. I could barely make out his face through the sheets of rain; it stretched and blurred the way Celia's did when it was reflected back to me on a curved surface—a bronze drinking fountain, a stainless steel teakettle. It frightened me. I was afraid to ride with him—but more afraid to stay.

"Sorry," I mouthed.

He turned back around. I put my feet up on the running board and looked at the rain hitting the messenger bag. I tapped his helmet again.

"You should let me hold that," I yelled, giving the bag a tug. "It's going to soak through."

I couldn't believe he wasn't being more careful with it. They were Mandy's notes, possibly the key to everything. We should be back in the roadhouse, studying them. They might be getting ruined as we sat there.

Maybe he'd scanned them in his computer to archive them. But still, there might be something about the originals— something on the originals—strands of hair, ash, magic juju powder—that he wouldn't be able to duplicate. The way he had crammed them in all higgledy-piggledy was incredibly careless. He couldn't give them back without her knowing that someone had taken them. Maybe he'd gotten her permission? Maybe she even knew we were out together.

I tapped his helmet again. "We should go back inside. The bag is soaking through."

The Vespa started rolling. Lightning flashed and I pulled on the messenger bag, trying to shield it with my hand, at least. As if to shake me off, he swooped the moped to the right, forcing me to grab onto him, and we zoomed off into the storm.

I was furious. He was going to regret this. Just like I was regretting my mean little swipe at him. Wow, he could dish it out, but he sure couldn't take it.

More lightning, more thunder, and I thought about the slickness on the road. I hoped he would calm down. At least we couldn't go very fast; if it had been a motorcycle, I might have rethought my plan to go with him.

We rounded a corner and he leaned far into it. I almost put my foot down to keep us upright, but at the last moment we straightened out. The road was dark; there were no overhead lights, and the Vespa's beam shone weakly against the storm. I couldn't see around his shoulders and I lost track of where we were.

Then three flashes of lightning flared one after another and I saw that we had reached the part of the road where I had seen the ghost girls screaming in my druggy dream. The wind whipped up and a low wail wrapped itself around us. I held him more tightly, leaning my head against his back as I stared out at the trees rising and falling in the wind. Blurs of white flickered through the skeletal silhouettes. Ghosts.

Not there, not there, I told myself. My heart was pounding. I wanted to get out of here.

Then his spine straightened, and he reared back against me. My grip was broken, and I flailed, fighting to hang on. I caught the messenger bag. The Vespa wobbled. He pulled back again, and I was afraid I was going to fall off the back of the bike. I craned to look around him.

Something white in the middle of the road, running at us—

The Vespa listed right, shooting for the trees, the ones filled with ghosts, and I screamed as I went flying, straight for a tree—

—and someone dangling from it, with a white face and black eyes—

"Lindsay," I heard.

Did I smell geraniums?

Blackness.

EIGHT

"*LINDSAY,*" THE VOICE murmured. "*Lindsay, get out of here. You're not safe.*"

My head clanged. Something dripped on my forehead and I opened my eyes, then let out a gasp when I saw a white blob. But it was the moon, only the moon. I had fallen off the Vespa at the side of the road, and it looked like I might have rolled down a little embankment, coming to rest in a circle of trees. My helmet was still on, but my clothes were sopping wet.

The voice . . . had it been my mom? Hope clutched my heart as I tried to raise myself up on my elbows. My body was rubbery. "Memmy?" I whispered.

But as I shook myself out of my confusion, I knew very well that it hadn't been my mom. It was Celia's voice.

So she was back—or else she had never left. I wanted to burst into tears. Except . . . I didn't feel her presence inside me.

"Celia?" I whispered aloud.

Silence.

Then I heard footsteps through wet leaves, and I forced

myself to sit up. Miles was shuffling toward me. His helmet was cradled against his hip.

"Oh, shit," he said, seeing me. He dropped to his knees beside me and searched my face. He pushed hair out of my eyes. "God, Lindsay, are you okay?"

"I—I think so. My head kind of hurts."

"Did you black out? You might have a concussion." He opened up my eyelid and practically pressed his eye against mine. I pulled back. "I can't see anything."

He pushed back onto his feet and began to straighten, bringing me up with him by wrapping his gloved hands around my wrists. I turned and saw the Vespa at the top of the berm. It hadn't slid down with us.

"What did we hit?" I asked him, glancing fearfully around as my teeth chattered together. "Was it a ghost?"

"I don't know," he said. "I don't think we *did* hit it. I think I veered in time. But it all happened so fast."

I exhaled shakily, and we began to walk back up to the road. Miles let go of my hand and grabbed the Vespa by the handlebars, balancing it and bending over to inspect it. He rolled it back and forth. Then he touched the key, which was still in the ignition, and turned it. The engine started.

"I'm buying stock in this company," he crowed. He waved me over and had me take his place, keeping the scooter idling, while he walked out to the center of the road. There was nothing there.

"I know I saw something," he said.

"I did too. But it was raining so hard."

"It was coming at us. In the middle of the road." He ran

his hands through his hair. His retro ducktail was long gone, and the wet strands were slicked against his skull. There was rainwater in his platinum eyebrows and his eyelashes glistened. He looked otherworldly.

"If it was an animal . . . " I began. He looked over at me and shook his head.

"We need to get out of here."

"We need the messenger bag," I pointed out.

"Shit." He nodded. "You stay here."

I was grateful that I had to stay with the Vespa to make sure it kept working but a little ashamed that I was wimping out and letting him do the searching. Jane had reinforced the notion that girls didn't need guys for anything. We wanted them, yes. But we were perfectly fine without them. It was an excellent strategy for getting them interested in us.

"Celia, was it you?" I asked aloud. There was no response. "Was it someone else, who found out that Miles had taken Mandy's notes?"

I pictured all of Mandy's notes scattered down the hillside, the ink run to illegibility, the paper nothing more than a pulpy mess. I was furious with him all over again. Yes, I had been tacky, but he had been incredibly stupid.

I studied the road, then walked the moped over and placed it so the headlight would shine on the strip of road where the figure had appeared. I saw nothing but rain.

A roll of thunder made me jerk. I was shaking with cold; my teeth were chattering, and I was starting to feel more bumps and bruises. I kept scanning the landscape. No ghosts, no anyone. No Miles.

"Hey!" I called out, and my voice echoed off the darkness. I tried again. "Miles!"

Wind wafted against my cheek like a kiss. I touched my skin, turning in a circle. All my nerve endings were crackling. Something was watching us. Something was here. And it meant us harm. We had to leave.

"Miles!" I yelled. "Miles, come now! *Now!*"

I clamped down on the handlebars, making the engine roar. Pressing on the horn, I gave it a good blast.

Nothing.

"Oh, God," I whispered. We were out here with nothing, not even flashlights. I reached in my pocket and pulled out my wet cell phone. It wouldn't turn on.

I looked up and down the road, hoping to see an approaching vehicle. We hadn't left the roadhouse that long ago.

Crickets chirped. Raindrops plopped off the trees in a steady rhythm, *plink, plink, plink,* as if they were counting time.

No Miles.

"Miles!" I shouted. "Can you hear me?" I got on the Vespa and gave the handlebar a roll, moving forward. I'd never ridden a moped before, but it was fairly easy to figure out. After a couple of jerking forward motions, I wheeled around in a wide circle and rode to the edge of the berm. I looked down.

It was pitch black. The wind rustled through the trees, but I heard nothing that sounded like a guy looking for a messenger bag. My throat tightened. If someone had run us off the road, had they gone after Miles? Had they knocked him out, or were they using him as bait to get to me?

Run, I thought, and it wasn't Celia talking—it was me. But never in a million years would I leave Miles out here by himself.

"Miles, damn it," I shouted. "Answer me!"

I hovered on the top of the incline and thought about walking the Vespa down. I was afraid to turn it off for fear it wouldn't turn back on—or if I had to start it up alone, I wouldn't know how. On the other hand, I had no idea how much gas it would take to get back to Marlwood.

First thing's first.

"Miles!" I shrieked his name.

"Oh, God, Lindsay, *God*," he managed, bursting through the trees. His face was scratched, and there were pine needles in his hair. He scrambled toward me, losing his balance, sliding, grabbing onto a tree branch and pulling himself up.

I jumped off the bike and held out a hand. He grabbed it. Then he threw himself into my arms, trembling.

"We have to get out of here *now*," he said.

"But the bag . . . "

"Screw the bag." He hopped onto the seat and gazed expectantly at me. I climbed on and threw my arms around him. He wasn't wearing his helmet.

"Miles?" I called to him.

He didn't answer. I held on, peering around him, almost breaking down and cheering when a car passed us, then another. We didn't stop and ask for help. We just flew back to school as fast as we could.

In the parking lot, Miles killed the engine. We would have to drive farther to get to the infirmary. But we were within walking distance of my dorm.

"I'll take you to Grose," he said. "You can change your clothes. Maybe get Julie to look at your head. If I take you back to the infirmary like this, Trina will have a fit." He was distracted, raking his hair, glancing over his shoulder.

"What did you see?" I demanded. "You have to tell me." I wanted to hear that he'd seen something—but I was afraid to know what it was. And I was afraid he'd have a breakdown, the way Shayna did. Tonight might be the only time we had to talk about it. I was desperate for help. We'd been so close to finding answers, and then he'd lost the bag.

He walked beside me, wheeling the scooter along rather than leaving it behind in the parking lot. He was panting and shivering. There was a cut over his right eye that I hadn't noticed before. And he was muddy.

"I don't know what I saw. It was what I *felt*." He looked at the ground for a long time. "It was . . . horrible." He grunted. "It's the shits, you know? You get clean so you can face life head-on, like a man, and life throws this kind of crap at you."

"What did you feel?" I pushed. He was falling apart. I had to know before he completely lost it.

Beneath the moon, he turned and looked at me, and his face floated in the darkness. His eyes were dark sockets. He looked like a ghost, and he scared me.

"I felt . . . I felt that if I didn't leave there then, I would never leave," he whispered. "I felt like I was . . . dead." He shook. "God."

I put my arms around him. His heart was pounding so fast I was afraid he would pass out. He hesitated, and then he put his arms around me. We clung to each other so hard I was afraid one of us would crack apart. I was holding Miles Winters. He cupped my head and leaned it against his chest. I heard his heart beating way too fast.

"I kept calling you," I said. "I didn't see you anywhere."

"I fell into . . . I think it was a grave. It was full of mud and rocks, but I just knew . . . I thought I was lying on bones . . . " He pressed his forehead against the top of my head.

Celia's grave? I thought. *The one I dreamed about? Body parts?*

"But why didn't you answer me?" My voice was shrill.

"I didn't hear you," he replied. "I couldn't hear anything. I was screaming at the top of my lungs, but I didn't even hear myself."

I couldn't imagine how terrifying that must have been for him. Even thinking about it made my stomach clench and my knees wobble.

"That place was haunted," he said. "Wasn't it?"

"Yes."

He shook his head. "It was . . . interesting. Fun. Ghost-busting. Another Miles and Mandy adventure. Until this."

"Welcome to my world," I said wanly.

He exhaled. "I need a cigarette. And a bottle." He smirked. "And a hookah and a bong and stuff you've never even heard of, Snow White."

"What happened to the messenger bag?" I asked him.

His smirk faded. "God, I screwed that up."

"Yeah, you did." I couldn't help my deep, red fury. "Miles, we had the answers. And you just freaked out and . . . "

"You freaked out too," he accused. "Okay, you pissed me off. I have anger management issues." He shook his head. "I sure could use that joint right now."

I batted at him, tears spilling. "Damn it, you're my backup. You're all I've got!"

He let me hit him. Then he grabbed my fist and said, "It's freezing out here. You'll get sick. Go inside."

"We have to go back to look for the bag," I said.

"Not tonight. Soon." He made a steeple with his fingers and pointed them at me. "Promise."

Then he turned and headed back toward the parking lot, and I pushed into the door. I shuffled down the hall as quietly as I could, whispers like the hushed conversations of ghosts following me every step of the way.

"Oh, my God, we have to tell Linz right away," Julie semi-shrieked.

Or maybe just the whispers of dorm mates.

I pushed open the door to the room I shared with Julie to find everyone there, sitting in the dark on my and Julie's bed. The white head glinted, as if it turned to look my way.

"What?" I asked.

Julie would have screamed if Marica hadn't slapped her hand over her mouth.

BOOK TWO: DEEP DARK SECRETS

Anger is a wound gone mad.

—Vanna Bonta

If you don't break your ropes while you're alive, do you think ghosts will do it after?

—Kabir, 1440–1519

NINE

February 24
possessions: me
  my shame
  my fear
  my secrets
  my hope: can we stop this? or will it stop us? do I have what it takes to see this through? or will I fall apart and bail? will they win?

  haunted by: knowing I could die at any second. Or I could go crazy. I could stop being me altogether—the worst fate I can imagine.
  listening to: the screams in the forest and the screams in my head.
  mood: freaked, confused, chaotic. hopeful.

possessions: them
  there are so many "thems" now, all having different things:

things they don't want
things they can't have
things that they are

haunted by: the distressed dead, the enraged, the infuriated.
listening to: the bumps in the night.
mood: bedeviled.

———

"GOD!" JULIE WHISPERED as Marica uncovered her mouth. "Linz, you scared me half to death." She leaned backward and flicked on the lamp on the nightstand between our beds. My friends stared at me as if I were a ghost, and I couldn't help but turn around and look behind myself to make sure there *wasn't* a ghost behind me.

Julie hopped up from the bed. "Linz, what happened to you?" she cried. "Did Mandy beat you up?"

"*What?* I had an accident," I said. I hadn't thought through what to tell them. I figured my outing with Miles had better stay a secret. But I didn't know what else to say.

"An *accident?* What kind of accident? Where did you go? Did you fall out of your hospital bed?" Claire asked me. The others shushed her, and I shut the door. Our housemother hardly ever checked up on us, but if she did investigate the ruckus, I would be busted.

"I . . . found a motor scooter," I said. "Outside the infirmary. And I took a ride. And I skidded."

"Your forehead is all bumpy," Julie said, reaching out to touch it. I instinctively pulled away, but she gently took my hand and walked me closer to the nightstand. I saw the white head, its porcelain forehead gleaming. Sometimes David Abernathy drilled right through the forehead to do the lobotomies. Had he believed the bone would grow back? Or did his victims have little holes there forever? Is that what killed them?

"Did you black out? Because blacking out is bad," Ida said. "Do you feel sick to your stomach?" She moved her hand in front of my face; and as she did so, I swore the head *moved*. I kept that to myself too. They hadn't seen it. They never saw things like that. And if I brought it up, they would take it as proof that I had some kind of brain injury.

"I just need to sit down," I said, and Julie eased me down onto my own bed, positioning me as if I had lost control over my arms and legs. I was shaking hard. I sneezed.

"You should get out of your wet clothes," Julie said. "I'll get your pajamas."

"What were you guys talking about? And why would Mandy beat me up?" I asked as she crossed to my dresser and Claire yanked up my bedspread and wrapped it around my shoulders. Though I acknowledged her kindness with a nod, inwardly I winced. Now my beautiful antique coverlet— compliments of Marlwood—was caked with mud. How would I explain that to our housemother?

I pulled back the covers and started to take off my sopping clothes. The layers peeled away like sheets of ice. There was a big bruise on my left forearm and a large scrape on my shoulder.

"Well, while you were out joyriding," Claire said, "so was Mandy. Well, not with any joy."

"No joy," Elvis agreed.

"I'm getting some bandages from the first aid kit in the kitchen," Julie announced, leaving the room.

I raised my brows and looked at Claire, waiting to hear the rest. The others girls were nodding at me, as if I had missed the dish of the century.

"Troy broke up with her," Claire said. "And she went cuckoo."

"He what?" I asked. My heart actually leapt. I felt it. He'd done it. I'd stopped believing that he actually would.

"Yeah. He said she was too messed up," Claire reported. She was grinning like a fox on a hunt, or a vampire contemplating a nice big neck vein filled with the blood of fantastic gossip. This was huge, and even better, it had happened to Mandy Winters. Extra bonus: they knew Troy and I were crushing and that only his lack of spine—his officially breaking up with Mandy—had kept us from being a couple.

Until now.

"Mandy left campus," Ida added. "We figure she went to cry on Miles's shoulder. Which is six kinds of skanky, but there it is."

"No," I began, almost telling them that Miles had been with me, but I stopped. I replayed what had happened: Miles had told me his car was in the shop. But what if Mandy had it? He had taken me to the roadhouse to paw through her things, but he'd been incredibly careless with them. What if there was nothing but a pile of fake "clues" that he and Mandy had created together?

And why drive over there in the first place? What if *she* had waited for us on the rainy, dark road and Miles had crashed on purpose? Would he deliberately risk getting hurt like that? *If he wanted to help his sister scare you to death, then yes, given how crazy he is,* I told myself. *Scare you, or . . .*

. . . kill you.

I shuddered even harder.

"How do you know all this?" I asked, and my voice cracked.

Claire raised her hand. "I was in the bathroom. I saw the light go on in her room. Lara was in there and Mandy was going just crazy, throwing things."

"No way," Julie said. "What about their housemother?"

Claire snorted. Our housemothers were legendary for doing as little as possible, especially if it came to getting in the way of rich girl self-expression.

"So I crawled out the bathroom window and snuck over there. I had made it to the hedge when they came outside. I hid and listened. And I heard *everything*."

"Go, Claire," Elvis said appreciatively.

"Mandy was completely freaking out. She said she was going to go kill someone."

"No," I whispered. By then I had stripped out of my wet clothes and pulled on my fleece bathrobe.

"Your name was not mentioned," Claire assured me. "I figured she was going to kill Troy."

"But we like Troy," Marica argued. "Now he can be Lindsay's *novio*."

"Well, we'd rather have her kill him instead of Lindsay,"

Claire said, and Marica nodded. "Anyway, then she split. I wasn't about to follow her in my pajamas and flip-flops."

Elvis huffed. "I don't know why not. I mean, we're all dying to know what she did next."

"No, we're not," Julie said firmly, returning with a roll of gauze, a box of bandages, some tape, and a pair of scissors. "I don't care at all what happens to her."

Julie did care. She had moved into Mandy's charmed circle for a time, then been tossed back out. Despite her loyalty to me, she had enjoyed her moment in the sun. But in the bipolar ways of mean queen bees, Mandy had abruptly yanked away the privileges she had bestowed on Julie. She ditched her to go skiing with Miles during winter break, and then she drove back to Marlwood without her, even though Julie—and her parents—had been counting on the ride.

As for me, I was grateful down to my soul that Mandy had dissed Julie. Because Julie had been full-on possessed, and now that she was free of Mandy, she was free of the possession. Hurt and embarrassed because of it, but Julie nonetheless.

"I wonder why Lara didn't go with her," Ida said. She stood up to help as Julie began to wrap gauze around my head. I wasn't sure what they were hoping to accomplish.

"Maybe she doesn't want to go to juvenile hall?" Julie asked, sniffing.

"Oh, please, as if any of them would ever get busted for anything they did," Claire said. "Look at Kiyoko." Everyone fell silent. I *had* looked at Kiyoko. I was the only person in the room who had seen her dead body. Her eyes had been shiny and silvery, like fish scales, a sure sign that she had drowned. But by the time she washed up onshore, she was frozen. Her hair was so brittle it broke off when they laid her in the body bag, zipped it up, and Life Flighted her away.

"*Chicas,* we are taking away from *Lindsay's* joy," Marica declared. She beamed at me. "Troy did it!"

"Yes." I finally let myself smile. Several of my layers of individuality were more thrilled about Troy's manning up than they were terrified about what happened earlier in the evening. Handsome, wealthy, funny, warm Troy, who had tried much harder than Riley ever had to be honest in his dealings with the fairer sex. Troy, who had whispered, "I love you," when he thought I was asleep. To *me.* After I had hit him with a hammer. That Troy.

"He's trying to talk his parents into spring break in San Diego," I told the others. A couple of them cheered softly, Ida and Julie doing the grinning-teasing-eyelash-fluttering thing girls did when one of their own moved from unrequited crush to victorious coupledom.

"We are *so* going to have to double-date," Julie crowed. "Spider wants to take me to a party at the Stinking Rose restaurant in Beverly Hills. It's all garlic. They have a private room called Dracula's Grotto."

"Cool," I said, beginning to shake off my fear in anticipation of good times to be had with Troy. This *could* end happily. I had almost stopped believing in the notion of a good time without a catch.

"There," she added, stepping away from her handiwork as

she cut the gauze with the scissors and tucked the loose end into the headband she had created for me. Then she frowned slightly at me. "Ooh, creepy."

Marica grimaced. "She's hurt worse than it looks."

"What's wrong?" I asked. I got up and moved to the mirror over my dresser—roses etched into the antique glass—and peered at myself. With the heavy bandage around my head, I looked like a wounded colonial soldier. Directly in the center of my forehead, a circle of bright red blood was seeping through the layers. The lobotomy zone. Did it *mean* anything?

I stared at it, bracing myself for a wave of fear and panic, but I felt . . . okay. Almost detached. I did have a bump on my forehead. It was bleeding. There was nothing supernatural about it.

"Maybe we should unwrap it," Julie suggested, handing me my cloud pajamas.

"No, it's okay." I took the pajamas. "Thanks."

I headed for the shower, bracing myself for a fresh wave of fear. I spent the majority of my days and nights at Marlwood in abject terror—either mine or Celia's—and we had shared many horrible moments in the Grose bathroom. But this time, as I put down my pj's and took off my bathrobe, I felt nothing. It was so odd and unexpected that I burst out laughing.

I showered, washing my hair, shaking it out as if I were some kind of poodle, remembering the bandage too late but leaving it on for the sake of my friends. My pajamas smelled like clean cotton.

I went back into my room, bundled up in the too-cute ski parka CJ had sent me (not even she could be right one hundred percent of the time when it came to clothes) and told everyone I was going to sneak back into the infirmary so I wouldn't get in trouble. Julie insisted on going with me. But I didn't want her to come back alone, so Marica volunteered to come too.

We headed out like the three Musketeers, tiptoeing around puddles and trying not to make any noise. I couldn't believe that Troy had finally done it. It was so amazing. This had been one of the most extreme nights of my life.

When we reached the door of the infirmary, my phone vibrated. So it hadn't been ruined after all. Life just kept getting better and better. I raised a gloved hand, and my escort halted. Pulling out my phone, I saw that I had four texts and a voice mail. The texts were from Troy, trying to get my attention, then telling me to check my voice mail.

This was it. My supreme moment of triumph. I looked at my two friends and whispered, "Troy." They lit up.

I hit voice mail and put the phone to my ear. Julie did a little dance and gave Marica a hug. Marica laughed silently and they both grinned at me, thrilled.

"Hello, Lindsay," it began. *"I—I'm sorry to do this over the phone but . . . "*

He didn't sound very happy. My stomach clenched.

" . . . I've been thinking and, I, well, the hammer thing did kind of bother me. A lot. So, I'm sorry, but . . . I . . . I'm just not ready . . . "

Then he was gone. I looked down at the phone to see if there was another message. If he'd been cut off and called back to tell me he was not ready to have his life ruined by Mandy. But some of my layers of individuality already knew that he wasn't ready to have his life ruined by *me*. I was a life ruiner. I'd hit him with a hammer.

But he said he loved me, I thought. I stood at the door, staring at Marica and Julie, numb and cold and shattered.

"No Troy," I managed. "For me."

Marica understood first. "He broke up with *you* too?" she asked.

I swallowed hard. Then I put my phone back in my pocket before I broke down and played it again just to hear his voice. Pathetic, lovesick girls did things like that.

My phone sat in my pocket like a burning piece of charcoal. My head pounded. I waited for Celia to say, *"See? I warned you about him. They're all the same."* But I still had no sense of her being anywhere around.

"Oh, Lin-Lin, I'm so sorry," Julie murmured, drawing me into her arms. "I'm sorry."

I let her hug me. She was five inches taller than me, and I closed my eyes and leaned against her.

"There must be a misunderstanding," Marica protested. "When he confided in me, I practically expected him to propose to you."

"Maybe Mandy made up some lies about you when he broke up with her," Julie ventured. "Trashed you because if she couldn't have him, she didn't want anyone to have him."

"But Troy is smart. He would see through that," Marica said.

Julie patted my back. "He wasn't smart enough not to go out with Mandy in the first place."

Maybe she told him that we're both possessed.

I didn't want to cry in front of them; I really didn't. Just as I was on the verge of losing it, the infirmary opened. Ms. Simonet stood there in her puffy coat and gloves, as startled to see us as we were to see her.

"Lindsay," she said. "I . . . what are you doing out here?"

I still didn't know if Miles had gotten her permission to spring me, or snuck me out, or what. Tears spilled down my cheeks and I wiped my nose with the back of my glove.

"This guy she likes broke up with her," Julie said. "On the phone. So she came to see us. And—and she tripped on her way."

"Oh. Oh, dear." To my surprise, Ms. Simonet put her hand on my shoulder. "I'm sorry, Lindsay." She stared at my bandage. "This thing is soaking wet. And you're bleeding. Let's go take a look."

"Thanks for walking me back, guys," I said, sniffling, wishing I could just disappear. I wanted to be alone, to absorb the shock. All this time, I had assumed that Mandy was all that stood in the way between Troy and me. But I was in the way too. I was my own worst enemy when it came to Troy.

Had Jane been there, she would have laughed at me. To her, guys were accessories—eye candy, arm candy, playthings, status symbols. She had lectured us over and over never to "cave" and actually *like* a guy. That gave them power over us . . . and we should never give up our power. Except to her, of course. She had even argued that she'd done me a favor by sleeping with Riley, as if it was just a reminder that no boy could be trusted.

Dejected, I followed Ms. Simonet back into the infirmary. She led me into the bathroom and unwound the bandage. There was a big scrape on my forehead. Considering the fall I'd taken off the bike, it was a pretty light injury. Red eyes and a few tears hid the major damage.

She gave me another pat. After she checked my pupils with a light, she had me hold an ice pack against my forehead. I climbed obediently back into bed, head swimming, heart breaking.

And wondering what Miles had seen—or pretended to see—in the middle of the road.

TEN

THE NEXT DAY, Dr. Steinberg examined me and told me that as far as he was concerned, I could resume my normal life. I wanted to tell him I didn't have one of those, but I nodded and thanked him.

Shortly after he left, Dr. Morehouse stopped in. His expression was a mixture of sympathy and mild disapproval—after all, I'd snuck out—but Ms. Simonet had told him why I'd done it—my wretchedly true cover story—and he had the decency not to ask me how I felt about having my heart ground into the dirt.

"Dr. Steinberg thinks you're well enough to return to your dorm," he said, sipping the coffee that "Trina" had brought him. It was early, and my dormies had not yet shown up with breakfast. "Do you?" Did I think I was well enough as in . . . *Oh*.

"You mean, am I going to freak out again?" I asked bluntly.

He regarded me. "You are so refreshing. Your lack of guile."

I wondered how much experience he had working with adolescents. I lowered my gaze and coughed to mask the growling of my stomach. Now that I was being sprung, I had mixed feelings about my freedom. I wanted to burrow in private and cry a lot, and I liked being safely squirreled away where no one could try to kill me. Celia appeared to be gone; therefore, I was out of the game. Wasn't I?

"I thought you'd be up and packing to go back," he said, sounding surprised.

To my dorm, he meant. Not San Diego. More mixed feelings.

"It's the boy thing, huh," he said. "It's thrown you."

I sighed. I really didn't want to go into it. That was the problem with therapists. Everything was fuel for analysis and rehashing and sometimes—

"*Oh,*" I said, getting it. He thought I was more thrown than most because I'd had a breakdown when my mom died, and then I'd found out that my boyfriend had had sex with another girl. I'd left San Diego in disgrace, at least socially, and Marlwood was supposed to be my safe haven. But here, Kiyoko had died, and the boy I liked had broken up with me before he'd even become my official boyfriend.

"It's hard getting past a hammer attack," I said, and we both smiled sadly at each other. "Hammer time."

His kind smile reached his eyes, giving him crow's-feet and smile lines; it was genuine, and I liked him even better than before.

"I'm okay," I said. "I do want to get out of here. I'll never make it to Harvard if I don't get back to my classes."

"I detect a note of sarcasm."

"This is the school that's supposed to make it happen."

"Yes, indeed. That's the mandate. Okay. You can go back

to your dorm on the condition that you come to see me once a week."

If he could keep Celia away, I'd see him every day. I paused, waiting to see if she had something to say to that. Nothing. Maybe I had only imagined that she'd warned me after the crash. I was so used to hearing her commentary on my life and her constant badgering to do what I needed to do to free her: kill Mandy.

"I'm in Dr. Ehrlenbach's office for the moment."

So she was still gone? "Not Dr. Melton's?"

He grimaced. "There were issues in his office. Black mold behind the walls. I'm not supposed to tell the students."

But he was confiding in me to help me feel special. I knew that trick. I figured I knew most of them.

"It's cool," I said, when I realized he was still looking at me.

"You're really all right, Lindsay," he said to me. "You've just had more to deal with than you should have had. Sometimes life's not fair that way."

Ya think? Saying that aloud would have been perceived as hostile, or whiny, or both, so I just smiled weakly at him.

He left, and I took a shower, poised to endure Celia's flashbacks and for seeing her reflection in the mirror. Still nothing.

"Thank you," I said aloud to Dr. Morehouse, even though he couldn't hear me.

My dormies, fabulous in cashmere and wool, leather and silk, came to bring me breakfast, carrying covered plates and trays and coffee carriers, and this time they brought Rose. Rose Hyde-Smith, my capering clown buddy, smart and sassy. . . and once very possessed.

"Linzita," she said, throwing her arms around me. She was decked out in her bad-pixie finery—fuchsia ruffle petticoat under a black skirt; black mock-turtleneck sweater, and an engraved copper pocket watch dangling on a chain around her neck. Her hair was slicked back, and I realized for the first time that she looked a little bit like the actress Emily Blunt.

"Hi, Rose, guys," I said. I had on my raggedy jeans and Doc Martens, Memmy's sweatshirt, and my army jacket. Quite a sight.

"Linz, Linz, who loves you best?" she cooed. "Oh, my God." She covered her mouth, giggling. "Listen to this. Troy broke up with Mandy."

I swallowed hard. "Yeah, wow."

"You already knew. How did you know?" She looked from me to the others, narrowing her eyes and pursing her lips. "Did you install webcams in Jessel?"

"In Mandy's laptop," I said. "Because we, y'know, really *care* about what she does." My voice sounded sharp and mean; I felt sharp and mean. I'd been broken up with too. I didn't want to be the subject of gossip, the way Mandy was, but I didn't want to hear about Troy the heartbreaker all day.

"Woof," Rose said. "High time you got out of there. Cabin fever made baby cranky." She leaned forward and scrutinized my forehead. She whistled. "How did *that* happen?"

"It just did, okay?" I stomped past her, suddenly feeling injuries I didn't know I had.

"Jeez, wait up," she called after me. Everyone else stayed quiet and kept their distance. I wished they wouldn't.

The sky was low and cloudy; the threat of imminent rain glowered over our heads as we walked toward the dining commons. Girls strode past us, heads together, giggling and chatting as if no one had seen each other for months instead of hours. A few came up to me and said hi and that they were glad I was better. No one seemed to know about the horrible scene in the operating theater. Stellar damage control. Or was Mandy just waiting for the exact right moment to use it against me?

"Hey, sorry," Rose said, catching up to me. "For whatever." She leaned around me and crossed her eyes at me in a gesture of endearment, but I could see that the love wasn't really there. In her eyes, I had slighted her by becoming friends with Shayna— and I had become friends with Shayna because Shayna knew what was going on.

We had excluded Rose because neither one of us could fully trust her. We were afraid she'd tell Mandy any secrets that we shared. Now Shayna was gone, Rose didn't know what had happened to her, and there was a dark void between us. She didn't remember texting me when Mandy and the others abandoned her in the lake house, didn't know that she'd gotten possessed that night and taunted me, promising that she was going to kill me.

"You know what, I'm—I'm not hungry," I said. "I think I'll go for a walk."

I walked back to Ida, who was carrying my coffee, and Claire, who had a muffin. I took them, murmuring my thanks, and hung a right, past the library and into the sculpture garden.

It was pretty crazy that I went there, and I really didn't want to. I just needed to be alone and it was the closest spot. I'd spent an entire week holed up in the infirmary—just me and my nightmares—but now, when I needed to roll up into a ball and cry, I was surrounded by chattering girls.

In the sculpture garden, not so much.

I looked at the sexy statues with their massive chests and barely covered "intimate areas" and lowered my head. I tried to force back the tears, but they came, hard. A hundred fragmented fantasies blipped through my mind. Troy lived in a world of private jets, shopping crawls, and surprise trips to Paris. He knew Prince Harry.

So did Mandy.

That would continue to be her world, even if she and Troy weren't together. And I had tried to hold that world in contempt—all those rich, snobby people, with their preoccupation with *things*—but the truth was, I had been looking forward to being treated like a princess—even if it was only for a little while. I was mad at him for breaking up with me and madder at myself because I felt like I deserved it. I had messed up again. I didn't measure up again.

And suddenly, as I was fuming over Troy, I found myself remembering how angry I had been with my father, because he had seemed so passive when my mother was dying. I found out about an online medical search engine called Medline, and I kept e-mailing my parents information about clinical trials and experimental procedures. But they didn't investigate any of them. They didn't even open up half the attachments.

"Memmy doesn't want to do that," he'd told me. "The cancer is too advanced. She just wants to spend the time she has with us."

When I tried to argue, he said, "It's her life, sweetie."

"But she's *my* mom," I'd argued with him, weeping. "She doesn't get to decide things like that when's she got a kid."

I couldn't believe that she'd chosen to give up and die. It was cowardly. And it was selfish. She should have fought with every ounce of strength she had to stay with us.

I'd kept collecting articles. I'd printed them out in a big file and got a huge shoulder bag to carry them around in. I would pull them out and read them every chance I got.

And the one time I'd been alone with her in the hospital, the one time I could have talked to her about it without my dad around, she'd started talking incessantly, just babbling, and I hadn't had the chance.

Didn't make the chance, Jane would have said.

But these tears weren't about my mom. They were about Troy. It was just that every time I was sad about anything, missing my mom came along for the ride. I didn't know if I could ever get rid of it. I didn't know if I wanted to. Missing her was almost like having her with me.

As I was wishing for a tissue, my phone rang. We didn't usually get phone coverage on this part of the campus, and I was startled. I jerked, grabbed it, and connected.

"Lindsay," Troy said.

I closed my swollen eyes. *He's changed his mind,* I thought. I felt as if someone had just strapped me into a roller coaster. I was so nervous I couldn't make a sound.

"Lindsay?"

I tried to clear my throat.

"I'm so sorry," he rushed on.

Yes. Yes, yes, yes.

"I hated doing that on voice mail."

I imploded. He hadn't changed his mind after all.

"But you did it," I said, and disconnected.

I turned around and saw Julie and Elvis heading toward me. The others were lagging behind, watching. Rose was swinging her petticoat in little half circles. I smelled bacon and coffee. And mud. I heard a bird trilling. I was hyperaware of everything, and I knew this was a moment I would never forget.

Then my phone rang again. I wasn't going to answer it. If he heard me crying, I would never forgive myself.

But I glanced down at the faceplate and saw that it was Heather again. I looked up at Julie and Elvis, just a few feet away, and held up a hand. Julie blinked and smiled, clearly assuming I was talking to Troy.

Turning my back, I swallowed hard, took a breath, and connected.

"Hey," I said hoarsely.

"Oh, my God, I'm so glad you picked up. My mom dropped me off early because I have this stupid yearbook meeting, which I did *not* want for my elective, but who cares because you are *not* and I mean *not* going to believe what happened two minutes ago."

I sniffled. "You gave birth."

"Fea!"

"Taylor Lautner asked you out."

"Are you *ten*? You won't guess. Lindsay, Riley threw down with Jane. In front of everyone. He dumped her and then he turned around to all their friends—you know, *your* old friends—and he told them that she was a poser and a user and she didn't really care about any of them. And that he was sick and tired of hearing her diss the world and he was sorry for every time she had said something mean about one of them and that he had not told her to shut the hell up."

"You shut up!" I cried.

"Are you *nine*? Who says that anymore?"

"What did she do?" I couldn't believe what I was hearing. Telling off Jane. I couldn't imagine doing it. It would be like standing in front of a tiger and telling it to shoo.

"She laughed and said he was lying because she wouldn't have sex with him anymore."

"What?" I wiped my eyes. Julie gave me a questioning look and I waved my hand to let her know it wasn't more bad news. I wasn't sure what kind of news it was.

"Well, you know they're all pretty free about admitting they're doing the deed. She started talking about how *bad* he was at it. I think she convinced a few people. You know Jane. A total actress."

"What did Riley do?"

"Walked away."

"Well," I managed, "good for him."

"The point is, Lindsay, that I think he did it because he still has feelings for *you*. I think he's been sorry ever since it happened. And then you had the breakdown, and you left. But when you came home for Christmas and he saw you again, you flipped out again. So I'm thinking he blames himself that you keep going crazy."

"Wouldn't that make you want to run if you were a guy?" I asked, thinking of Troy.

"Not if you really cared," she replied firmly. "It might make a *nice* guy feel guilty. He really did like you."

"I thought," I began, and then I faltered. I had never told anyone what I thought. I lowered my voice. This was one of my deep dark secrets.

"I thought maybe Jane ordered him to hang out with me. Like, give the nerd a thrill. Or maybe to test his loyalty or something."

"Oh, my God, you have no self-esteem."

"This is news?" I asked. She was Heather. She had known me best. She'd understood when I started being so horrible. She'd known I'd been driven by the crazy promise of acceptance by Jane and her golden elite. Driven, and driven crazy. If she could see me now, in my jeans and my hair, surrounded by *Teen Vogue* models and bona fide, professional actresses, she'd know how hard I was fighting to prove that I was over and done with all that nonsense.

Troy. No more walks, or photography sessions, or meeting at my house for Monopoly and movies. Ever. *Troy.*

"Heather," I said, "this guy I really liked up here? He just broke up with me. I mean, we hung up and then you called."

Heather was quiet for a moment.

"That is entirely freaky, *fea*," she said. "But maybe it's fate. Maybe you're supposed to end up with Riley."

"A cheater."

"He made a bad mistake. But I think he regrets it, Linz."

Julie came forward and pulled out her cell, tapping the faceplate and frowning. Rose zoomed up and darted around her and swung her pocket watch back and forth, back and forth. Julie mouthed, *Going to be late.* I nodded at her.

"Maybe you'll come home *now*?" Heather asked me.

"Maybe," I said. If Celia was gone and Mandy—or someone else—had staged that accident . . . maybe I could just leave. Maybe the nightmare was finally over.

ELEVEN

THE GIRLS AND I walked into the commons for breakfast, and I made a concerted effort not to look in the direction of Mandy's table. Jessel sat together: Mandy, Lara, Alis, and Sangeeta. There had been five, with Kiyoko. Five of the possessed girls:

Belle Johnson

Lydia Jenkins

Anna Gomez

Martha St. Pierre

Henrietta Fortescu

First Kiyoko, and then Julie, and then Rose had been possessed by number six, Pearl Magnusen, the nicest of the batch. I didn't know where she was now. Neither Julie nor Rose remembered anything about it. And Kiyoko was dead.

I heard Mandy laugh, and Julie said under her breath, "She's pretending everything is fine."

"She's trying to retain some dignity, no?" Marica said, which was fairly close to defending Mandy. But Marica was a perpetual defender of class under pressure. Mandy *was* retaining her dignity.

"Everybody stay close to Lindsay," Julie ordered. "Mandy might not know . . . the circumstances."

"You mean that they're mutual dumpees," Rose said. "Might blame Lindsay for the breakup and challenge her to a topless whip duel." She flounced in her skirt.

Julie frowned and started to say something, but Rose jetted off for the serving lines. We sat down at our table and I could feel my head—and my heart—spinning.

I felt disoriented for the rest of the day, as if I were the new girl all over again—the irony being that we were all new. Marlwood had reopened after a century of serving as a retreat for the descendants of Edwin Marlwood. I wondered who they were and where they lived. If they minded that their school was back in session.

If I wasn't the only new girl, I was the newest. I had arrived later than everyone else, wait-listed until someone else decided not to stay. I had arrived academically behind everyone, and now, because of my time in the infirmary, I was desperately behind.

I lost track during discussions about all the academic camps and summer enrichment courses my fellow students were already enrolled in, both because they were so unattainable and because I was unfocused and dizzy. I didn't respond to the glossy gossip that Jilly Maguire, the actress who was in my biology class, was having some major plastic surgery done during break. I didn't even blink when someone mentioned that Lourdes Caprio had gotten a Porsche Boxter for her sweet sixteen.

All this was their version of normal. It was like watching a movie; I felt strangely detached. I grinned to myself when I thought of Riley calling Jane out. And then I found myself aching and heartsick when I remembered that Troy's message was still on my phone and that I should erase it.

But I couldn't—not yet.

———

ONE WEEK TO the night since the accident and the break-up, I was studying in the library. Rose was due to help me with math. We were doing probability theory, which I did not understand at all.

She darted over to my study carrel and leaned over me. I showed her the problems I was working on and she said, "Hmm, hmm," like a doctor examining my tonsils. "Okay, good. Keep going."

"Thanks." Most of our tutoring sessions were like that.

"Guess who wants to see me," she said in a low voice.

Troy? I almost blurted. But I just raised my eyebrows.

"Dr. Morehouse." She made a face. "Is this because you went loony on Valentine's, do you think?"

Of course she knew what had happened in the operating room even though she hadn't been there. Rose was a first-class observer and spy.

"It probably is," I told her. "Or else he wants to know if you still believe you're the lost princess of Atlantis."

"Or a virgin," she said, snickering. "Whoops, sorry, *you've* still got the white hat, huh. Troy didn't—"

"Rose, please, let's not talk about it." I picked up my pen.

"I'm sure Dr. Morehouse just wants to make sure everything's okay."

She scrunched up her face. "You can't like Dr. Freud, Lindsay. He sounds like a Norwegian. And he's so weird."

"You think so? I *do* kind of like him," I ventured, waiting to see her reaction. I was surprised that she thought he was weird. He seemed nice, even though he was a therapist.

"Eww." She made a show of shivering. "He's got you fooled, baby. Didn't you notice his eyes? Dead." She made her face go slack, and a chill ran down my spine. She did look dead.

"Well, anyway, don't worry. I won't say a word." She mimicked zipping her mouth shut and throwing away the key.

"A word about . . . ?" I looked up at her, and she blinked as if I were being deliberately clueless.

"Like, how, well, let's call it all the pure and total dysfunction." Mine or everybody's?

Rose ticked her gaze from me down to my hands. I was clenching the ends of the pen in my fists, as if I were going to snap it in two. My knuckles were white.

"Don't worry," she said. "Like I said, I'll cover for you."

"But you don't need to cover for me," I insisted.

"Okay." She patted the top of my head. "It's all good."

She turned to go.

"Rose," I said, and she turned back. "When's your appointment? I have to see him too. Maybe we'll run into each other there."

She sneered. "Tomorrow during free period. Does that not suck? I have to see him on my own time."

"That sucks," I affirmed. "Suckily."

"They're probably charging the parents. Not us, of course. But if money is involved, those super-rich moms and dads are going to want to see results." She made claws of her hands. "No more wackadoo, baby."

"Thank God we're poor. We can still be wackadoo," I replied.

I made a point of going back to my studying. She danced away, disappearing among the stacks. The library was busy, filled with other girls studying and whispering, catching up on e-mail on the library's computers. Even their after-school clothes were beautiful—cashmere sweats and hoodies, Italian silk scarves draped around their necks, diamond bangle bracelets and perfect, perfect nails.

About two minutes later, Mandy walked out of the same area of the library where Rose had gone. I ducked my head, avoiding contact, but I watched her. Mandy bore watching, always.

She was dressed in ghostly, foggy gray—gray sweats, gray turtleneck, gray hoodie lined with what I hoped was faux fur. Her hair hung like a platinum veil, concealing her profile, and she was walking stiffly, like someone who had been bedridden—like me this past week, like Memmy was before we knew what was wrong with her. Everything about her snapped into hypersharp focus. My heart pounded, and I shivered. I was afraid that if Mandy pulled back her hair, I would see Belle's face—white and dead, like Celia's.

She sailed past, unaware of my presence.

That's not Mandy, I thought, my stomach pulling at my backbone. *And whoever it is, she's done something to Rose.*

I stood. Mandy's back was to me, with her perfectly straight, shiny, silky hair. *If she turns around, I'll scream,* I thought.

She walked away.

My face tingled with cold, then heat, and I felt my forehead to see if I had a fever. My skin was cool.

I hurried to the row where I'd seen Rose disappear. There she was, at the other end. She was standing still, a mirror of Mandy, with her back to me. There was nothing unnatural about it, nothing scary, but I was uneasy, and I tiptoed away before she could see me.

Everything is fine, I told myself, sitting down. But how could that be? We were at Marlwood.

THE NEXT DAY, Rose dressed in what I had come to refer to as her "catering clothes"—white blouse, black skirt, black stockings. and black flats—her attempt to look, as she called it, "mundane." She paraded around at breakfast, talking fast. She was nervous. I knew she didn't like being summoned to the admin building for any reason. Rose wasn't exactly poor, but her family had significantly less money since her father's company had fallen apart during the recession. Besides me, Rose was the only other scholarship student that she and I knew about. She was positive they were itching to boot her because she had no looks, no clothes, and although she had a framed Cirque du Soleil poster in her room, her favorite group was the Dresden Dolls. One look at their website, she figured, and Dr. Ehrlenbach would boot her. Ehrlenbach was not a fan of people without money.

As Rose passed by our table, she gave me a little conspiratorial wink. It made me as nervous as she was.

At free period, I joined my dorm mates in the newly renovated "conservatory," which was a gift from Sangheeta Shankar's family. The conservatory was a Victorian structure made of glass, hunter green wood, and iron, though mostly of glass—lots and lots of small panes—and the interior was brimming with palm trees in black urns, trellises of ivy, and large, overstuffed furniture upholstered in thick green brocade that didn't quite match. There was also a fireplace with a white wood mantel.

The conservatory had opened while I was living in the infirmary, and each dorm was going to get use of it one day a month. Today was our day, and I was looking forward to the novelty. At ten-thirty, the beginning of free period, it began to rain, and we whooped and laughed as we trundled inside the glass jewel box. There was a fire crackling in the brick fireplace and we'd all brought cups of hot chocolate.

"Sangeeta, this is so cool," Julie said. "Your parents are angels."

Sangeeta smiled at Julie, flushed and proud. She sat in a chair with a flourish and sipped her chocolate. Then she gazed up toward the glass ceiling, at the rain.

"It rains as much here as in India," she said, "only it's much colder."

"Lindsay?" a voice said at the doorway. It was the new part-time clerical person who was helping the school secretary,

Ms. Shelley, in the admin building. I couldn't remember her name. "Ms. Shelley needs to see you. Something about a form for you to sign."

Everyone groaned for me. I was going to miss our conservatory time.

"Okay." I picked up my chocolate, jumping a little as thunder rolled around the glass building. Before she'd left, Dr. Ehrlenbach had decreed that I needed an extracurricular, even though my scholarship didn't cover it. She was trying to make me more college-worthy.

The woman turned on her heel and left. Marica handed me her umbrella. It was beige, navy, and red plaid. Burberry, maybe.

"Thanks," I said. "I'll bring it back."

I left, darting beneath a stand of pine trees. As I looked over my shoulder, Julie waved; then she flopped into one of the chairs and stretched out her arms, as if she were embracing the whole world.

I wasn't all that good with an umbrella; it hardly ever rained in San Diego, and we all had cars, so we never carried umbrellas around. I ran to avoid getting soaked to the skin, darting up the hill toward the admin building. It stood dark and stark against the clouds. I thought of Miles and wondered what he was doing.

I slogged along the wet path and through the front door. Steamy warm air greeted me as I neared Ms. Shelley's empty desk. There was a folder on the dark green blotter with a white Post-It on it. *FOR LINDSAY CAVANAUGH* was written on it.

I hesitated. Did she mean for me to take it?

Then I heard muffled voices coming from the hall. I listened. Rose and Dr. Morehouse. I wondered what they were saying.

I opened the file. There was another Post-It.

Lindsay, I had to step out. Please fill out the form and photocopy it. Copier is in the storage room.

I glanced down at the form. Ms. Shelley had filled in my name, birth date, and some other basic facts. Then I had to initial a form about when I entered the infirmary, who had "attended" to me," etc.

A little miffed that I had had to miss our time in the conservatory to spend thirty seconds filling out a silly form, I nevertheless took it with me and looked for the storage room, where the copier was located. Dr. Morehouse and Rose's voices grew louder as I tiptoed down the hall. I thought Rose might be crying.

What if she was telling him about some of the conversations she and I had about the wrongness of things here? Or if she confessed that we had broken into Mandy's room during Thanksgiving break?

Down the hall past the glaring statue of Edwin Marlwood was a door marked *No Admittance*. It was locked. There were no other doors to try.

I went out the front door, onto the porch, and walked it around to the left, where I recalled seeing a door during my first trip to the admin building, in October. I stepped off the porch, and saw that a door was hanging open. A sign below an old-fashioned brass knocker read *Storage*.

I reached the door and cautiously peered around it.

There was a small room, clean, lined with wooden shelves that reached from floor to ceiling. Reams of photocopy paper and plastic bins with neatly typed labels filled the shelves. At eye level, there were some framed photographs separated by clear bubble wrap. The top picture was a head shot of Dr. Melton smiling at the camera. Out with the old, in with the new.

There was a large photocopy machine pushed against the far wall. And beside it, a tiny elevator, in a shaft about as wide as my shoulders, with a wooden base and top, and nothing else but the rope and pulley system that would be used to raise it. I wondered if it was operational. Like the rest of the room, it was very clean.

Out of curiosity, I set my papers on the photocopy machine and leaned in to examine the dumbwaiter. A glint of light caught my eye, and I leaned in farther. There was a crack in the wall, at least two inches wide.

"Rose," said a muffled voice. "I'm here to help you." Dr. Morehouse.

Rose was crying. I remained stock-still. I knew I should go; I shouldn't intrude on her privacy, but I had secrets I needed to pry out of Marlwood. What if she knew something, said something that would help me? If it could put an end to the madness, I should hear it.

Guiltily, I edged back to the door and pulled it shut. Against the contrasting darkness, light streamed in from the crack and shadows splayed across my body.

I put my hand on the wooden floor of the dumbwaiter. It didn't move. I placed my other hand beside it and pushed down experimentally. It remained in place.

Rose said something that I couldn't hear. I bent forward and planted my hands. Amazed that I was being so reckless—or else, more interested in what Rose might say than afraid of plunging down the shaft—I crawled into the tight space. Arching my back, I pressed my face against the crack in the wall. I could see a pair of men's hands, resting on the polished wood surface of Dr. Ehrlenbach's desk.

"You know I'm here for you, Rose," he said. "You don't need to carry such a burden alone."

"I don't know," Rose said, so quietly I could barely hear her. "It's just so . . . *hard*."

"You have to trust me, Rose. When it's your time, I'll let you know."

His cadence was calm and soothing, the vocal equivalent of a fish tank. I had no idea what he was talking about. Rose's time?

She whispered something. His hands moved on the desk, flattening against the wood. A shadow fell over the backs of hands. The backs of his hands . . . the backs . . .

Ice water poured through me. Starting at the crown of my head, it cascaded over my brain, into my forehead, down my skull. I gasped; cold throbbed through me in a steady slow pulse. My vision started to cloud.

It was Celia. She hadn't left me. I was still possessed. I wanted to scream, I was so devastated. I was shivering. The cold had never been this bad before. It made me ache.

"Leave me," I whispered, in my own voice. "*Stop*."

She didn't answer, but I could feel her moving my hands,

making me push backward, forcing myself to crawl out of the dumbwaiter. I couldn't hear Dr. Morehouse anymore. I didn't know if he could hear me fighting her, trying to stay in control. She was forcing me to leave because he'd been helping me get free of her. I was surer of that than of anything else that had happened since I'd come home from break.

"I hate you. I hate you," I whispered, as I grabbed my form off the copier. I was shaking. I wanted to cry out to Dr. Morehouse, let him know I was there and I needed his help.

But then I was walking stiff-legged to the door, like a robot or a monster. I was walking like a stalker.

Like the Marlwood Stalker.

I pushed the door open and staggered outside into the pouring rain. It wasn't noon, but it was as gray as twilight; rain poured down in buckets. I was so cold already that I felt no difference. My teeth chattered.

Lightning jagged overhead, and I shambled back onto the porch and rushed into the admin building. I put the form on Ms. Shelley's desk and wrote on the Post-It, *Sorry, couldn't find copier.* Now she'd think I was an idiot.

I walked back around on the porch, making sure I'd shut the door. There was a back porch, too, sided by two small columns with a triangular overhang. Something was sitting on it. The driving rain washed the image out, making it impossible to figure out what it was. But suddenly I knew it was bad. I knew I had to stay away from it.

I knew I should run back to the conservatory.

And yet, I walked toward it. I couldn't stop myself.

I couldn't breathe. Shivering in the cold, nearly paralyzed with fear, I kept lurching toward the thing on the porch. I had the sure sensation that someone was watching me. It was like a laser beam at the nape of my neck.

"No," I told Celia "I won't do this."

We were getting closer. A white blob was sitting on the porch, about two feet tall. I didn't want to see it. My heartbeat was hammering in my eardrums. My throat had closed so tightly I couldn't even swallow.

Something was still watching me. It was behind me. I didn't know how close, but it was there. I knew it was there.

If I fainted, what would happen to me? I looked down, completely mute. My eyes bulged and the rain smacked my face.

The thing on the porch was the white head from our room.

Did it *move*? Did its blank eyes gaze up at me?

"God!" I finally forced out, swaying, reaching out to grab onto something, anything. But there was nothing, just the freestanding porch and the head sitting on it.

I staggered backward.

Something was behind me.

I couldn't turn around. I couldn't move forward.

The scent of wet geraniums filled my nose—my mom's favorite flower, the borders of my walk with Dr. Morehouse. I had friends in this world, connections, people who cared about me and could save me.

No one's coming. I stood in the rain and I knew it.

I was at Marlwood, an isolated world unto itself. Brimming

with ghosts and danger. I was drowning in terror. If that head moved, if it came near me . . .

"No, please, help me, please," I whispered.

Did someone take my hand? Did someone lead me away?

Because everything went hazy and blurry; I floated away; I wasn't there. Time passed without me, as it had when I woke up in my pajamas and found Kiyoko's body in the lake. What had happened to me while I was "gone"?

I came to outside the conservatory. The shrieks of my friends must have snapped me out of my catatonia.

"Lindsay, what are you doing?" Julie cried, racing up to me. She was carrying a dark blue umbrella with white stars on it and she shielded me from the downpour as she grabbed my wrist and dragged me into the airy glass-and-iron room. Marica, Elvis, and Claire were seated at a glass table that was perched on a base of weathered turquoise-streaked copper. They'd been playing cards; Julie had thrown her hand down when she'd come to get me.

"Oh, my God, you look like you've seen a ghost," Julie said, then blanched. I had tried to tell her that there were ghosts at Marlwood, but she hadn't believed me. What did I say now? What did I do now? "Here. We were drinking hot chocolate. Drink mine." Julie sat, pushing me down in one of the stuffed chairs and picking up a white china Marlwood academy mug.

The other three watched me warily, and when I peered through my lashes at Marica, she knit her brows.

"I forgot your umbrella," I said, sounding dazed. "I left it in the admin office."

"It's all right," Marica said, her frown transforming into a reassuring smile. "I'll get it later."

"Take off your jacket. Jeez, what have you been doing? What did Shelley want?" Elvis asked.

"I had paperwork. I—I lost something on the way back," I lied. "I dropped it in the grass and it was too precious to lose."

"What was it? An earring?" Marica asked.

"Something . . . that belonged to my mom."

The four of them groaned sadly.

"A . . . a ring," I said. "Just a simple silver band with a piece of turquoise shaped like a wolf's head." Actually, my cousin Jason owned a ring like that. Jason was the one who had given me my army jacket.

"I think you showed it to me once," Julie said, although I hadn't. She was so suggestible. Ordinarily, that bothered me; at the moment, it was very convenient.

"Yes," I said. "When I put away my necklace from Troy." My voice caught, and I sneezed. I had a thought: did I have to give back the crocheted silk choker decorated with the crescent moon charm that Troy had given me for Christmas?

"You should go change," Claire said. "We'll help you look after it stops raining. And be sure to tell Ms. Krige about it. She can get the groundskeepers to keep an eye out for it."

"Thanks," I said, but my voice cracked again. I still felt as if I were being watched.

I looked down at the glass in the table. And I saw Celia's reflection. White face, black eyes, black mouth.

I rose from my chair and stumbled to the fireplace. I looked from the table to the glass panes of the conservatory.

Her white face floated in the air, black eye sockets, black hollows in the cheeks. Giddy hysteria welled up in me: *"What do you want from me?"* I wanted to scream.

The head moved its mouth, talking, but the excited girls obviously didn't see her. I felt so entirely defeated, completely and totally conquered. The ghosts of Marlwood had closed in, and Celia, not Belle, was their leader.

Julie looked at me. I hugged myself, saying, "I'm cold. And I'm upset about the ring. I don't have a lot of things of my mother's."

"Did your stepmother take them?" Claire asked me. "Stepmothers can be like that. Greedy."

"When people pass away, other people fight over their stuff," Elvis said. "It's disgusting."

"No." I leaned my face in my hands, cold and exhausted. I'd thought it was over. I'd thought I was free. "My stepmother is nice." My voice cracked.

Julie came over beside me and took my hand, rubbing it. She reached down and pushed layers of corkscrews away from my face.

"I know it's hard," she said quietly. "Spider and I texted and he says Troy is stumbling around like a sleepwalker. I'm sure he's having second thoughts. You guys will get back together."

I didn't react.

"As far as I know, he's never had a nice, normal girlfriend. He's never dated anyone but Mandy. So you can see why he's not so great at this kind of thing." Julie licked her lips. "Give it time."

Time was not something I had control of. I was out of control. Or Celia was.

I need to see Dr. Morehouse, I thought. Celia didn't respond. She had gone dormant again, or taken a time-out, or I didn't know what. But one thing I had to face: she hadn't gone away.

"Oh, Julie," I moaned. I laid my head on her shoulder. "Julie."

"I'm here," she soothed.

And that helped, a little bit.

TWELVE

DR. DAVID ABERNATHY gathered Celia up in his arms and kissed the side of her face. Next her forehead, then her lips. He touched her neck, and she stiffened and caught her breath. She loved him so, but she was a poor girl, and sometimes gentlemen made assumptions about the lower classes.

Smiling gently, raising his brows, he stopped. "Are you afraid of me, my love? Never, never be afraid. I will take all fear from you."

"How can you?" she asked him, searching his face. "My father has sent me here. He signed the papers. I'm his. Only he can set me free."

"I will marry you. Then you'll be mine. And he'll have no say over what's mine."

To be his, to be his . . .

———

I HEARD MYSELF sighing as I woke up. My first thought was disappointment—I was dreaming Celia's dreams, or sharing her memories. But as Celia's dreams went, it hadn't been a bad one. What it represented—trusting that horrible guy—was worse than the dream itself.

Rubbing my eyes, I looked over at Julie, who was still fast asleep. Moonlight fell on her cheeks, and she was faintly smiling. The little stuffed corgi, Panda, was cradled in her arms. Julie was fifteen, a year younger than me, with her first serious boyfriend newly acquired, and living in a shark tank. I felt a rush of tenderness and smiled faintly back at her. I had wanted a little sister with all my heart. They had discovered my mom's cancer because she couldn't get pregnant. Julie and I weren't sister close, but it was still nice to share a room.

The moon glowed on the white head, which was perched on the windowsill. I had found it back in our room when I'd ducked in before dinner. No one else had been in Grose. They'd been taking full advantage of our day to use the conservatory.

Julie had taken to putting it on the night stand, afraid it would fall and break if it was on the sill. But when I had come in that evening, it had been in its original position. And it had been wet.

By the time Julie had seen it, it was dry. She said she hadn't moved it. And when I asked her about it, she had looked at me strangely, as if to say, *Not again. Don't start this up.*

So, had someone seen me going into the admin building and tried to scare me? Because of course the head couldn't have gotten there by itself—there, or back here.

I didn't want to walk across the room in the dark, but I had to pee. I pulled back my covers and winced for a second as I put my feet on the floor. When you saw ghosts and moving porcelain heads, it didn't seem outlandish to imagine something under your bed, just waiting to grab you.

I held my breath as I tiptoed over the bare wood, and then the soft cabbage-rose carpet, and opened our door. Gritting my teeth, I snaked my hand along the wall in search of the light switch. The miniature overhead chandeliers flicked on at my touch, casting down-ward beams on the bad art from our bad art students, and pooled on the floor. I tried not to look at anything for too long. If I saw Celia's face, I was afraid I'd scream.

Besides, the bathroom was a much more terrifying place than the hall. I had to save up my courage.

In the center of the tiled room sat five enormous bathtubs, where they used to force the worst girls to lie up to their necks in water, with wooden lids bolted over to hold them there. Through me, Celia had relived one of her private torture sessions, when Belle had nearly drowned her in one of those tubs, demanding that she give up David Abernathy, screaming, *"He is mine!"*

But he had been no one's.

I turned on the bathroom light and hesitated, standing on the threshold, holding my breath. Then I rushed past the tubs and went straight into the nearest stall. I did my thing, then ran back into the hall without washing my hands.

When I came back to our room, the outline of the head was cut sharply by light glowing behind it. The light was on in Mandy's turret room. I didn't want to look there either, but I moved forward in the shadows.

A row of white tapir candles—six—was lined up along the sill, and I took an involuntary step backward. Mandy had conducted rituals disguised as pranks in her room, designed to help her pick five willing girls to allow Belle's dead friends to possess them. Mandy had let me watch them from my window, in the hopes that I'd become one of those girls— never dreaming, at the time, that I was already possessed by the seventh victim of that horrible fire—Celia Reaves, the girl who had started it. The girl they all wanted to kill.

It was so insane. They were dead. But their fury was burning in their souls as strongly as the flames that had consumed their earthly bodies. They couldn't get past their rage.

So was Mandy back to her old tricks, collecting live girls so that the dead girls could finally get their payback? I had to stay alert. Or their madness would swallow me alive.

The outline of Jessel rose like a medieval castle above Searle Lake, its inky blackness spreading below the horizon. I wanted to sneak down into Jessel's basement and do some exploring. I was angry with Miles all over again for losing the messenger bag.

Mandy walked into my view. She was dressed in a long white nightgown with her hair pulled back, and she was holding a glass of wine. I knew I had to watch to protect myself, but I couldn't stop wondering if Celia and Belle were watching too. If they made us do things we weren't aware of. If we had entire other lives we lived in secret.

For them.

Mandy moved through the room, gesturing, drinking her wine. She was talking to someone. Belle?

Then a shadow loomed behind her. It was a figure, taller than she. A guy.

Miles, I thought, clenching my fists. Was he her partner in crime? Or was he spilling his guts, telling her he had stolen her papers and lost them?

Or was the figure Troy? Maybe Belle had given her some kind of power over him, and she'd compelled him to row across the lake. Miles and the other guys took the old Lakewood rowboats and came over to our side all the time. I'd once thought he'd been possessed by David Abernathy. Maybe he had been. Maybe he was now.

The shadow moved toward her. I could see the outline approaching—definitely a guy, and I craned my neck forward to see who it was. Closer, closer, I could almost see who it was . . . then Mandy rushed back to the window, threw out her arms, and looked straight at me. I stiffened.

She stood still for a moment. Then she grabbed the edges of her beautiful damask curtains and yanked them closed.

The show was over.

I remained by the window, frozen, replaying everything I had seen. Going over the details, trying to figure out what had been going on. Mandy had looked frightened. I could almost swear she'd been asking me for help. What should I do? Sound the alarm? Would anyone believe me, the crazy girl? Mandy was in a building filled with dorm mates and a housemother. But what if something happened?

What if something was happening right now?

Wine, candles, nightgown. Oh, yeah, something was probably happening.

I walked back around Julie's bed to my own, and as I started to climb back in, my foot came down on something soft. I cried out.

"What?" Julie half-shouted, bolting upright.

The nightstand light came on. I looked down. I had stepped on Panda, the stuffed corgi. How had he gotten all the way over by my bed? Taking a step backward, I scooped it up and showed it to Julie, whose hand was still wound around the lamp.

"Sorry," I said, holding him out to her. My scalp was prickling; the hair on the back of my neck stood straight up. "You must have dropped him."

Julie yawned and blinked at me. "Or thrown him." She took him from me and smiled down at him, tugging on one of his big ears. "Panda, did you miss Lin-Lin?" She gave him a little kiss, then turned him around toward me and made air kisses. "He still loves you, Linz. You want to sleep with him?"

"Jules, he's not alive," I blurted. She flushed, because she was just having fun, being girlie and silly. "I mean, I'm sorry, Panda." I pursed my lips as if to give him a kiss.

"What are you doing up anyway?" she said, a little strained. She picked up her cell phone to check. "It's one in the morning."

"I had to pee."

"Do you want one of my French sleeping pills?"

I felt a terrible sense of déjà vu. At the beginning of last semester, she had offered me a pill. I hadn't taken it, but I'd wandered around the dorm and finally dozed off in our living room. When I had awakened in the morning, I'd discovered that someone had been in our room. They'd raked the side of Julie's mattress, leaving a pile of wadding on the floor. I'd blamed Mandy and her clique, insisting they were trying to prank her. She'd suspected I'd done it, to make them look bad. It had never been resolved.

"Did you put the head back on the sill?" I asked her now. I hadn't planned to. It just came out.

She placed Panda on her pillow and folded her hands. "Marica came by to study. We made some tea and we needed more room for our books. *Okay?*"

Maybe I winced. Her face softened. "I'm sorry, Linz. I know you're under a lot of stress . . . "

I'm not crazy. Believe me. Believe in me.

"Yeah, no kidding," I said. "I'm still not caught up. By the way, Rose? Not such a great math tutor."

"I didn't think that was going to work out. Maybe Marica?"

"That'd be great."

I climbed back into bed, resisting the urge to look underneath it first. Julie lay back down, leaving on the light.

She said sweetly, "Maybe we can leave it like this for a little while."

"It's okay," I told her.

"It's kind of for me," she admitted. "I had a bad dream."

Oh? "Would you like to talk about it?" I asked her, trying to keep the tremor out of my voice. Both of us with bad dreams—what were the odds?

"Not really. I want to forget about it," she replied. "You know, if you go over and over things, they make a bigger impression on you. I like to move on."

"You're right." I smiled at her.

"When you brood about something, you give it power over yourself," she continued, in case I wasn't getting the message.

"Yes. Well, *sweet* dreams."

She dimpled. "The same to you."

———

IF I DREAMED anything after that, I didn't remember it. We got up, did the usual tango with all six of us vying for the showers and the sinks, got dressed, and I walked with the group down to breakfast. Claire mentioned something about not sleeping well. Hearing noises. I figured that might have been me, using the bathroom, except Claire's room was farther down the hall in the opposite direction.

"You're just nervous because Dr. Morehouse wants to see you," Elvis advised her.

"What does she have to be nervous about?" Ida asked, her voice a little tense. "He's seeing all of us, to see how we're coping with things."

"Yeah." Claire gave her head a toss. "It's not like there's anything *wrong*."

Elvis cleared her throat, as if to remind everyone that I, a veteran of shrinks, was present, and that there likely was something wrong with me.

The air pushed down, heavy and filled with moisture, and a morning fog boiled up from the walkways like a smoky, fluffy carpet. Julie swooped her boots through it in a playful gesture. The mist curled around the statues in the garden, dressing them in robes and capes. I thought of Mandy's white nightgown and the figure in her room.

We went into the commons, grabbing trays and going through the food line as girls around us laughed and chatted. We had a bet going that when Dr. Ehrlenbach came back (and she'd been gone for a while), they'd close the lines and have people serve us. Many of the parents had complained that their daughters had to fetch their own meals. For the prices they were paying, they expected their children to be a bit more pampered.

That struck me as ironic, because few of the girls actually ate much of the food. There were a lot of egg-white omelets and cups of organic green tea on the wooden tables beneath hanging copper pots of ferns, washed with soft colors by stained glass windows. Rose, as usual, was getting extra servings of hash browns and grabbing a fistful of creamers for her coffee.

Seeing me behind her, she smiled and said, "What is the *probability* that it will rain today?"

"Did you take the white head out of our room? For some reason?" I replied.

She raised her brows in mild surprise. "Busted. How did you know? And why do you care?"

"I had to go to the admin building around the time of your appointment with Dr. Morehouse." I felt guilty all over again. "Ms. Shelley wanted me to fill out a bunch of paperwork, from when I was in the infirmary."

"Probably documentation in case your grades go bad," Rose said wisely. "Yeah, I hauled it over to show Morehouse. He said they used to be really common about a century ago. Did you know doctors used to measure people's skulls to find out what personality type they were?"

"They did a lot of things they don't do anymore." I nodded at the breakfast server, who was a young, trim woman who also taught yoga. Her name was Moon. No dumpy lunch ladies at Marlwood. Moon added some cheese and scrambled eggs and a ladle of hash browns on a white china plate embossed with the Marlwood crest. I could have asked for brown rice and an egg-white omelet, but no.

"I'd sure have hated to be insane when this place first opened up," Rose agreed.

"Are you insane now?"

"Dr. Morehouse says I'm holding up pretty well, considering all the trash that's being spread all over the internet about my parents' divorce." She caught the inside of her cheek between her teeth. "My mom was *never* a hooker."

"They said 'party girl.'"

She feigned being shot through the heart, pressing her fingertips against her chest and pulling in her shoulders. "Lindsayama, how *could* you read that stuff?"

"How could you take Julie's head without asking?"

"I think she said I could," Rose shot back in a singsong voice. "I didn't realize I had to make sure it was okay with you too. Jeez. Did you have it appraised or something? Is it a valuable antique?"

"Sorry," I said, fully aware that I had overstepped, not really caring if she answered my question.

"Whatever." She smiled crookedly. "Anyway, I like Morehouse. He's not starstruck, the way Melton was. Melton just loved listening to the lifestyles of the rich and infamous. But Morehouse is Harvard. Less to prove." She leaned toward me and gave me a noisy kiss on my cheek. "We should hang. Later, babe."

"By our necks until dead," I promised her as she pirouetted away.

Starstruck. Yes, it would be easy to be that way at Marlwood. I hoped the divorce wouldn't shake up her world too badly. Rose hardly ever saw her parents, and she didn't seem to like them very much. Maybe her life post-divorce would just be more of the same, with a few subtle twists.

I poured myself some coffee and carried my tray to my table. Smiles all around; a few yawns.

"We're deconstructing Claire's nightmare," Elvis informed me.

"Yes." She mocked-shivered. "Bad nightmare. Did you happen to open my door last night, Lindsay?" she asked. "I woke up and—"

Whatever she had planned to say was ignored as the door to the commons burst open. Lara walked Mandy in, holding her up as if she would collapse to the floor under her own steam. Swathed all in black—black turtleneck sweater, black maxicoat, black trousers and boots—Mandy had a huge bandage wrapped around her head, identical to the one I'd had. There were huge dark circles under her eyes, like purple bruises, and a gauze bandage on her chin.

"Whoa," Elvis said.

The last time I had seen Mandy was when she was shutting her curtains and a guy was walking up behind her. I put two and two together . . . and didn't like the conclusion I was drawing. At all.

"God, *God*," Mandy wailed, and Lara patted her shoulder. She walked Mandy over to their table and the rest of Jessel gathered around her. They bent around her like football players huddling around their quarterback.

"Nothing!" she bellowed. *"I can't eat!"*

Everyone in the room stopped pretending they weren't watching and stared quietly at her. She looked around as if she were suddenly aware of that fact, and she raised her chin and stared us down.

"I was in an accident, okay?" she shouted.

Approaching our table, Elvis set down her Diet Coke and piece of dry rye bread. "Yikes. What is up with that? She looks like she's copying your head injury."

"Lindsay had hers first," Claire declared. "She wins."

Mandy cradled her head in her hands. Then she pushed back her chair and stood. Lara hadn't yet sat down; she took Mandy's arm and spoke to her softly. Mandy burst into tears and Lara put her arm around her.

They both turned to go. As they did, Mandy craned her neck over her shoulder and looked at me. Our gazes met. Locked. Held. With tears rolling down her cheeks, she looked just as frightened as she had last night, when she had closed the curtains.

The room was hushed. Lara opened the door, ushered Mandy out, and shut it behind her. We all heard the click.

"What the heck?" Elvis said.

Everybody began talking at once. Except me. I kept staring at the door, my heart pounding.

THIRTEEN

"I HAVE TO go back to the dorm to get my antibiotic out of the fridge," I told the table. It was only a partial lie. I did have to get it, but not until dinner. My timing was beyond obvious; Mandy and Lara had left the commons just minutes before. But I didn't really care what anybody thought. I just wanted answers.

"If you find out anything, you have to share," Claire said.

"I'll tweet," I promised, with a tinge of sarcasm.

"Also because I think Mandy was in my nightmare," Claire added.

I started. Looked at her.

"Figures," Elvis said. "She *is* highly scary."

Ears buzzing, I pulled on my army jacket as I left the commons. Claire was having nightmares about Mandy? This warranted a discussion. Later.

More fog blanketed the blacktop pathway; the horse heads floated, staring at me. The oversized white chain links in their mouths glistened, as if they were bobbing, moving. As I forked left and walked toward Jessel, I thought I heard a clink. I looked.

Nothing.

By then I was walking through Academy Quad. Jessel was on my left, down a slope, its red door flanked by columns. Weak sunlight glinted off the brass knocker of a lion's head in the center of the crimson wood. I lifted it and let it clang. No one came. I knocked, maybe a little too softly.

No answer.

It was possible that their housemother was out—they visited each other, and they had staff meetings and things like that. Maybe Mandy had told Lara not to answer the door. Or maybe whoever had been in her room wouldn't let her open the door.

Miles, I thought. *King of Freakdonia.* I couldn't believe he was living on campus. And that he and I had hugged each other. And that I hadn't melted or burst into flames when he kissed me.

And that I had liked that kiss, the teeniest tiniest bit.

I am mentally ill, I thought.

I had to go; classes were due to start and it was hard to explain being tardy when you lived on campus. I walked back off the porch and looked up at Mandy's turret room. The curtains were closed.

Did they move?

I took another step back, studying the drapes, wondering what was going on behind them. Anxiety slid across my shoulders like a wet towel; someone was watching me. Through the peephole? Behind me?

I looked around, making a little circle. The fog swirled with me, like a miniature tornado, then broke apart as I headed back toward our classroom buildings, on the far side of the commons. Girls were streaming out of the commons; I saw Julie and hurried to catch up with her.

"Find anything out?" she asked me.

I shook my head.

"It's just freaky that she has an injury like yours." Julie cocked her head. "I wonder if she went to the infirmary. Maybe Ms. Simonet wrapped her up."

"Maybe." I shrugged. "It doesn't seem like she'd copy my injury just to get attention."

"*Copy* it?" Julie echoed incredulously.

"Never mind."

It sounded crazy even to say it. Take away the supernatural and we were still in two camps—Mandy and the trendsetters in one and the closest thing to emo we had, that being me, in the other. It had bugged Mandy since the beginning that I had refused to play her games. It still bothered her that I wouldn't succumb to her charms and join her privileged circle.

And privileged they were—the dots that connected her life were Paris, Rome, private islands, billionaire kids, the royals—Prince Harry, specifically—and movie stars. Mandy wasn't old money; her father was a ruthless financial genius and he had taught her well how to make herself powerful. Daddy's little girl.

Miles's sister.

But she would never resort to something so obvious . . . or so self-destructive as getting hurt to take back the spotlight. She wasn't the self-destructive kind. Except for willingly getting possessed . . .

"You're right. She wouldn't do that," I said.

"Well, she'll be the center of attention all day," Julie pointed out. "Look at all of us. What are we talking about?"

She was right. The trek to first period was rife with gossip and innuendo. Mandy, hysterical *and* injured. What was up with that?

I went to American Lit, the class where I'd met Kiyoko and Shayna. Neither of them was here anymore. Neither of them had come to a good end. People used to speculate about them. How had Kiyoko wound up in the lake? Did she jump in on purpose? Did she fall? Had she been pushed?

Had *I* pushed her?

I'd been the one to find her. Somehow, people forgot that. No one had ever accused me of having anything to do with it. But still, I wondered.

I wondered.

We had free period, and it was Claire's turn to see Dr. Morehouse. Other girls had to be going at different times; there weren't enough free periods left in the school year to see all of us before June. Then lunch, then afternoon classes, then we split up for various activities. Julie was delighted that spring soccer tryouts had commenced. Unlike Julie, I had no sports or extracurriculars, so I went back to our room to get some work done before dinner. The catch-up seemed endless.

I wondered if someone had called Dr. Ehrlenbach about Mandy's injury. The school had to keep the Winters family happy. Not to imply that they were happy to start with. Unless he was skulking around us, Miles was always in rehab, and surely they noticed that their little princess was an imperious bitch.

As I sat at my little study desk, on my side of the room beside my closet, I saw that a message had come in on my cell. It had blipped in during the morning. I'd had a new message all day and hadn't known it. I'd turned the ringer off in preparation for classes—if your phone went off, you lost it for a week. Not that anyone's did, with our patchy cell cover. I hadn't felt it vibrate in my backpack, either. Judging by the time—just after eight—it must have come in when I was on Jessel's porch. I had always been able to get good reception there.

I thumbed over to the message in-box on my phone. My heart skipped a beat. Another beat. I stared at the faceplate. The message was from Riley.

I pressed listen.

"Hi, Lindsay? If you get this, I hope you'll call me back..."

There was a pause.

"Heather and I were talking today, and she said you and she are in touch. And, well, she misses you as much as . . . as I do, Lindsay."

My mouth dropped open.

"I don't know if you'll ever be able to forgive me for what I did to you. I've regretted it ever since it happened. God, I wish I could go back in time and have a do-over."

Was this actually happening?

"I want you to know that if you could possibly give me another chance, I'd like that. If you're coming home for spring break, please let me see you. And if you could call me back . . . Heather

says your reception is bad. You might not even get this. Please let me know if you do. Bye."

I stared at my phone as if it were a foreign object. I was tingling all over. He had broken up with Jane and called me.

He called *me.*

I tried to fully grasp it.

He called *me.*

Troy had broken up with Mandy and called me too. What was the probability of that? And of Riley, who had cheated, turning out to be the happier ending of the two? "Whoa, slow down," I said aloud. We weren't even at the starting gate of a relationship. And what was it they said? Once a cheater, always a cheater.

What if *Troy* had been in Mandy's room last night?

"Are you talking to yourself?" Julie asked as she opened the door to our room and chugged on in, still wearing her shin guards and gym uniform—dark green sweatshirt, black shorts. She must be freezing. "God, I have, like, fifteen minutes before I see Dr. Morehouse. I have to take a shower and get dressed and—"

"This is so amazing. You're not going to believe this," I said, registering that she was seeing the good doctor at a time other than free period. I held up the phone.

"What?" She smiled hopefully. "Did Troy call?"

As she took off her sweatshirt, revealing her dark green Marlwood T-shirt, she hustled over and perched on the edge of my desk. Maybe someone less thoughtful would have flopped onto my bed in their muddy clothes, but not Julie.

I played the message on speakerphone. Julie giggled with

pure joy and threw her arms around me. Of course she knew the whole Riley soap opera.

"That's so great! Oh, Lindsay, he sounds so nice!"

"He sounds like a moron," said a voice from the doorway. It was Miles, wearing all black, like his sister—black sweater and trousers and a long, black coat. With his ducktail in place, he looked like an edgy European model. The unlit cigarette dangling from his mouth only added to the effect.

Julie looked at him in abject terror. I hadn't told her he was on campus. Or about our trip to the roadhouse. How could I? She would know without a doubt that I had gone completely insane. And if I told her why I'd done it—talked about possession—she'd probably have me committed.

"Riley's not a moron," I said steadily. "He's very smart."

Did you hurt your sister last night?

"Riley can't even string two sentences together. C'*mon*, Lindsay. That's the competition?"

What did he mean by that? Troy's competition? Miles couldn't be saying . . . his own competition? *No.* He was just being snarky. Still, my cheeks went hot and I made a show of setting down my phone.

"I have to get ready," Julie said, sounding stricken. She gave Miles a look. "We're not supposed to have boys in here." She picked up her sweatshirt and held it against her chest. "She can get expelled for it."

"She won't," Miles said. "Trust me on that one."

All the color drained from Julie's face as she scowled at him. Miles was on all of our America's Most Wacko lists.

"Do you want me to get Ms. Krige?" she asked me.

"No, it's okay. Go take your shower. Really, it's okay," I added when she shifted her weight from foot to foot, like a soccer goalie preparing to take down the enemy if he just got close enough. I loved her for it. When I first met her, she would never have stared anyone down, least of all Miles Winters.

Miles made a show of moving away from the door, arching backward like a bullfighter so she could dart past him. He smiled as he did it, not in a mean way, but she didn't budge.

"Lindsay," she said. "We should call someone."

Miles pulled the cigarette out of his mouth and toyed with it. "I'm not a bad guy, like the Marlwood Stalker. Lindsay knows that."

Julie looked at me, eyes wide with astonishment. When Miles smiled more brightly, she glanced nervously over at him, then back at me.

"I do not know that," I replied.

"Neither do I," Julie said. She shifted her weight again.

"Look." Miles cocked his head. "If I really wanted to do something evil to her, would I actually come to your room?"

She huffed. Someone had attacked Julie at the beach house last fall, and we still didn't know who. There were strict rules about boys on campus, but the rules didn't apply to the Winterses. I wasn't sure they even knew what rules were.

I gave Julie a little wave, telling her not to even bother with him. Obviously freaking, she crossed to her closet and pulled out some dark brown wool trousers, a wide belt, and a purple top, then a beautiful brown and gold brocade jacket. From her dresser she palmed what I imagined was some underwear, a bra, and some socks. She also grabbed her makeup bag. Throwing me one more questioning look, she left.

"How's Mandy?" I asked him as soon as we were alone.

"Oh, God." He slumped and walked to my window. From there he looked down at Jessel, the last rays of the sun etching his profile into the glass. "How is she? Well, she's been better."

He lifted his hands and rested them on the top of the white head. Jerking, he glanced down at it, then ran his hands down along the sides to the temples.

"Let's see . . . "

He picked up the head and carried it toward me. I fought to hide my revulsion. He tapped a marked-off section above the forehead marked with a large 7.

"She has contusions of the 7. Bruises," he said. Raising his hands, he caressed the 7, then moved along the left and right sides of the head toward the temples, marked 11 and 12. "And some scrapes at the *undecim* and the *duodecem*. Not bad or deep, but painful." Then he led with the back of his hand, allowing his fingernails to glide over the lips. "A tiny cut here. Just a nick."

He ran his thumb along the outside line of the upper lip. It was sickening to realize he was fondling the head like some huge weird love object while he was talking about his own sister. His outrage at my comment at the roadhouse seemed even more off given how much he was baiting me.

He carried the head over to my bed and sat down, his back pushed up against the wall, and cradled it on his lap. He tapped the forehead. "Right there at the bull's-eye. That was where Abernathy would aim the ice pick sometimes. But he also went through the eye socket. A few wiggles, taps of the hammer..." He set the head on the nightstand and tsk-tsked.

"Why do you do it?" I asked him. "Work so hard at acting like a freak?"

He grunted. "Did you do group therapy when you had your breakdown? You have that same sort of confrontational style."

"What happened to Mandy?" I asked him. "Did you beat her up?"

"*What?*" He whipped his head toward me.

I waited. He folded his arms across his chest and frowned at me. A silence grew between us. After a few seconds, he unfolded his arms and chewed on his lower lip.

"I thought *you* knew what happened to her," he said. "She won't tell me. But she wants to see you. Alone."

I jerked, startled. "Why?"

He lowered his head and looked up at me through his lashes. "You two have so much in common, no?" His voice shook. "And she and I ... don't."

He sounded jealous, as though there had been a rift in their force. I didn't understand him. I trusted him less. "Why are you acting so weird? Are you actually saying you're jealous that you aren't possessed? Were you in her room last night?" I asked.

His surprise seemed genuine as he shook his head.

"Excuse me, are you asking me why I'm upset? Have you completely forgotten what's happened to us in the last twenty-four hours? Have you *seen* my sister? She's hurt."

I didn't stop to point out that *upset* and *weird* were not synonyms.

"There was a guy in her room last night. I thought it might have been you."

A beat. "A *guy*?" He looked astonished.

"And today she's got contusions of the seven," I said.

A red flush washed up his neck and spread across his face. He pushed up off my bed, straightening, feeling in his pockets as if he were assuring himself that he had something. What? A gun?

"I'll kill him."

"I didn't see who it was," I said quickly. "Don't jump to conclusions."

In a fury, he headed for the door. "Oh, please."

"Miles, don't." I got up and followed him. He kept going. I reached out and tugged on his sleeve. *"Don't."*

He shook me off. "Why not? He charmed you too. Mr. Charming, stringing everyone along, so tortured and nicey-nice-nice, confusing her, *hurting* her."

I reached out and tugged again. "Miles, wait! Stop!"

He whirled on me. "Why? Why should I?"

A high-pitched scream shattered the fury between us. It came from down the hall, toward the front door. We looked at each other, then bolted out of the room, racing like one person toward the sound.

FOURTEEN

I STOPPED THINKING as I ran in the direction of the scream. I operated on pure adrenaline, my only aim to help whoever was screaming. I pushed around Miles in the narrow hall; he bashed against the wall, sending bad art flying, the frames clattering on the hardwood floor. If he yelled, I didn't hear him.

I was all about the scream.

Wheeling left, I burst into a room to find Claire on her knees, doubling over, making retching sounds. I fell to the floor beside her, cupping the sides of her head and bending low to peer into her face.

Her eyes were bulging and she was gagging. In case she was choking, I formed a fist and pounded on her back. She shook her head wildly.

"Get me out of here, oh, God," she whispered.

Miles took both her hands and urged her to her feet. I stood too, trailing after her as Miles dragged her out of the room.

She was hiccuping and crying, and her free hand was around her wrist. At first I thought she was trying to get free of him, but then I saw that she was clinging to him. I followed, gazing back into the room. Once we were out, I shut the door.

"Ms. Krige!" I shouted.

"She's not here," Miles said. He pulled Claire down the hall, toward our front door, then stopped and bent his knees so he could look into her eyes. "What happened? Are you all right?"

Claire couldn't stop shaking. I wanted to get her some cold water or find her a place to sit down, but as I moved, she let go of Miles and grabbed onto my forearm. Her eyes were enormous and pleading. She was shaking, and tears were cascading down her face. When I tried to speak, her fingernails dug painfully into my skin.

I walked her toward the door. Miles held it open and we burst out onto our porch. Claire practically propelled me down the path that led to Academy Quad. I gave Miles a stern look to back off and he slowed, then stopped, and Claire and I kept on going without him.

She leaned forward and made more heaving noises. Then she groped for me, as if she were blind. I held her tightly.

"Claire, you have to tell me what's wrong," I insisted. She was sagging against me. My back was spasming from the effort of trying to keep her from sliding into a puddle beside us. "Tell me *now*."

"G-ghost," she whispered. She choked back another scream. "In my room."

I caught my breath. Before I could say anything, she went on in a rush. "Dr. Morehouse said it's because I'm too stressed, but I really saw it. It wasn't just a—a dream." She grabbed at my shoulders as if she were going to climb up my body. "Lindsay, it was . . . " She shut her eyes.

I pried her hands off my shoulders and gave them a squeeze. She wept hard, each sob a sharp contraction of her stomach. I glanced up at Miles, who was loitering about thirty feet away, watching us closely. My gaze drifted past him to Grose, my dorm. I couldn't see into Claire's room—it was on the opposite side of the hall, the windowless side—and at the moment, I was glad I couldn't.

Then I looked over my shoulder at Jessel. My line of sight led directly into Mandy's turret room. The curtains were open, and she was staring down at us. The white bandage looked like a ski headband. In the dim light, I couldn't make out her expression. Then she moved away, disappearing from view.

A ghost. In Grose. That someone else had seen. More proof.

There was another long silence between us. As Claire cried, my mind raced. Thunder rumbled and I glanced up. Gray clouds were scudding across the sky, smothering the last of the sunlight and casting us in nickel-plated shadow. A sharp wind schussed, stinging my face, and I shivered.

That seemed to trigger something in Claire. She wiped her face with the back of her hand and exhaled sharply.

"Dr. Morehouse says I externalize my fears," she ventured. "That's why I'm having the nightmares and I—I'm sleepwalking."

Alarm bells clanged, but I kept calm. I counted to ten before I spoke again.

"But you were awake just now."

"Oh, my God, it was horrible!" she screamed. "I really saw it, I did. It was there. I don't care what he says!" She pawed at me, as if she could climb inside me and hide.

The way that Celia had.

"Please, tell me what it looked like," I said. "Because . . . I've seen things too."

She jerked as if someone had shocked her. She looked away from me and stared hard at the ground. She caught her breath again and I looked down too. She was staring into the puddle.

My hair rose straight up. I saw nothing in the water, but that didn't mean that there was nothing there. Something that Claire could see. Was she possessed? When she looked back at me, would I see that her eyes had turned completely black?

I was afraid of her. But she was in such anguish that I made myself stay planted beside her. I cleared my throat.

"Claire," I pressed gently.

"She was floating in the air," Claire whispered. "She was white, everything white, except her eyes, and she had a hole in her head."

"A hole." My voice was hoarse. I tried to clear it again, but my throat was so tight I was afraid I wouldn't be able to breathe.

"She was there," Claire said. "He says it's stress. He's seeing a lot of it. Because of Kiyoko. There's so much pressure on us, from our families . . . " Could I confide in her? She was so terrified, torn between her own reality and what shouldn't, couldn't be real. Was it better to know there really were vengeful ghosts that could possess you and force you to do evil, horrible things?

You don't know that, I thought. *You don't know if Celia made you do anything bad.*

"I just want to scream," Claire whispered, holding on to me. "I want to go home."

As I hugged her, more wind whipped up, blowing straight through me, as if I weren't solid. Miles was scowling at the empty turret room window.

"We'll go get a security guard," I suggested.

"No." She grabbed my hand. "They won't see anything. *You* didn't." Squeezing so hard that my knucklebones scraped together, she searched my face. "Did you?"

"I'll go back and take a look," I said, sounding far calmer than I was. "Why don't you go somewhere where there's people?" Night was settling around us. "The commons might be open for dinner. Or you could go to the library."

"I don't want to go anywhere," she said. "I can't move."

"I'll check it out," I promised.

She looked through her hair at Miles. Her face changed into a hard mask of anger. "He did it. The Winterses think it's so funny to scare people. I'm sure it's something he worked out with Mandy. That's why he was in our dorm."

I realized then that my offer to call for help could backfire. The grown-ups didn't know what was happening or, if they did, could never admit it. They might just get in my way.

"Go ask Miles if they were pranking me." Her voice was a hoarse croak. "Make him admit it."

I turned to go; she grabbed me hard, shaking. Her hands were like ice, but so were mine. The air was frigid. She had no jacket. Neither did I.

"I'll go ask him," I told her. "Stay here."

I worked at her fingers; she couldn't seem to let go. Her lips were gray, her face very white. She almost looked like a ghost herself.

Aware that she was watching and that Mandy might have been too, I crossed back to Miles. He had just lit a cigarette. He drew in, held it, exhaled.

"Where does Mandy want to meet me?"

"In the conservatory." He held out the cigarette to me. "During study period." Smoke trailed upward, meeting the last moments of sunlight.

He gestured with his head at Claire. "Did she really see anything? Or is that an existential question best left for the sages among us?"

"Oh, my God, you're so screwed up," I said, sounding as angry as Claire. "I'll go see Mandy on one condition."

He raised a brow, as if he had any power in this situation, as if he could grant favors. He took another puff on his cigarette.

"You have to tell me right now if you did anything to Claire's room to make her see things."

He frowned. I held up my hand.

"You're her brother. I'm sure she sent you pictures of the haunted house Jessel made for our Halloween carnival. She had help from friends at Disney, for God's sake."

"It was spectacular," he murmured, smiling faintly.

"How can you smile?" I demanded. "Look at Claire. She's losing it."

"How can you not smile?" he countered. "Don't you feel more than one thing at a time? That's what insanity is, trying to feel one way. That's why it feels good to go crazy. Or to be addicted. It's so much easier than feeling several things at once."

"You, you're . . . " I said. I looked away from him. "Tell Mandy I'll meet her."

"Yes, ma'am," he replied, sweeping a little bow.

"And stay in your guest bungalow," I ordered him. "You can't creep around all the time. It's scaring everyone."

"They should be scared. But not of me."

I walked past him and headed back to Grose. I didn't want to do it; I was scared too. As I reached the door, Marica and Elvis sauntered up. One glance at me and they traded a look.

"What's wrong?" Elvis asked me.

I pointed down the hill at Claire. "She thought she saw something in her room. She's scared. I told her I'd check it out."

Elvis and Marica glanced in Claire's direction. Elvis did a double take. "Hello? Marlwood Stalker? Could it by chance have been *Miles* in her room?"

"Don't think so," I replied, hedging.

"Oh, my God, are you insane?" Elvis stared at me, then took off back down the path toward Claire, who had moved to the center of Academy Quad, huddling against the cold. Keeping his distance, Miles was smoking. Marica stayed with me.

"If there's someone in her room, we should call for help," she said reasonably.

"Marica, she thought she saw a ghost," I told her.

Marica sighed. "She's been very worried about the meeting that she had with Dr. Morehouse. She talked a little bit about the stories that Marlwood is haunted. She wants to go to Harvard, and she's afraid they'll think she's too unstable."

She made a slicing motion across her neck. "I told her next time just to say that she is great."

Next time? Stories? I wondered if I had been mentioned. Lindsay Anne Cavanaugh, freak show. The weird poor girl who kept flinching at the reflections of mirrors and windows.

"So it's best not to call security," she finished.

"Okay," I said. "Then let's go."

I was grateful that she was willing to come with me and that she didn't ask any questions, or remind me that I had been raving about ghosts and possessions during my breakdown in the operating theater—a Valentine's Day prank gone horribly wrong.

Valentine's Day was my birthday. My mom had always said I was the best valentine she could have ever asked for. That was one thing I had—my mom's eternal love.

We entered the dorm, striding past the little table where a figure of a saint or a shepherd or something kept watch over our incoming and outgoing mail. On the whiteboard, Ms. Krige had scrawled, *Ms. Shelley ill. I am covering phones.*

I was striding down the hall, propelled by fierce emotions I couldn't even name. Marica kept up with me. I smelled her perfume; she was always made up, even in the middle of a crisis.

"In here," I said, opening the door.

As I entered Claire's room, I was hit with the scent of geraniums. I took a step backward in surprise, bumping into Marica. She caught me by the shoulders and walked around me, looking around the room and then at me.

The scent grew stronger. Was Memmy with us? Had Claire actually seen my mother?

But Memmy didn't have a hole in her head, I thought.

"You smell it too, don't you?" I asked, and when she inhaled deeply, her forehead wrinkling, I knew her answer. She didn't.

Did I hear a sigh brush my ear?

Did someone touch my cheek? "My perfume is awfully strong," Marica said, apologizing.

She wasn't aware of the presence in the room. I didn't know what to say or do. If it was my mom, oh, *God*, if it was my mom . . .

"Lindsay?" Marica said.

Then it was over. All I smelled was Marica's perfume. All I sensed was her presence.

My throat tightened, my chest constricted, and I made a show of walking around the room, calling out to Memmy in my mind, and in my heart, to come back. Marica trailed after me, tilting her chin thoughtfully as she came to Claire's framed hideous Hawaiian art. She said nothing, only moved on, picking up a book, setting it down.

"There's nothing here," she announced.

My mind was racing. In my fantasies, I was already offering to come stay with Claire, getting a Ouija board, trying to contact my mother. I felt totally out of control. I could call back my *mom*. Maybe even become possessed by her.

Marica walked out of the room. Trembling, I lingered, furious with Miles all over again for losing Mandy's notes.

Then I realized what I was thinking: They were *Mandy's* notes. Mandy was the one who had contacted the dead in the first place. The one who knew how.

I walked out of the room. The door clicked sensibly shut, and I looked at Marica. Then I leaned against the door as if to force it to stay shut.

There were other doors that I could open.

I would keep that date with Mandy.

FIFTEEN

JULIE CAME BACK from her meeting with Dr. Morehouse to announce that she was the captain of the Blues, an exalted position considering that she was only a freshman. The list had been posted while she was in session. If we'd had juniors and seniors, that might have been even more exalted, but I kept that thought to myself and toasted her in the commons with sparkling apple cider provided by the staff. There would be Cristal champagne later, after we were supposed to be snug in our beds. Most of the girls had the most incredible stashes of liquor, chocolates, and munchies. There was a seemingly endless supply.

But first there was dinner, and then it was study time. Mandy time. I told Julie I was going to the library and scooted out of the front door. But I remembered the scent of geraniums, and felt the tender bruises on my forehead, as I walked in the direction of the conservatory. Crickets scraped, and an owl hooted a melancholy warning to nearby rodents.

As if in reply, there was scurrying in the dirt behind me. Maybe what I was doing was foolhardy. I hadn't told anyone that I was meeting with the great Satan, but maybe Mandy's posse of evil knew. Maybe this was an ambush.

Wind whistled hard, pushing away some of the layers of clotted mist. I kicked up piles of it as I walked past the staring horse heads. Above me, to my left, the iron, tulip shaped cupola of Founder's Hall stood out in bold relief; behind it, the admin building floated gauzy and dreamlike.

After a few minutes I stood outside the conservatory, in the same location where I had stood before after I'd spied on Dr. Morehouse and Rose. Yes, spied. That was the only word for it. Then Celia had come out to play. A chill shot down my spine. Maybe this wasn't the best of my ideas. Not that any of them of late had been much good.

A small light flared inside the Victorian-style structure of glass and wood. I glimpsed a strand of platinum hair behind the yellow flicker. Mandy's face glowed as she set the candle in a black candleholder on the same glass table where Julie, Claire, and Ida had played cards. There were other things on the table, but I couldn't tell what they were.

Moving back into the shadows, I found the outer door to the conservatory and turned the knob. It was locked.

There was a click. The door opened, and Mandy faced me on the threshold. She was wearing pencil-leg jeans, heeled boots, an emerald cashmere sweater, and a black leather jacket. A candle flickered beneath her chin, casting goblin angles and hollows on her face. Bruises splotched her fabulous complexion—on her forehead and high on her left cheekbone.

She actually looked glad to see me.

"I thought you weren't coming," she said. Her voice was high, shrill. Scared. I wasn't sure if I should find that comforting. Probably only if it was me she was scared of.

"Who else knows you're here?" I asked her.

She frowned at me. "Why?"

"Everyone knows I'm here." That was a lie, but I wasn't about to tell her that. "They've got the place surrounded. One false move and they're taking you out."

Rolling her eyes, she reached around me and shut the door. I was a bit dashed that she seemed unconcerned about my nonexistent backup.

Soundlessly she led the way back to the table. There was a Ouija board with the letters of the alphabet, *A* through *Z*, in a semicircle. The numbers from one to nine were printed in a straight line below. *GOODBYE* was printed beneath the numbers; *YES* in the left-hand corner, and *NO* in the right. In a black votive candleholder, another candle sat—unlit, and some books stacked beside a bottle of red wine and two glasses. Both were full.

She set down the lit candle and picked up the wine. Handed one to me and raised hers in a toast. I was already a little queasy and I had no idea if Mandy had maybe drugged my glass. Or filled it with arsenic.

Seeing my hesitation, she took back my glass and sipped from it, then took a drink from her own. I crossed my arms and she set both goblets down.

"Who beat you up?" I asked.

"No one."

With a heavy sigh, she sank into her chair and raked back her hair with her hands. Her little finger caught in the bandage and she jerked on it. The gauzy strip lifted up on her forehead and I saw a dark circle, like a deep bruise, directly in the center.

"I think," she added.

I sat down across from her. Mandy Winters and me, alone in the conservatory. Alone anywhere. By choice. Unbelievable.

She leaned toward me. "I went for a walk at the lake. And I guess . . . I must have gotten dizzy and fallen . . . " Her voice grew faint. I heard what she wasn't saying. She didn't know how it had happened. And she had lost time, as I had.

"Who was in your room last night?" I asked her. "When you had on your nightgown and the wine and all?"

"What are you talking about?" She took a hefty swallow from her glass.

"Last night, when you were in your nightgown. You looked straight at me before you closed the curtains."

She looked dumbfounded. I had never been able to tell how much she knew about her own possession. If she remembered what Belle said and did when she took Mandy over and if nightmares and visions of the past dogged her the way they did me.

"Are you sure that was me?" she asked.

"No, actually. I'm not."

She exhaled slowly and looked down at the Ouija board. I picked up the little putty-colored triangle used to point to the letters and examined it. She shifted uncomfortably, as if she thought I might be struck by lightning for daring to touch the sacred plastic, and I set the triangle back down.

"You did this to us both," I said. "With all your mumbo jumbo."

"I didn't think it would work." She drank more wine. Her hands were shaking. "I—I had a dream about it and it seemed, well, interesting, and then it was like someone was guiding me to the answers . . . "

"To the things that were needed. In the basement."

She rolled her eyes. "Miles told me he took all my notes and journals. And lost them."

"He thinks Troy beat you up. He said he was going to kill him."

She was silent for a long time. Then she reached down at her side and picked something up. It was in her fist.

She turned her hand over and opened it. Inside lay the black knitted silk choker Troy had given me for my birthday. The silver crescent moon that had been attached to it was missing.

"Where did you get this?" I asked her.

"It was lying next to me on the ground when I came to." She set the choker on her Ouija board and fumbled with the bandages on her head, trying to pull them back over her forehead. She was trembling, hard.

"I know Troy gave it to you. He told me about it when he broke up with me." She sounded more like her old self—kind of perpetually pissed off, and always better than me.

"Why would he tell you that?" I picked up the choker. The

last time I had seen it, it had been in the top drawer of my dresser in my dorm room. And Troy had *never* been in my dorm room.

But Miles had.

"So, you think he might have left it beside you to rub it in?" I persisted. I had a thought. "Or do you think *I* was the one who came after you?" I went on high alert. Was that why I was here?

She put the Ouija board triangle on the board. Studying it, she finished her glass of wine and reached down again, hefting the bottle onto the table. She poured herself another full glass. I decided to drink mine. Jane had taught me how to appreciate wine, and we'd preferred the astringent reds. In Jane's circle, getting drunk was hugely uncool.

"You planted Troy's ID bracelet on Julie's skirt," I said, "when she was attacked on the beach."

"No." She shook her head. "You assumed I did, because he gave it to me. But someone took it from my room."

Her room was usually locked. I knew that from personal experience.

"And someone took *this* from *my* room," I said, holding up the choker like a dead rat. "I didn't give it back to him."

"Oh, my God," she said.

"It would be just like you to fake all this. To get back at me, and him, or just to mix it up."

"The good old days." Her eyes sparkled as she readjusted her bandage. "When all I did was terrorize the peasants."

"And troll for five unsuspecting accomplices for your

murderous little plans. To kill *me*." Before she could argue, I grabbed her wrist. "To *kill* me."

"I didn't know that was what Belle was really after, I swear I didn't." She looked away and gave her arm a wiggle, to break contact. "She just said that she wanted to experience life again. She envied us for being alive. And for having so many great things."

"And you believed her?"

"Why wouldn't I?" She lifted her chin. "I *do* have a lot of great things."

"You'd think someone who was dead would be less shallow," I declared.

"Maybe, but I . . . my mind was on something else." She sat back, resting her hands on the arms of the chair, looking regal. I let go of her.

"On your own brother."

Her eyes narrowed and her face went hard. "I know your mom died. She was sick for a long time."

"Keep her out of this," I warned her, even though it would be a good moment to bring up my questions about getting in touch with her.

Mandy nodded, staring at the board. "My family was like that. Any kind part of us, any good part, died slowly, year after year."

I grew quiet. Maybe she would tell me something true. Or at least useful.

"I read everything I could to figure out what was going wrong. I did find out that families pick out someone to blame when that happens. Suddenly one of the kids is the problem, or the mom, or the dad. In our family, it was Miles."

She placed her two forefingers on the plastic triangle. It scooted toward the *D*. I wasn't sure that she was moving it.

"Our family therapist helped it happen," she went on. "Helped it be Miles's fault. I think Dr. Greene liked the big checks Daddy wrote out. Or maybe Greene got pissed off when Miles asked him about the complaint that had been lodged against him when he worked in a group home."

The triangle moved to the *I*.

"On his recommendation, Miles was sent to a residential care facility. They cut off all his hair. He tried to escape. So they medicated him and tied him into a wheelchair. I could smell the pee on him."

"God," I said.

"They said he was resistant to treatment. So they sent him to a different facility. I wasn't allowed to see him at that one. My mom would cry when she'd come back. And then she'd drink."

My father had gotten drunk once, when the doctors told us my mom's disease was terminal. The next morning, he apologized to us and threw out all the alcohol in the house.

"She's been on all kinds of antidepressants and sleeping pills ever since," Mandy continued. "She OD'd. Everyone said it was an accident. The first time."

The triangle began to drift across the board.

"The second time, they said that it was Miles's fault."

The triangle rested on the *E*.

DIE.

I pushed away from the table.

"Whatever happened, I wasn't a part of it," I said. "And whatever deal you made with *Belle* had nothing to do with me or my life." I picked up the Ouija board and tipped it toward myself, grabbing the triangle and throwing it on the ground. "And you came after me, all of you, after you got rid of Kiyoko."

"I don't remember coming after you," she insisted. "God, Lindsay, honest, I didn't know what was going to happen. And I did not have anything to do with Kiyoko."

She leaned forward again, tears welling in her eyes. Maybe they were real.

"I don't remember trying to hurt you."

Because you don't want to, I thought. But how many times had I been unsure that it was actually happening? I'd come to in all kinds of places—the operating theater, the old library— not sure about what had really happened, or what I'd dreamed, or maybe even imagined.

"I know I'm in too deep," she said. "I'm looking for a way out."

Me too. And Celia had told me that the only way out was to kill Mandy. Had Belle been equally informative?

"Miles told me what happened with the scooter," she went on. "That there was something in the road."

"Maybe it was you."

She shook her head. "Lindsay, I think someone is trying to kill us. I mean, like a person. Like the Stalker. And I'm really, really scared."

"Welcome to my world," I said coldly.

"Lindsay, *please*." She looked younger than I had ever seen her look. She was my age. Sometimes I forgot that. All her money and power gave her the illusion of maturity, but she was only sixteen years old.

I looked at the choker in my hand. I thought about the ID bracelet. In both instances, Troy had been involved.

"I think we should confront our ex. See if he knows anything," Mandy said, also looking at the choker.

"At the very least we could tell him what a dirtbag he is," I suggested.

"That's the spirit." She grinned, and a ghost of the queen bee I knew and loathed shone through her misery. "We'll go over there and tell him."

"Seeing us together would totally freak him out."

"So we'll freak him out. Together."

Maybe this could be my way out. Working with Mandy, who had started the possessions in the first place. If anyone could figure out how to end them, it would be her.

Could I actually be insane enough to trust her?

Desperate enough?

"Seal our pact," she said. "With a drink."

I put my glass to my lips and drank. Drank it all down. I loved the bitterness. The bite.

In sync, we threw our glasses against the stone fireplace. It seemed like a crazy, OOC thing to do. But we did it together, without a moment's hesitation.

"We'll go tonight," she said. "Late."

"*Not* on the scooter."

"We've got a boat at Jessel," she said. "We can row over."

I guffawed. "I knew it. Oh, my God, do you think I'm an idiot?" When she just looked at me, I snickered. "Like last time, and I got in the boat with the hole in the bottom? And I went out to get away from all of you when . . . " I trailed off. She had been possessed when it had happened, and evidently she really didn't remember.

"What?" she said. "Are you still talking about Kiyoko? I swear to you, Lindsay, I'm not going to drown you."

Maybe she didn't know that water rendered the spirits powerless. When Belle Johnson and the others had raced after me, the lake had protected me from them. As I rowed away, one of them had jumped in after me, dissolved, and faded away. If anything happened out on the water . . . if Belle decided that it was a good time to put Celia out of her misery . . . all I had to do was push Mandy in.

That was a good thing to keep to myself.

"I *swear* to you I won't kill you in the next twenty-four hours," Mandy said.

"The sad thing is, in our world, that sentence makes sense," I said.

"Ours is a wider world," she agreed. "So, let's go over after everyone goes to bed. Say, elevenish?"

"Sure." More sneaking out. I doubted I'd get expelled if I had a Winters with me. "But it's just us two. If you bring anybody along, I'm leaving."

That made the lake an even better choice—we'd be landing on Lakewood property. I didn't know the layout of the boys' campus, but I was willing to bet it'd be harder to sneak a bunch of girls in via the land route. Less chance of a trap.

"Just us two," she agreed.

"No Miles." I had a thought. "He won't *really* try to kill Troy, will he?"

She laughed. "My brother's a big teddy bear."

"Hardly."

"He only acts scary. I think it was his way of pushing back in all the psycho wards."

"That's comforting."

"I'll meet you down at the water. Do you know where the tie-up is? By the no-trespassing sign?"

"I do. Elevenish," I said.

"This will be fun." She hoisted the bottle of wine in the air. "Wait and see."

And she drank it down.

SIXTEEN

AFTER I LEFT Mandy, I started back to my dorm in the increasingly heavy fog. Nobody kept tabs on us during study time, but almost everyone studied, because getting good grades was not a given and most of the parents expected a good return on their investment of fifty thousand dollars a year. As for me, I was expected to earn my keep with a sky-high GPA.

But as I walked along the path and gazed into the fog, my body flooded with cold. From the top of my head, ice seeped into my brain and ran down the bones of my skull. I could feel it behind my eyes, aching in my cheekbones, freezing my chin. My chest hurt; my ribs felt as if they had crystallized and would shatter if I breathed too hard.

"Celia, no," I whispered.

The cold increased, stiffening my muscles, and I shuffled forward like an old woman. I tried to work my jaw, but it clamped shut.

"Rigor mortis," she whispered.

Then I was walking toward the admin building, just as cold,

but able to move. Grunting in protest, I was propelled up the walk; then I moved to the left—she *moved* me to the left—and I lurched past the porch where I had seen the head. Then past the wall and down the side of the building to the door that led to the storage area. My icy hand grasped the knob; I was trembling all over. My head tipped back and I saw the bone-white moon in deepest, frozen blue velvet. Fog, as if out of nowhere, began to tumble down, and when I exhaled, it was as if more fog was rising to join the falling mist. I was surrounded by milky white. I couldn't see a thing.

My forehead throbbed as if someone were stabbing me with an icicle. The center ached, deeper than bone deep, as deeply as it could go.

Celia was thrashing like a frantic animal inside me. Was this her pain or mine? Her fear? Or ours? I couldn't tell what she wanted—to leave? To go inside?

The door opened. I couldn't tell if I was the one who opened it. I was numb. I didn't know if I stepped forward or if I fell on my back. I was completely disoriented.

"Death," Celia whispered to me. *"Do you see? Do you feel it? This is death."*

"No," I replied, but the word echoed inside my head. It was unbearable. I had never felt so isolated, so alone, so . . . nothing.

"Where I am," she said.

Then warmth hit my face and moisture beaded on my cheeks and chin. The light from the crack in the wall gleamed through the fog, which evaporated in an instant, leaving me standing in a little puddle. My blood pumped, circulating. My heart beat. I was alive.

"God," I whispered. I heard my own voice. I swayed left, right, dizzy; I grabbed onto the wooden rail of the dumbwaiter and breathed slowly in and out. Wet fabric, and the smell of wood.

Voices drifted from the crack and I tilted my head. I thought I heard crying. I concentrated, but the sounds were just beyond my reach.

Cold poured through me again, and my eyes lost focus. Panicking, I took a step forward, toward the dumbwaiter. Celia urged me closer to the wall, forcing my feet forward. Next she tried to get me into the dumbwaiter, folding myself up, cramming myself in. I held back, and sleet washed through my lungs. I was afraid the rope would snap under my weight. But as I crawled on in, the cold lessened.

"It's all right to admit your real feelings," Dr. Morehouse said, over soft weeping. "This is a safe place."

"But . . . she's just my friend." It was Ida. There was more weeping. "I . . . I think."

"Do you think she may have . . . feelings for you?"

"That's not how I was brought up," Ida murmured. I could barely hear her. Before I realized what I was doing, I was placing my ear directly over the crack. "I mean, I have gay friends. But I'm . . . I can't be."

"You'd know best." His voice was soothing. "And . . . would it be so awful?"

"Why do you keep asking me if it's true?" she asked. "If it's not so awful, why do you care so much if we're—if she's . . . " She trailed off.

"You just seemed very tense when you walked in. And the first thing you talked about is Claire."

"She had a fright today. *Oh.*"

"'*Oh*'?"

"She doesn't want . . . she asked me not to talk about it."

"Really? Why?"

Harvard, I thought, biting my lower lip. *Ida, shut up.*

"I don't know." A pause. "Oh, because I think she wants to talk to you about it herself."

Her voice was falsely bright. She was trying to flatter him.

"But she confided in *you.*" A pause as well. "Because you're special to her. Her special friend."

"Well, I'm her *best* friend."

"It's okay, Ida."

"But I don't feel that way about her. Honestly." I could hear the edginess returning to her voice. She was on the verge of tears again.

"What if I told you that Claire herself has indicated that she feels that way?" My mouth dropped open. I had been to enough therapists to know that what he was doing was completely and totally unethical. What a patient said to a therapist was confidential. And you sure didn't *hint* about what another patient might or might not have said in a session.

"Would that make you feel safer?" His voice was gentle, kind. "Before you answer, please understand that I would never, ever divulge anything Claire said to me when she's in this office. Nor would I tell her what you said. But what did you feel just now, when you thought she might have told me that she's attracted to you?"

"Um," Ida said.

"Hopeful? Shocked? Happy?"

"I don't remember how I felt."

"Just a few seconds ago. How did that strike you, Ida? Shall we try counting backward again? That seemed to help before." There was a long silence.

"You won't tell anyone what I say."

"No, of course not. Never."

"Not for college placement, or anything like that."

"It's confidential. I promise."

"Okay."

"Good. Now, here's a light. Let's put it on the wall and look into it. You're walking along a path . . . "

Geraniums. The smell of the ocean.

"Ten."

Seagulls calling overhead.

"Nine."

The warmth of the sand between my toes.

"Eight."

The rolling waves.

I CAME TO as I was leaving the building. Celia, if she was still with me, was quiet. I felt . . . content. Calm. It was puzzling, but I would take it. I was so often *not* content or calm.

The fog rolled along with me like churning waves as I headed back to the dorm. Everyone was getting ready for bed.

Ms. Krige had said good night and shut her door. That was the signal to pop the cork on a bottle of Cristal champagne to celebrate Julie's captainship.

We got a little wasted, and then one by one, people dropped off to sleep. Ida, who had arrived a few minutes after I had, stuck close to Claire. Claire, announcing that she was too freaked to stay in her own room, went off to sleep in Ida's room.

"Yeah, baby, I kissed a girl and I liked it!" Elvis whispered loudly after them.

"Do you think they're, y'know, girlfriends?" Julie sipped more champagne. "Not that there's anything wrong with that."

"Don't know. But I'm totally jealous." Elvis thrust out her lower lip. "I want Ida for myself."

"You do not!" Julie cried, scandalized.

"Not that there's anything wrong with that," Elvis drawled.

I waited Julie out. It was easy; she was tired from her tryouts and the champagne went straight to her head. Throwing back the covers, I quickly dressed in the dark clothes I had laid out—black sweater, knitted cap, jeans, Doc Martens, and my army jacket. I scooted into the bathroom, avoiding the mirrors and shiny tiles, racing to the window that we always kept slightly open. I climbed up on the wicker laundry hamper and pushed up the sill, gazing out in surprise.

The fog was worse. It had completely filled the bowl of our campus, white on white on white. Layers of it, blankets of it, thick as cream. I couldn't see a thing, not even Jessel or the trees of Academy Quad. The boulder that we used to climb down from the window had sunk into the murk of liquid porcelain. As I hovered on the ledge, I felt my resolve evaporate. The last time the fog had poured over us like this, I had wound up in lockdown with pneumonia.

Payback for Troy, I thought. *And answers. I am going.*

I extended my leg into the fog, feeling with my toes for the rock face. I found it and eased myself onto it. I tried to ignore the images of hands waiting to grab me, of someone with a knife, a hammer, or an ice pick. Or ghost girls, shrieking in rage because I was alive and they were not.

I kept one hand on the rock, trying to orient myself. In times past, Celia had guided me through the fog and darkness, but now, as I braced myself to feel her presence, there was nothing.

Then someone tapped me on the shoulder, and I jerked hard, stumbling into the fog. They laid a hand on my forearm. Judging by the size, I figured it was a girl's hand.

"Mandy?" I whispered.

"Sssh," the voice answered, tugging gently at me.

Freaking out, I reached out my hands to find the boulder. I was going to forget the whole thing and go back inside my dorm.

Except . . . I couldn't find the boulder.

I couldn't understand it. I hadn't moved that far away from it. It should be at most two steps away . . .

Adrenaline shot through me as I began to panic. Swallowing my impulse to pant, I kept my ears open for the sounds of someone nearby. My mysterious escort. It had to be Mandy.

The wind picked up and thinned the mists. I could see a few

feet in all directions, and I had to stifle a grunt as I saw that somehow, I had managed to squeeze behind the boulder, as if I had deliberately hidden behind it. I looked everywhere, seeing nothing but the curling white billows, some pine trees, and the horse-head-lined paths.

"You freak," I said loudly. "Forget it."

"Oh, come on, can't you take a joke?" Mandy said, bounding from behind the nearest tree.

She laughed and pointed at me and then at herself, voguing a bit with one gloved hand on her hip and sucking her cheeks in tight. She was dressed like me, from the black sweater to a black cap with a bill. But where I had on absolutely no makeup and had made a point of doing nothing with my hair but stuffing it into my cap, she had on tons of smoky, glimmery makeup and her hair hung in buoyant, fat curls around her shoulders.

It hadn't dawned on me until that moment that Troy might still be undecided about his decision to break up with us. We looked like Fashion Woman and her schlumpy sidekick, Emo Girl. He'd be playing against type if he picked me.

Not that I wanted him to, much.

"I can take a joke from anyone but you," I retorted.

She took my hand and swung it playfully. Then she began to trot through the fog as if she could see perfectly well. I was afraid we were going to break our necks.

"You should have saved me some champagne." The running was making her breathless. "I love champagne."

"Jeez, Mandy, were you spying on us?"

"Why not? You spy on me." She waggled my hand. "Let's not argue. We're having an adventure."

I forced the air out of my cheeks.

We galloped down the path that led to the lake, Mandy in the lead. I was beginning to tense up. Many times, I had looked into that lake and seen someone else's reflection—Celia. And I had seen Mandy bent over the water, arguing with Belle. We were here together. What if Celia and Belle came out to play?

"Maybe this isn't such a good idea," I said.

She cupped my cheek. "We're not going to let them win." Her smile was faint, but I found myself responding to it. It was incredible; I'd been on the receiving end of so much abuse from her. I'd seen her humiliate girls willing to endure just about anything for the long shot of being her friend; she'd ridicule them over their weight and their clothes. But now, when she smiled, I warmed to her. I didn't want to. It just . . . happened.

And I smiled back.

She fluttered her lashes. "You like me. You really, really like me."

"Yeah-huh." It was the best I could manage.

I noticed she kept looking at me as we skirted the water's edge. I saw the rowboat—it was one of Lakewood's castoffs, white with *LAKEWOOD* painted in dark green. It was wide, with three wood benches, one in the center, for rowing, and one on either side, for more passengers. Green and white oars lay on the floor, plus two orange life preservers and a silver flask. The initials MCW were scrolled on the side.

"Miles Clemson Winters," she said, following my line of vision. "My great-grandfather."

"Is Miles named after him?"

"Yes. Poor thing. No one's supposed to know that he was a baker." She snorted. "Didn't own a bakery, didn't create some amazing recipe, didn't discover oil on his property. Didn't make millions. Made cakes. Died."

"Is that on his gravestone?"

She opened the flask, took a swig, and handed it to me. "Single-malt scotch," she told me. "It'll keep you warm at night, pumpkin."

I sipped. It was like drinking fire.

She stuck out her hand, gesturing for me to hang on to her while she climbed into the boat. She kept her stance wide, like a seasoned sailor, then eased down onto the bench.

"Cast us off," she ordered.

SEVENTEEN

I LOOKED AT the white rope wrapped around the no-trespassing sign. Mandy wanted me to untie it, then hop into the rowboat.

I loomed over her. "Shouldn't you do this? You're the one with the experience."

"I'm already sitting down," she said sweetly.

I reached out with my boot and pushed on the side of the boat. To my delight, it rocked, and Mandy splayed out her arms for purchase. I laughed at her. Then I did untie the line and hop in, sitting on the bench in front of her, facing her.

"You're supposed to help me row," she protested as she grabbed one of the oars with both hands and slid it into the brass oarlock.

"I'm already sitting down." I took another swig from the flask.

She frowned at me and reached for the other oar. I made no move to help her. "The bottle that came from," she said as she fitted the oar into the lock, "would pay for three months of your tuition."

"You can afford it."

"Yes, we can." She reached for it and took a swig.

"C'mon, row, row, row my boat."

In the dark, she grinned like the Cheshire cat. Her white teeth were perfect, the best that money could buy. She was skinny-wiry. Rowing across the lake by herself would take her forever. I relented, moving beside her, lifting the left oar out of the oarlock and pushing against the lake bank. We began to move.

"I'm not a big fan of this lake," I muttered as I looked up at the back of Jessel. A light was on. Second floor, on the right— probably Alis and Sangeeta's room.

"Did we tell you the story about the school bus?" she asked me. "Rolling around down there, all the kids frozen . . . "

"It's an urban legend. They tell the same story about Lake Tahoe." I had been so disturbed by the story that I had checked it out on the internet. "And why on earth would you tell me such a freaky story when we're both already wigging out? What drives you?"

"I like to get a reaction out of you." She pulled off my cap with her free hand. "You're just so easy, flopsy top."

"Hey." What was up with her? If this was what happened to her after a little bit of alcohol, I was all for it. "If you'd been this nice in the first place, I would have joined your coven."

Mandy guffawed. "Wrong. You came here with a chip on your shoulder the size of a surfboard. You were too good for Marlwood. Because you are a decent, honest, poor person and we are spoiled bitches." She fluttered her lashes. "God bless us every one."

I began to deny it, but she was right. That was how I'd felt. Still felt, mostly.

"My dorm mates are very nice." I sounded like a prim and proper librarian.

"Coo, lovey," she said in a Cockney accent. "You just ain't done nuffin' to piss 'em off. Blimey, guvnah." She dipped her oar in the water, lifted it, and watched the droplets plink into the cold, black lake. "I came here pissed off to start with." She took off her cap and gave her shiny hair a toss. "I admit it freely."

"And you thought you-know-who could help with that."

"*Belle,*" she mouthed. "Yeah, I did."

"So I guess it's true that blondes are stupid."

"Me-*ow*."

"Whatevs."

"We should row. Put your back into it, Linz."

We glided across the water, working out a rhythm. Mandy didn't shirk. Fog clumped in bunches on the surface, then floated away, swanlike. Swan ghosts.

A bird cawed. The water rippled and I tensed, remembering times it had seemed as if Celia would rise from the lake. Or from the depths of my mind.

In less time than I would have expected, we made it to the center of the lake. I stuck my feet through the neck hole of one of the orange life vests and gazed out at Marlwood. The other time I'd rowed across the lake, I'd been too intent on saving my own life to take in the view. Victorian silhouettes, treetops, the cupola of Founder's Hall, and, on the highest rise, the admin building. Lights were blazing on the upper floors of the admin building, as if to reassure us that the grown-ups were on duty. That did nothing to make me feel better.

Lights were out in Jessel and Grose, our dorms. Ghosts walked there at night. Tormented us, watched us—envied us. Wore our faces and played make-believe. Plotted and planned.

"I hate this place," Mandy whispered. "I wish it would all burn down."

"I could help with that."

"We'd never get away with it." She sounded as if she'd already thought it through. "Even my dad's lawyers have their limits."

"Scruples. How refreshing."

My arms were getting tired and I wanted to get off the lake. I felt like we were tempting fate, rowing along, laughing and joking. The oars dipped in layers of white fog and then black water. The moonlight leeched all the color from us, as if we were one of the old sepia prints on the fireplace mantel at Jessel—of inmates, I now knew. Of Belle.

The boat rocked, and I caught hold of the bench with my non-rowing hand. Then I accidentally glanced into the water, bracing myself for seeing Celia's face. But she wasn't there. Mandy raised up and looked down beside me. No Belle, either.

Mandy patted my shoulder. "Who knows? Maybe after this, we'll become friends. We have all these villas and things—"

"Sure, yeah, okay," I said blandly. "It'll be supercool fun."

"*Why* are you always so sarcastic?"

"*Why* are you always so full of it? Julie had to find alternate transportation back here, thanks to you."

"You don't know that whole story. I—" Her voice changed. "Lindsay, look, there's something in the water. It's swimming toward us."

I jerked and raised my oar out of the water. "Where?" I cried, half rising.

"Stay down." She raised her oar too and pointed at the stern. "Eleven o'clock, on your side. See it?"

I stared hard. Fog rolled toward us, obscuring the moonlight, making it harder to see. I craned my neck as my heart jackhammered against my ribs. The water was obsidian shadow against ebony depths with no variation, except . . .

"Wait. Yeah," I said under my breath. "I see it."

A streak in the water, streaming straight at the boat. Reflexively, I lifted my feet and swallowed, hard.

Mandy shrieked with laughter.

"Psych!"

Livid, I balled my fist and socked her on the arm.

"Ow, ow!" she shouted. "Child abuse! Child abuse!"

"Shut up!" I hissed. "Oh, my God, Mandy!"

"I'm sorry." Chortling, she rubbed her shoulder. "It was just . . . there. Waiting to be done. It would have been a waste of a good prank not to have done it."

"What *is* it with you and pranking?" I asked, clenching my jaw. "Some kind of fetish?"

"I don't know. It's sick." She sighed and picked up her oar. "I first contacted you-know-who as a prank."

"And that went well."

She was quiet for a moment. "It did, for a while."

The bottom of the boat made a scraping sound; we'd

reached the other side of the lake. I was so relived I nearly wet my pants. Without waiting for my orders, I jumped out and dragged the boat farther onto land. I couldn't wait to get out of the boat. I'd give anything to hitch a car ride back.

"Come on," Mandy said, putting on her cap as we doubled over and crawled from the loamy earth into a stand of pine trees. Beyond that, there was a crumbling stone wall, very picturesque. Mandy led the way along it, then stepped over a ruined heap of rubble. A well-worn trail through wild grasses proved the popularity of our route.

"Voila," she said.

Across a vast lawn dotted with semicircular benches of white marble, brick walkways, and a large fountain sprawled a three-story white and brick colonial-style building. It was topped with a rotunda, like the White House, and white columns held up an overhang that sheltered the entrance. The glass doors formed a panorama window, and through it, ferns in marble urns flanked a reception desk that looked like it belonged in a posh hotel.

"*Sacrebleu*, it's so cheerful," I said.

"Whisper, tea leaf."

She gestured for me to follow her as she darted to the right, feet crunching on white gravel. There was no fog on their ground. We ran past brick walls covered with ivy, turned left into an alley, and exploded out of the darkness onto what appeared to be a soccer field. Overhead lights beamed down on lush grass; Mandy skirted the yellow circles, zooming along the perimeter. She was a blur of black, like a cat.

It had occurred to me when we'd left Marlwood that if

Mandy and I had a fight, I'd have to get back to campus on my own. But now, as we cruised the warren of miniature alleys and identical brick buildings, I knew I would have to stay on her good side. Short of a GPS or ghostly intervention, I would never find my way out of Lakewood alone.

About midway down our sixth or seventh alley, Mandy screeched to a halt and put one of her boots on the rung of a ladder obscured by ivy. It clanged. She giggled and began climbing like Spider-Man. I knew I was supposed to follow, and I wondered if Miles had been wrong about my physical condition. I was winded, and my lungs hurt. It seemed to me that my pneumonia had been real enough.

With hardly any pauses, Mandy rocketed all the way to the top of the three-story building. Then she hung over the side of the building, calling sotto voce for me to hurry up. I was wheezing. I made the mistake—only once—of looking down, and even though I had farther to go up than down, a rush of vertigo hit me.

Mandy kept gesturing at me and I finally made it up. As I swung my leg over the wall on the roof, sweat congealed into ice and I shivered. But Mandy was already headed for a door. She squatted beside it, pulled out a loose brick, and showed me a swipe card inside a plastic bag. She ran it through the door's card reader and the lock yielded with a click.

I held the door open while she put the key back in the bag and replaced the brick. I'd have been happier if we'd kept it. Then Mandy scooted around me and headed down a pitch-black staircase. I could hardly hear her footfalls. Stealth Mandy.

She'd already told me the plan. As an honor senior, Troy

got his own little suite, with a sitting room, a bathroom, and a separate bedroom. And most importantly a balcony, which was how we would enter without being detected.

Troy usually stayed up very late, at least until one, because he was a night owl with a sweet final-semester schedule that allowed him to sleep in. I could verify that much—I'd talked to him on the phone late, whenever I could get a connection.

We went out the back door of the building to a landing. Facing us, Troy's white balcony jutted toward us. There was a space between our landing and his of approximately two feet. All we had to do was climb up onto the rail, balance for one terrifying moment, take one giant step, then grab the white wrought-iron wall of the balcony and climb down.

Mandy went first. She scrambled up onto the railing and opened her arms for balance. As she hovered, I looked down at the rectangle of crushed white rock below. If you fell three stories onto gravel, would you die?

I thought of the hours of begging and demanding Celia had subjected me to, insisting that the only way I would ever be free of her was to kill Mandy Winters. I braced myself for another barrage now.

Nothing.

Mandy extended one leg, balancing like a gymnast. The wind picked up. I held my breath, wondering why she was taking so long. I still didn't trust her. And now, on this crazy night, I wasn't sure I trusted myself. I stayed back, arms folded, and waited.

"Oh, *God*," Mandy whispered.

I gasped, running toward her, arms extended in case I had

to catch her. And then, just as I reached the rail, she pushed off, cleared the space, and balanced on the balcony wall. Then she stepped gracefully down.

She'd faked me out again.

She gestured for me to hurry up, mouthing, *"I'll catch you."*

The wind blew harder. A cloud crossed the moon, dimming my vision. Not sure, not sure at all.

And then suddenly, wildly, I climbed up, stepped into thin air, and found the balcony with my Doc Marten. I fell into Mandy's arms and she caught me. Then she lowered me to the balcony deck and kissed me on the lips.

"Blech, Mandy," I managed, but I was so pumped from making it across the gap alive that I smiled as I pushed her away. She put her finger to her lips, reminding me to be quiet.

Then she crooked her finger and we tiptoed around the side of the balcony. A light beamed brightly, and I could hear Troy's voice. He was talking to someone.

"His bedroom," she said.

"This is stalkerish," I whispered, and she nodded happily.

We reached the window. The curtains were pulled back. A dim light shone. Mandy bent beneath the glass, staying out of range. I did too. On a silent count of three, we raised our heads.

Mandy pointed downward. Troy's bed was up against the wall beneath us. He sat with his back against it, wearing a white T-shirt, gray sweats, and bare feet, and he was on the phone. From my vantage point, I could see the faceplate. There was a picture of a girl with short reddish-brown hair.

"Yeah, I got it today," Troy said. He reached down beside

himself on the bed and picked up a sheer piece of red fabric. I gaped. It was a *thong*. "Under my pillow, you know it."

"That *pig*," Mandy whispered fiercely. She reached up as if to knock on the window. I grabbed her hand.

"Not worth it," I whispered. I was crushed. Troy was a pig. Troy. He'd just broken up with us, and he was getting underwear from another girl?

Were all guys just one guy? A handsome jerk who pretended to like you, then cheated on you?

While I pondered, Mandy pounded on the window, hard. I collapsed into a little ball.

"Yeah, *you*!" she shouted.

"Oh, God," I muttered, lifting my head and resting it against the wall.

A few seconds later, I heard a sliding glass door. Then Troy emerged, without the phone, his face a mixture of guilt, embarrassment, and anger. He was looking at Mandy. But as I got to my feet, he stared at me. He looked like a fish. If I could have laughed, I would have.

"Hi, *Thongboy*," Mandy said, stomping over to him. "So I got pushed down by the lake and I passed out, and when I woke up, the choker you gave *Lindsay* for her birthday was lying on the ground next to me."

"Oh, my God, Mandy, are you okay?" he asked, peering at her forehead. He looked at me. "What happened to you guys?"

"I told you, I was pushed. She fell off a motor scooter. But someone jumped out so she would swerve. And we think it's you."

"What? Why?"

We were clearly light-years ahead of him.

"Because when *I* woke up, there was a red thong lying on the ground," I deadpanned.

Mandy whooped with impressed delight. She high-fived me as Troy stood there, sputtering.

"Oh, my God, you're one of those sex addicts," Mandy said. "Or else just an immoral, horny little teenage boy." She batted her lashes at me. "Must make you feel like a loser to know that he left you out of his harem, Lindsay." I squawked out a protest. I'd thought we were bonding. I tried to think of an appropriately snarky comment, but I had nothing. I kept thinking about Riley and Jane, and how hurt I had been. How naive I still was. Because in all my scenarios about Troy, I had never figured him for a player.

Because he kept telling me over and over that he wasn't.

"We're coming through your crappy dive to go home," Mandy told him. "And I'm taking everything I ever gave you. Including the pass to our suite at the ballpark."

"Mandy," he said, "listen."

She pushed past him and walked into his suite. I followed, her unwitting, unwilling accomplice. His living room furniture was leather, with brass studs and dark bookcases crammed with lots of books. A gym bag sat in the middle of the floor and there was a sleek laptop beside it. Without missing a beat, Mandy walked to a bookcase and grabbed a hardback book. She handed it to me.

Tantric Sex Secrets.

Ewwww.

His bedroom was significantly more lived in, piled with

things. Jeans, T-shirts, and shoes were strewn everywhere. How many pairs of athletic shoes did one need? How many socks? There were posters on the wall, mostly forested landscapes, but there was also a large glossy picture of Emily Blunt, signed. Mandy reached up and ripped it down. She dropped it to the floor and walked over it.

I walked around it.

Mandy grabbed up his bomber jacket—the one he'd placed so sweetly around my shoulders more than once—and pulled open the top drawer of a dark wood dresser. She grabbed up tighty whities, socks, coins, and leather necklaces with things dangling from them and tossed them over her shoulder. She reached in and handed me a Rolex watch. A scattering of cuff links and rings that went flying like comets. And an embossed journal. And a fancy pen. A cashmere scarf.

She picked up speed, showering his floor with his stuff.

"Mandy," he said.

She flew into his closet and grabbed a black silk shirt. A snowboard. A pair of skis. She handed me the snowboard and started to pick up the skis.

She clearly had not thought about how to get all this back to Marlwood.

"Box the rest," she commanded him. "Ship it to our place in San Francisco."

Then she led me out of the bedroom, through the living room, toward a front door. My arms were full. It didn't matter if she took these things. He had more things. And he could buy whatever he wanted to replace the things we took.

She was heaving with exertion as she maneuvered to open

the front door without dropping the skis. I followed, wanting to die.

"Lindsay," he said.

She got the door open. We were standing in a carpeted hallway with walnut paneling. She charged to the right, hoisting the skis over her shoulder. I dropped a few things. I didn't stop to see what they were.

I looked over my shoulder at Troy. He looked like he'd forgotten who he was. That might have been nice for him.

We went into the elevator, went down, went out, and crossed to a side door. She opened it, blasted outside, and held it for me.

"Have you got everything?" she asked. "Because once I shut it, we can't get back in."

I nodded. We hiked back to the lake, staggering under the weight of Troy's possessions.

Once there, she stood at the water's edge and threw it all in. Skis, snowboard, jacket, Rolex. Rings, coins, cuff links.

"Some ghost is going to be very happy with all this crap," she told me.

And then we rowed back to Marlwood, screaming with laughter, so loudly our voices scared the birds off the water.

EIGHTEEN

THE NEXT MORNING, Mandy walked up to me in the breakfast line, which was such an event that people stopped talking to observe it. Mandy was haggard and pale, and she hadn't changed her clothes. Her hair was a mess, and I didn't think she'd even washed her face.

Granted, we hadn't gotten back to Marlwood until nearly after three, but we'd had at least four hours to clean up and get some sleep. And Mandy had often bragged that she thought sleeping was a waste of time. That she would sleep when she was dead, and not a minute before.

"Linz," she said, taking my arm and pulling me out of the line, which was annoying. I was tired and hungry. But the fear in her eyes trumped my low blood sugar. Something else had happened.

"Someone was in my room while we were gone," she said. "And they trashed it. My clothes are slashed. It's like they took a hammer to my jewelry."

"God, Mandy. Who?" I kept my voice low. Everyone was

dying to know what the great enemies Lindsay Cavanaugh and Mandy Winters were talking about in such hushed, earnest voices.

She took a deep breath. "I locked the door. I made sure. No one else has a key."

I tried to keep my face neutral. Rose and I had broken into her room with ease, using Rose's lock pick kit. Later, during a séance, Rose stole a key for me to use. We'd snuck it back, but maybe someone else had taken it without Mandy's noticing. Her room was usually as much of a disaster as Troy's had been.

"Is anything missing?" Could she tell?

"My Ouija board," she said. "And my picture of Belle."

"That thing with the half-eaten face?" I said. It was so faded and moldy. I didn't know how she slept with it in her room.

"And Belle's locket," she concluded.

I'd had Celia's locket, but I'd lost it in the snow. The inventory made it obvious that someone else knew about the possessions. And the only person *I* knew who fit that description was Miles.

"What about Miles?" I asked, keeping my voice neutral. "He carted off all that other stuff. Your research."

"But he just *took* it. He didn't destroy my belongings. Whoever did this was . . . crazy. Really enraged." She went even paler. Her skin was tinged with blue. And she was trembling.

"It could be one of your coven chicks," I whispered. "The ones you tricked into getting possessed. Or one of them *while* they were possessed."

"Yes," she mused, showing no remorse over having done so.

"That would make sense. We know it wasn't Troy. But there's the key issue again."

"Key issue. Maybe someone can pick locks." I had to say it. She looked so scared. Now that we were frenemies, it fell on me to help her out if I could.

"Are you going to tell security?" I asked her.

"I don't think so," she said slowly. "I think we need to keep it on the down low and figure it out ourselves. There would be too many questions that I wouldn't be willing to answer."

I heard the "we."

"We've got to be careful." She wiped her face with her hands and dropped her hands to her sides.

I heard the second "we." But she was right. We did have to be careful.

Oh, my God, I thought, *how is this happening?*

"Body part," I said. "The hair in the locket."

"But that was David Abernathy's hair, not Belle's," she said. "I still have the mourning brooch with her hair in it."

I remembered my wish to contact my mother. Did I have anything of hers? I'd washed her UCSD sweatshirt a million times. Maybe her fingerprints were on the framed picture of her, my dad, and me on our last family vacation. We'd gone to Vegas. She wouldn't gamble for her life, but she'd doubled down for free drinks and potato chips.

I had my mom's DNA. Could *I* be her body part?

"Well, it is what it is," Mandy replied. "Later, yes?"

"Sure," I replied as a default, not really because I was saying yes to anything.

As I went through the rest of the day, I got a lot of looks.

Everyone knew that I loathed and despised Mandy Winters. Clearly that had changed, and a big question mark was dangling over my head. Plus, by coming to me, she had outed me to whoever had hurt her and ruined her stuff. It was possible, although not likely, that Miles and I had had a genuine accident. But Mandy had dragged me into the sights of who ever was targeting her. Maybe she'd done it on purpose, to advertise the fact that she had backup.

Her sidekick, Emo Girl.

I gave as many looks as I got, although I was far more discreet. If Miles hadn't ruined Mandy's things, who had?

I didn't rule out Belle. Mandy didn't remember entertaining a male visitor, so maybe Belle had. Maybe he had wanted to punish Belle for going to see another guy, even if she had done it while hitchhiking in someone else's body. Just as he had hitchhiked in some guy's.

I pondered all the pieces as I went jogging after dinner. I knew I was supposed to take a buddy for safety, but I told myself I'd stay in plain sight and stick to the main paths. I didn't want to fend off any more questions about Mandy.

I needed downtime, desperately. Maybe everyone else had forgotten that I'd come to Marlwood shortly after having a nervous breakdown, but I hadn't. I was a master at disguising my anxiety, but at dinner, I'd come close to having a full-blown panic attack. In the din, no one had heard my shortness of breath. No one had seen my quivering lip and shaking hands, wrapped in a napkin underneath the table. But I was in serious danger of losing it, and I had to burn off the adrenaline in my system. Dilute the stress hormone known as cortisol.

So I began my run, listening to myself pant, watching my breath puff like a steam engine. I heard the rhythm of my footfalls. I began to feel grounded again. I had come a long way from the days when my panic had overwhelmed me to the point where I was lurching from the ice cream case to the frozen vegetables in our local Vons.

Mandy. I listened to the cadence of her name as I jogged. *Man-dy. Man-dy.*

I felt myself disengage from all my worries. My footfalls changed to *Lind-say. Lind-say.* Lindsay Anne Cavanaugh, starting over in the middle of the weirdest weirdness on the planet. Hitting reset. Putting myself back together with superglue. Finding myself in the maze that was Marlwood, all the other little rats and me.

Don't think that way, I thought, and then I blinked and looked around.

I caught my breath. I was standing outside the door to the admin building storage room. I turned and looked back, recalling nothing about running up the path, past the porch, around the wall. I had lost time, and I was shivering with cold.

Equally icy and aware, Celia shivered inside me. She had taken me over and brought me here.

My hand was on the doorknob and I knew she wanted me to go inside. Someone must be having a session with Dr. Morehouse.

I cringed at how excited that made me feel. But I had a

good reason. I had to know if any of them were after Mandy. I doubted they'd come out and confess to our shrink, but he was good at pulling things out of people. And maybe I'd figure it out, even if he didn't.

I went in and pulled the door closed. On the balls of my feet, I crossed to the dumbwaiter and crawled inside. As before, I winced, afraid my weight would snap the rope, but stubbornly remained.

"I don't know *why* I like to eat dead birds," someone was saying.

"Oh, *God*," I blurted, revolted. I covered my mouth and pushed on the door. I was going to be sick.

I flew out of the room.

BUT I WENT back again. I was just so astonished that someone (Claudette Hurst) could eat dead birds that I had to find out more. Maybe after I bolted, she confessed to destroying Mandy's possessions, and I had missed it. Maybe Claudette was the Marlwood Stalker, killing small animals for her own twisted needs.

So I went back again. My stealth was rewarded, but not in the way I expected. Instead of discovering what I wanted to know, I listened in on Charlotte Davidson's admission that she tried to shrink her feet by wrapping them in Ace bandages every night. Then I heard elegant Susi Maitland's confession that she was a bed wetter. In on the secret, her housemother stripped and washed her sheets every morning, with no one else knowing.

I learned that when Gretchen Cabot was home, she spent nights folding and refolding all her clothes. She hated to touch anything that was pink. When she touched any hue of blue, she tasted citrus.

Maeve Spitzer was contemplating a sex change operation.

I still didn't find out what I wanted to know, but my own weirdness was that I got kind of addicted to spying on my fellow Marlwoodians. Each time I eavesdropped on someone else's misery, I somehow felt better about myself. As if I didn't have to work so hard to feel normal, because being normal wasn't all that common. The other girls were as haunted by their obsessions and quirks as Celia haunted me. Maybe one of them was unhinged enough to murder Mandy and me, just because.

I was shocked. Marlwood was still an asylum for wayward girls. I just hadn't known it until now. Even though they had everything they could want—emphasis on *thing*—they really were under enormous pressure to live up to expectations. Their moms were PhDs or trophy wives. Their fathers were movie stars or billionaires. How could they hope to measure up to that? To surpass it? But they had better do it. Their parents were paying for private schools, enrichment camps, tutors, mentors, nutritionists, stylists, and therapists. And because they paid, they made their children pay it all back in accomplishments, awards, and Ivy League acceptances. These girls had to be the best that money could buy.

Dr. Morehouse seemed to know how to turn on the safety valve and help them let off steam. It worked on me, too. While

I collected secrets and Dr. Morehouse soothed tortured psyches, Celia would grow calmer during each and every session that we spied on. He was a great shrink.

I had battles of conscience, but I had to know what else I could find out. Who else was gripped by a neurotic need to binge and purge (Gigi Martinez), or an obsession with collecting the entire fall collection of Manolo Blahnick heels (Mia Thomassen). And the more I listened, the quieter Celia got. Maybe he was healing her. Maybe she knew it. Besides, if I let too much time lapse between observations, Celia would force me to walk up the hill, open the door, and climb into the dumbwaiter. If I continued to eavesdrop, maybe she would leave me alone, resting in peace at last.

But of course, my own sessions were the best. We spoke of inconsequential things, mostly small talk, but they reminded me that I wasn't alone. We ended each "chat," as he called them, with a walk along my geranium-strewn path. I left refreshed and joyful, and each time, hope bloomed that Celia had left for good.

A week went by, then two. Mandy and I got together to compare notes, but we had nothing. There were no more stories about the Marlwood Stalker. And I hadn't seen Miles in all that time, despite his claim that he was living on campus. It was as if he had dissolved into thin air, literally. I couldn't say that I missed him, because it would be way too twisted to miss Miles Winters. But when I finally broke down and asked Mandy where he was, she said he'd gone back to San Francisco. But I had the feeling that she didn't really know;

that it would be embarrassing for her to admit that she'd lost track of him.

Maybe it didn't matter. Now that she and I were air-quote friends, perhaps we could fix whatever there was left to fix. If anything.

Dr. Morehouse had to have a session with every single student at Marlwood—the damage control that Dr. Ehrlenbach had ordered. And speaking of Ehrlenbach, why didn't she come back? How could she monitor our well-being, see if we were accomplishing all the things the glossy school brochure had promised? I could write up my findings, I thought sarcastically. Let her know that beneath the surface, most of her star pupils were suffering from too much pressure. They were buckling beneath the weight of clutter, their many layers more like debris fields from battles they hadn't really won. They just pretended to be winners.

One night, I eavesdropped on a girl named Barbara, who had confided in Dr. Morehouse that her mother was having an affair with her stepbrother. Lightweight stuff, compared to other things I'd heard. Dr. Morehouse worked his magic, soothing her and helping her decide if she should tell her stepfather or not.

I headed back to my dorm feeling oddly lighthearted, given the agony I'd overheard. The night, though cold, was clear. It hadn't rained in days. I heard cheering from the illuminated soccer field. Team captain Julie would be over there, giving the Red team hell.

I let myself into Grose, saluted the statue that was blessing our mail, and wandered down the hall. The TV was on in Ms. Krige's housemother apartment. I smelled microwaved popcorn. Normal life. *My* normal life.

I pushed open the door to my room and flicked on the light.

The white head was lying faceup on my bed. Except . . . it didn't have a face. It had been smashed in. The nose was gone. The mouth, shattered.

And it lay on *my* bed.

My heart skipped beats as I walked across the room. Tingling, I peered down at it, holding myself stiffly, braced for . . . *what*?

"I'm glad," I whispered to it, half expecting it to move. In my world, that wasn't crazy. I had hated it for so long, feared it for longer.

Then I noticed that something was glinting inside, among the porcelain shards. I didn't dare reach in, but I turned on the lamp on the nightstand and raised it slightly to get a better look.

I gasped.

It was the silver crescent moon that had been missing from my black silk knitted choker.

Fear flooded through me. Whatever calm we had been blessed with, it was over.

I went back outside, meaning to rush over to Jessel and bring Mandy to show her. But when I snapped back into awareness, I was inside the storage room again as someone else poured out her heart to Dr. Morehouse.

"I—I didn't mean to take it," a girl whispered, weeping. "I was going to pay for it."

There was a pause. "We found quite a few things, Lara. From the school store, and . . . things that belong to other people. Your classmates."

I was agog. Lara was a thief. Was she *the* thief? The person who had taken our things?

Of course. She would have easy access to Mandy's room. She went in and out of there all the time. She might even have a key that Mandy didn't know about.

"I—I was . . . I *needed* them," she said. She sniffled.

"You have every possession you could possibly want. This is actually a problem with impulse control." He stopped speaking, and Lara cried even harder.

"I . . . I start thinking about it." She sobbed, hard. "I think about what it would be like to be caught. I'm so nervous by the time I do it. "

"Yes."

"And then, when I get away with it, the relief is . . . "

There was a silence. It stretched out over several seconds.

"It's the best drug there is," Lara said finally.

"So you do it for the pleasure that the relief brings you."

"I guess. I don't know. I get so scared when I'm getting ready. So I tell myself I won't take anything else. It's usually little stuff, but . . . but I know I won't get in trouble for that. People just look the other way. Because of who we are. Y'know, rich and all.

"So sometimes I steal bigger stuff. It's riskier."

Trashing Mandy's room was past risky. It was suicidal.

"We think such impulse challenges may be genetic. Meaning that it's not your fault. We've also found that it can be combined with some other sort of impulse situation. Such as bingeing." He paused again.

"I don't do that," she said in a rush. "That's disgusting."

"Or depression." His voice was soft, low, coaxing.

"I'm not depressed. I don't have anything to be depressed about." She was shrill. Defensive.

"You have an older sister at Yale. She's a world-class fencer." Another beat, and then he added, "Depression can be defined as anger turned inward."

"No sibling rivalry here." She blew her nose. "I'm not mad at Linette. She's away at school. I never even see her."

"Lara, I'm here to help you. Some kind of stress is manifesting itself as kleptomania. Is there a secret that you have, something you haven't been able to tell anyone?"

Like, you're possessed? I thought. But I didn't think Lara herself knew.

"No," she said firmly. "I just do it, okay?"

"You know you have to have six sessions with me, or the school board will be notified and you'll be asked to leave."

"My parents already said they'd pay you guys off. And nobody even missed that stuff. It was just little crap."

"Claire mentioned to me that Lindsay Cavanaugh lost a ring that belonged to her mother."

I went on alert. What else had Claire mentioned?

"Probably some piece of cheesy junk."

I jerked.

"It has value to Lindsay. Her mother is dead."

"I don't know why you people let her in here. If you want

to talk crazy, Lindsay's picture is beside the definition in the dictionary."

Nice. But I had a thought—she could have easily taken my choker and left the black silk beside Mandy. Then smashed in the head and dropped the moon inside.

"Celia," I thought, talking to her, *"did one of them force Lara to take my choker and break the head?"*

She stirred inside me, but she didn't answer. I took that to mean she didn't know.

"Let's look at this light on the wall," Dr. Morehouse suggested. "Now, clear your mind, and imagine yourself walking along a path."

I saw the glow through the crack in the wall. I listened to his gentle voice. And I smelled geraniums. I really smelled them.

I drifted.

Celia grew still.

"Ten," he said.

———

I DIDN'T KNOW how much time had passed when I opened my eyes again. But I felt refreshed, if stunned by what I'd learned. I had to tell Mandy right away.

I crawled back out of the dumbwaiter and headed across the room. Without looking where I was going, I opened the door.

And slammed hard into someone's chest.

"Lindsay," Miles said warmly, putting his arms around me. "Fancy meeting you here."

NINETEEN

"MILES," I SAID, trying move out of his arms as he smiled down on me. But he held me tightly against his chest.

"Come here often?" he said, looking meaningfully from me to the door and back again. "Peekie, peekie, peeping Tomette?"

"Wh-what do you mean?" I asked, but even I could hear the lie in my stammer. I knew exactly what he meant.

"Getting dirt on all the girls."

"Researching," I shot back.

"Yeah. Okay."

"Did you leave me a present on my bed?"

The warmth from his body was seeping into my cold bones. He smelled like cigarettes and cinnamon. There was a dimple in the center of his chin that I hadn't noticed before, and his blue eyes were beautiful. He was wearing a black hoodie and slouchy jeans, not the suave Euro-model of times past, but almost a regular guy. Except that there was something about him that made him different.

Something I responded to.

"I didn't leave you a present on your bed," he said, walking me backward. My back touched the side of the building. Flattened. "But I could. Or in it."

He cupped my chin and smiled down at me, his lush, long lashes brushing his cheeks. My stomach clenched and little chills fanned out from the small of my back. I tried to remind myself that this was Miles Winters, who had, speaking of beds, been seen in bed in the Lincoln Bedroom at the White House with his own sister

—*that could just be gossip*—

and who had been in rehab centers all over the world—

—*not his fault*—

—and who might have staged an accident to kill me.

Maybe he was in on it with *Lara*. What if he'd heard about our visit to Lakewood and trashed all Mandy's stuff with Lara's help in an act of mutual revenge? Mandy loved to hint around that Lara was gay. Maybe she and Miles were pissed off at her for going to see Troy.

I had assumed being a lesbian would be the deep dark secret that she might one day reveal in a shrink's office, if it even bothered her. Not that she was a kleptomaniac.

Maybe *he* was possessed. I looked at his ice-blue eyes. Not black. Not possessed at the moment. So warm, and I was so cold. And he was a guy who was, what? Coming on to me? After Thongboy had just so thoroughly dissed me that I still couldn't believe it?

"C'mon, Lindsay," he whispered. "Haven't you had enough swimming in the baby pool? The world's an ocean. Let me show it to you."

"I would drown," I said unsteadily.

"I'll breathe for you," he promised.

He leaned down. He was going to kiss me again. I tried to remind myself that the first time had been very unpleasant. But that wasn't true. As brief and surprising as it had been, it had been a great kiss.

"We've teamed up, remember?" He rubbed the sides of my chin with his fingers. His thumb pulled down on my lower lip.

"Miles, stop, okay?" I said. "This kind of stuff doesn't work on me."

"You haven't had very good luck with guys," he said. "Wily Riley hooked up with someone else at your party. Troy the Boy Toy, well, let's just say you two should have taken me with. I'd have helped you dump his T-bird in the lake."

That was so unexpected that I guffawed. Right in his face. He made a good-natured show of wiping nonexistent spittle off his nose.

If he knew about that, maybe he knew about Mandy's trashed room. So I told him. He was completely caught off guard. She hadn't mentioned a word of it to him.

"Maybe she didn't want to worry you," I said. Then I added, "Where have you been?"

"Sorry, I had business." His voice was tight. "Probation meeting."

"Must have gone well. You might have mentioned it."

He relaxed a little, his shoulders coming down. Lines in his face softened. He was incredibly good-looking, in a quirky way.

"You missed me."

"I just couldn't keep tabs on you. "

His smile was triumphant. "But I didn't come back empty-handed. I've got something for you."

What was this, hitting on Lindsay round two? I couldn't back away; he had me pressed against the wall. He was tall; he loomed over me, smiling like he knew the best secret. His body heat seemed to be melting me. The warmer I got, the more aware I was of how cold I had been.

"Something you will like," he murmured.

He lowered his head toward mine, and I felt my lips parting. I was going to kiss Miles Winter. I actually wanted to.

Then Celia roared to life inside me. I felt her thrashing, her coldness washing over my bones. Her screams echoed in my mind: *"Not him! Not him!"*

I grunted.

"Not him!"

As he sighed against my mouth, Miles brought his hand around my neck. I flared with fear. He put his other hand around my neck and eased his weight against me.

"Not him!"

I looked into his eyes . . . I tried to look into his eyes. His head was blocking the moon and his features were masked by shadow. His breathing sounded different.

His hands around my neck tightened.

Oh, my God, oh, God. I whimpered.

A little tighter. He was beginning to cut off my air, and he lowered his face toward me. He was humming under his breath. I tried to knee him, but I was pinned.

He put his mouth over mine.

In my mind, Celia screamed, and screamed, and screamed.

"Not him!"

And I bit him.

"Ow!" he yelled, letting go of me, stumbling backward. He put his hands over his mouth and pivoted in a circle. "Ow!"

I pushed past him, flying down the path. I knew I should scream, but I couldn't utter a sound. *God, God, God* . . . I was heaving, running faster than I ever had in my life, faster even than when Belle and the other spirits had come after me outside the operating theater, hell-bent on murdering me.

And Miles shouted after me, "Why the hell did you do that?"

I kept running.

"I found the messenger bag, you ninny! That was my surprise. And I found something else!"

"I don't care!"

I thought I was yelling, but not even I could hear myself. I was crying and stumbling over my feet, racing back to the dorm.

"I want out of here, I want out," I whispered. I tasted Miles's blood on my lip and spit on the back of my hand.

I stumbled onto our porch and pushed open our front door. Julie was standing with Ms. Krige, holding the remains of the white head in her arms. Both of them stared at me as I skidded to a stop. Ms. Krige looked alarmed, and Julie was near tears.

"How could you do it?" she demanded.

I looked from her to Ms. Krige, then back to her. I took a step toward her.

"Julie, I didn't break that."

"I found this." She held up the crescent moon pendant.

"Yeah, I lost it. Someone took it," I emphasized. "Probably whoever broke the head. And I—"

"I don't care about the stupid head," she said, cutting me off. "But of course you knew that. How *could* you?" Her eyes were glittering. Our housemother stood a little closer to her.

I was baffled. Then Julie held the head out to me, and I reluctantly peered inside.

Her little stuffed corgi, Panda, lay in tatters. He looked like a bird's nest. One little black eye stared up at me.

"Why on earth would I do that?" I said. "*Rose* took your head without asking."

Julie turned away, sniffing. I held out my hand to her. When she ignored it, I put it on her shoulder. She stiffened as if at a horrible violation. Like me with Miles.

Ms. Krige said, "I told Julie you would never do something like this."

"But she would," Julie shouted, whirling back around. "She's crazy! Everyone knows it!"

"No." Wounded, I folded my arms across my chest. Hugged myself.

"I don't want to share a room with her anymore," Julie said. "I want her to move out!"

She turned on her heel and ran toward our room. Correction: her room. She had invited me to share it with her when I'd gotten accepted late. It was her first time away from home and she was anxious. Plus, her parents would get a rate reduction. But it was her room. She could kick me out if she wanted.

"Ms. Krige," I said, "I didn't ruin her things. I swear it."

"I know, honey," Ms. Krige assured me. She liked me. She'd

tried to warn me about how mean some of my classmates could be, especially toward an outsider like me. But Julie had always been there, sweet and thoughtful, my friend.

"Do you know who did do it?" I asked the older woman.

She hesitated. "No. But I'm sure we'll find out, and the guilty will be punished."

I almost told her then that Miles Winters had been in our room. But it was Julie's room now.

"Claire has asked if she can move into Ida's room," she said, in a tone that said she didn't entirely approve. "Would you like to move into hers?" The haunted room. But weren't all the rooms in our dorm haunted?

"Sure," I said.

My housemother looked relieved. I'm sure she didn't want any of this happening on her watch.

"Thank you, dear," she said. "I'll have someone help you pack."

———

I SKIPPED DINNER and Ms. Krige herself helped me pack. I was moving from a room with a perfect view of Jessel and the quad to a room with no view at all. No windows. It was unbelievably dark.

Luckily, I didn't have that much to move—I had brought everything in a couple of suitcases and a cheesy plastic backpack, while the other girls had sent large trunks ahead. They were called steamer trunks, and in some cases, they had been in their families for generations. Marlwood might be a new boarding school, but most of my schoolmates had been to boarding schools before. People were trying Marlwood out.

I wondered how many would come back next year, with all our bad press. That had to be why Dr. Ehrlenbach had still not returned.

Ms. Krige and I finished carrying the last of my books into the dreary room. Claire hadn't taken down her Hawaiian art prints from her mother's gallery yet, but I didn't mind them, no matter that they were kitschy. I didn't have any posters for my walls.

"Can I help you unpack?" Ms. Krige asked as we set down the box of books. She looked sweaty and tired. She was getting up there.

"No, that's okay," I said.

She smiled and walked out of the room and I sat on the bed. I knew it was dark outside, but it was as dark as a basement in my new room. I wanted to close my eyes, see if I could smell geraniums, but I was afraid to. I had no idea how I would ever get to sleep.

Then Ms. Krige walked back in. She knocked gently on the door and poked in her head.

"Dr. Morehouse says he's had a cancellation and he'd like to see you tonight," she said.

I wondered if he'd been informed of what had happened. If I were being summoned to explain why, under stress, I destroyed other people's property.

I put on my army jacket and went outside. As I headed up the path, I saw Mandy walking with the rest of the Jessel girls. Spotting me, she gave me a wave. Other girls—Jessel and non-Jessel girls alike—took note and elbowed each other, surreptitiously watching us.

I wished that we had ESP, instead of being possessed by each other's mortal enemies. And just as I wished that, Mandy broke from her pack and trotted up the hill, to me.

"I heard what happened," she said breathlessly. "You broke that head and Julie booted you."

"That's not what happened. Booted me, yes, but I didn't do it. And I didn't shred her little stuffed dog. But I have some big news for you."

"Hey, Mandy, c'mon." Lara climbed the hill, making a show of huffing, and put her hands on her hips. "We'll start the movie without you."

"Go ahead," Mandy told her, gazing regally at her over her shoulder. "I care not." She turned back to me. "What?"

Lara hadn't budged. She stared straight at me, as if she still couldn't believe that this month, I was in. As far as social acceptability at Mandy's lofty level went, I bounced in and out like a pogo stick. With all the cozying up and whispering we were doing, Lara's position as Mandy's second in command looked to be less stable than before.

"Can't tell you now," I said. "But we've got to talk."

"Conservatory, elevenish," she whispered.

"Okay."

Then I turned and headed for the admin building, wondering if Miles was still there.

Wondering what I would do if he was.

TWENTY

WIND WHIPPED THE trees and threw shadows on the walls of the admin building as I walked to my appointment. The shape of a man appeared here, there, but no one was really there. I began to wonder if I'd actually seen a man in Mandy's room. Stare into the abyss long enough, and it stared back at you.

Professionally pleasant, Dr. Morehouse let me in and walked me into Dr. Ehrlenbach's office. He was wearing a dark green sweater with the Marlwood logo embroidered on the front. She'd kept the office very cold; he had a space heater, and I settled in as it dissipated my chill.

"Would you like some tea?" he asked me.

I said yes; he went to get it. I leaned forward and cocked my head to the left, trying to see the crack in the wall where I did my spying. It wasn't visible; I relaxed a little, assuring myself that he wasn't on to me.

He brought in the tea—peppermint, and then sat behind Dr. Ehrlenbach's highly polished wood desk. I saw that my hand was shaking, set the tea down, and folded my hands in my lap.

"Bad day," he said.

"Yours or mine?"

He pulled a sympathetic adult-as-friend expression. "I know Julie asked you to move out."

"I didn't break her head or rip up her dog."

"I didn't think you had," he said. "It hurts to be unjustly accused, no?" He wasn't going to waste any time with small talk tonight. Maybe he was tired. Or he figured I needed extra help stat.

I inhaled the scent of peppermint. "Yes," I said. "It sucks."

"Especially when people who do terrible things seem to get away with them repeatedly." He drank his tea. "You're one of the smartest girls in this school, Lindsay. If I ever seem to patronize you, I apologize."

Accepting what amounted to a compliment, I managed to steady my hand enough to pick up my tea. I was hurting. Scared.

"You've had a lot of disappointments. Losses. Boys, your mom, now Julie. None of it through anything you did." I set down my cup and watched the steam. Evaporation was what I was all about.

"Julie wanted a roommate because she was scared to be alone," I said. "But I just made her more scared."

"And you're wounded by that." He regarded me over the rim of his teacup. "And if these wounds aren't taken care of, they become scars. So let's take care of them."

That sounded ominous. Cupping my hands around my cup, I resettled in my chair. "Okay."

"Let's begin at the beginning." He smiled kindly. "Get it out in the open, so you can move on. I know you've been to other therapists, and you've done a lot of work. So this should be easy."

"Okay," I said again.

"I want to take you back to when your mother was sick. You tried very hard to get her to try more aggressive treatment. You live in San Diego. There are all kinds of high-tech biomed companies there, running experimental drug trials, inventing new surgical methods."

"She didn't want to," I murmured, but a flash of anger ran across the backs of my eyelids.

"Your father said that she didn't want to, am I right?" He drank his tea. "He told you not to bring it up."

She would have listened to me if she'd had the chance, I thought. *But she let him take over. She did what he said. And he said not to try.*

He said not to try. I was trembling.

"Do you think that if your mother had stood up to your father, she'd be alive today?"

"Whoa." I took a breath and sat back. "My dad is a good guy."

"It's what you think," he said gently. "Deep down. How you feel. It doesn't matter if it's true or not. It's your reality, inside your mind."

"He did what he thought was right," I said, but we both knew that was what I thought I was supposed to say. What my other therapists had told me. Dr. Morehouse was the only one who actually listened.

"You couldn't save her. From the cancer. From him." I drank more tea. It was too hot. I drank it anyway.

"They wanted us to talk about our anger," I said. "Especially the social worker at the hospital."

"Who probably used all the finesse of a cattle prod."

He was proud, my Dr. Morehouse. He thought he was better than that social worker. And he was. I had listened to him draw out the secrets of the other girls and make them deal with them. He would help me. Maybe he could exorcise me. Celia had picked me because I matched her in so many ways. But if I changed, would she move on?

"So, your mother dies. And then, you try to put your life together. You're mad at your father, but you can't say that. So you turn away and try to start over. You make new friends. You have a new boyfriend. Riley. And let's talk about what he did."

I sat in silence. I didn't want to talk about it. It was too humiliating.

"This is what you're haunted by," he said. "You think your anger at your father is acceptable, even admirable, because it's on behalf of your mother. But being mad at Riley seems, what?" He opened his hand to me, as if to say, *You're on*. It was time for me to make him look even better.

"Pointless. It was just a crush."

"It was a betrayal."

"People our age hook up. They move on." I tried to sound philosophical. It was what Jane had told me, afterward. She had expected me to get over it. All her lectures about using boys and never caring for them had zinged right over my head. I had unleashed my inner drama queen when I found out that she'd slept with him just for fun.

People hook up. They move on. That was what she'd said to me when we ran into each other at the park, after my breakdown.

She also said that people who had breakdowns were weak. They bailed out of their problems by going crazy and forced other people to pick up their pieces. My breakdown annoyed her. And it cast doubt on her ability to pick the right people to allow in her presence.

"You really liked him. You gave him your heart."

"*Yes,*" Celia said inside me. I jerked. He noticed.

"Are you all right?"

I cleared my throat. "Yes."

"Tell me about that night." He leaned forward, giving me his attention.

"Jane wanted me to throw a party. I didn't want to, but I did it."

And I told him all the rest. About worrying about the broken glassware, and the carpet, and the noise. Knowing my dad hadn't really wanted me to throw a party but was happy that I had a social life, so he let me do it. But people were OOC. At Jane's, they followed the rules: cleaning up as they went, being respectful of her family's things. At my house, not so much.

Someone had announced that my dad's car was in the driveway, so the partyers had to terminate any nonapproved activity, including the couple—whoever they were—who had locked themselves in my parents' bedroom.

When the bedroom door had opened and Jane and Riley stood there arm in arm, Jane had tittered and said, "Whoops." She had slept with him in my parents' room, on the throw I had knitted for my mother. Riley had the decency to look shocked and ashamed, as if he couldn't believe what he'd just done.

But I had heard laughter through the door, before I'd known who was doing the deed. He hadn't been shocked and ashamed then.

I had known I was supposed to step aside and let Jane have him if she wanted him. But she didn't want him. Wanting a boy implied you thought they had value.

"You fault yourself for taking this relationship seriously," Dr. Morehouse said. "You weren't sophisticated enough not to care."

Jane had laughed at me. All the girls had. She'd said I was too young to hang out with "her babies." And when I had refused to speak to Riley, she said I didn't really care about him. If I had, I would have fought to get him back.

"You equate not fighting for this boy with the battle your father refused to fight for your mother. You think that if he'd loved her enough, he'd have done more to keep her."

"Whoa," I said again.

"And this disappointment runs very deeply. It's a wound you've been ridiculed for having, and that you've been told is inappropriate.

"And now, another boy has betrayed you."

He meant Troy. "Not really," I murmured. "All he did was break up with me."

"To the heart, that's a betrayal," he said. "We're dealing with feelings, not rationale."

"Betrayal," Celia said. *"By men."* I felt itchy, as if Celia were scratching from the inside, trying to burrow her way out.

He raised a brow and cocked his head. "I'm sorry. I didn't catch that."

"I—I didn't say anything."

Itchy, and overloaded. Too full. Brimming over.

"It's all right," he said. "You're safe in here."

"I am not safe."

And something in me blew. Everything I had been dealing with—or trying to deal with—overwhelmed me. It was too much, all too much; I started sobbing. My mind jumped from my father to Riley to Troy to Miles.

And from there, to David Abernathy:

It was December, and there was snow. The girls were freezing. They had no blankets. They were dressed in linen shifts, in preparation for the operation. They were moved through the tunnels so they wouldn't sound the alarm. There were secret tunnels everywhere, to make them disappear. So the other girls, the lucky girls, wouldn't panic and scream.

David and Celia had planned the escape. She would start the fire, as a diversion. They would help everyone out, he and the orderly, Mr. Truscott. And the horrible lobotomies and the starvation and the inhuman living conditions would end. There would be no stain on his record of service, and she would be spared.

He and she would escape together and be married, and no one would take her from him. Because she would be his, plucked like a rose from her father's garden.

"My love is like a red, red rose," he sang as they made their plans. As he kissed her and promised her that true love would win the day.

Stealthily, she stole the lamp oil that was left out—not realizing at the time that he was the one who left it for her—and the oily rags, and she hid them in her cell. She and the others were scheduled for the surgeries the next morning—Belle Johnson would be first, and Celia would be number seven.

But Celia would start the fires and save them all, even Belle, whom she despised for trying to take her David from her. Belle, who had tried to murder her in the hydrotherapy bath because she stood between Belle herself and David.

Soon the oily rags began to smolder, then to burn. But the fire traveled too quickly; drugged for the surgeries, the seven girls were having trouble staying in advance of the flames.

Then the door flew open and David appeared on the threshold. Celia held out her arms to him, joyful, terrorized—

And he pushed her back in.

To make her burn.

"Oh, God, oh, my God," I gasped, snapping out of the vision. I was gripping the sides of the chair, rocking back and forth.

Across the desk, Dr. Morehouse held a box of tissues. When he saw that I was looking at him, he pulled a few sheets out of the box and passed them to me.

I twisted them in my hands. I couldn't stop crying. Every part of my body ached. My head was throbbing. Even my teeth hurt.

He didn't soothe me or tell me that everything was all right.

He let me cry, and I wept as I had never, ever cried before. Deep, low, soul-shattering, heartbreaking.

Celia's hair on fire, she burst through the tunnel wall beneath the operating theater. The tunnel wall was blazing, but she dared to run through the flames. The world was falling down into ash.

The sky shook with smoke and screaming.

"Damn you, Celia Reaves!" Belle shouted, left behind to die. "I'll send your soul to hell for this!"

And Celia, on fire, every inch of her burning, ran.

To the forest, to the ground, to sizzle in the snow. And he found her there, and buried her . . .

"Let me out, let me out!"

Celia pounded hard against the prison of my flesh. I coughed and bent forward so that I could look into the polished wood of the desk to check my reflection. My eyes were chocolate brown. I was myself. Still, she kept fighting. I could feel her.

"When we've been traumatized," he said, "we try to find a pattern. It's human nature to look for a cause so that we can avoid it in the future."

"Men," I heard myself say. Celia's word, my voice.

"I'm afraid we haven't given a very good accounting of ourselves." He handed me more tissues. "I doubt you trust even me."

"I'm sorry," I blurted. I didn't know what to do. He started to reach for my hand, then stopped. I knew about therapists and the no-touching rule.

"No need to apologize," he said. "Now that we know where we stand, we can move forward. That's a step in the right direction." He smiled at his little pun. "We have to find ways for you to learn to trust me. And then I can help you. Are you willing to give it a shot?"

"Help me! Help me help me help me!" Celia screamed inside my head.

Could he help us both?

"I'll give it a shot," I said.

"Good." He turned on his flashlight and aimed it at the wall. I gazed at it.

"There is a path," he prompted.

Fire! Fire!

"With geraniums," I said loudly. "*My* path."

"Yours," he assured me. "Let's count together. Ten."

Nine.

TWENTY-ONE

"ONE," I SAID, and opened my eyes. Across the desk, Dr. Morehouse gave me a concerned-therapist face.

"Better?" he asked.

I paused, and checked. Celia's frenzy was over. So was mine. I felt calm and relaxed. Safe. And not quite so wounded.

"We'll work on this together, once a week," he reminded me. "We can't do it all in one day, so you need to be patient. Today we just got started."

"It's just . . . " I tried to find the words to describe how badly I needed this to be fixed, *now*. It could be a matter of life and death. Correction: it already was.

"Healing takes time," he said. "It's not like we can do something once and be done with it. There's no shortcut. No pill, no shock therapy. No special surgery—"

"Like a lobotomy," I blurted.

He looked at me strangely. "Miles Winters was just discussing that with me. It seems Marlwood has a sordid history on that subject."

"He told me too," I said. I cleared my throat. This was risky territory. I wasn't sure how much Dr. Morehouse knew about the night I had lost it. *Why* had I brought it up?

"Well, luckily we don't do that kind of thing anymore."

"No kidding."

"It was barbaric," he said. "What makes it problematic is that in some cases, it did work."

"A quiet zombie is a happy zombie."

He dipped his head. "The people of that time suffering with severe incurable schizophrenia and chronic deep depression might agree with that statement." He made as if to rise. That was my cue to leave.

"But that's not you. You're a runner, yes? You can't run one time and be done with it. You have to run every day. You're training your mind to think a different way."

"Got it."

"We need to substitute new habits for the old ones." He smiled wearily. "Which can be pretty tough."

I went outside into the fresh air. I didn't realize that I'd smelled smoke in Dr. Marlwood's office until I was outside. Or dreamed that I'd smelled smoke. It had rained while I was inside, and Marlwood smelled clean. I looked for Miles and didn't see him.

I went back to my deeply depressing room and unpacked. Claire told me I was crazy to move in there. She stayed in the doorway and wouldn't come in.

"They should clear out one of the extra rooms and let you move in there," she said.

"It's not exactly wonderful," I agreed.

"I'll leave the art for you. It's original, from our gallery in Maui."

"That's sweet." I smiled at her. "Thanks."

Julie didn't make an appearance. Marica told me everyone was mad at her. No one else believed I had broken the head and torn Panda apart.

"It's like . . . she was picking a fight," Marica said. "Just *looking* for something to blame on you." I agreed with that. Julie had wanted to dump me. Her destroyed possessions provided an excellent reason to do it.

"THEY THINK *YOU* broke the head," I told Mandy when I met her in the conservatory. "You or one of your hench-persons."

Mandy wrinkled her bruised forehead as she poured us each a glass of wine. She had given up on wearing a bandage, and the bumps and purple blotches were spectacular. It amazed me how much abuse a body could take and still function.

The goblets we were using were cut glass, with flat bevels bearing an *M* in the center—for Marlwood or Mandy, I wasn't certain. Someone must have swept up the evidence of our last meeting. No one said a word about shattered glasses or drips of Bordeaux red on the fireplace stone.

"We did rip up the mattress last semester. Actually, Kiyoko did it." She grimaced. "I told her it was going too far. She was OOC." I thought it was convenient that she could pin the blame on someone who was no longer here. But I glossed over it. I had more pressing matters to discuss. I just wasn't sure how to explain what I knew.

"I got sent to see Dr. Morehouse," I continued. "After Julie found the head."

She nodded. "I'm scheduled for tomorrow."

I filed that away. "I mean, it was an extra visit, because Julie threw me out. Anyway, I was in the hall, and I heard him talking to someone in his office. And whoever it was, was freaking out. So . . . " I trailed off.

"So you put your ear to the door. You got an earful." She grinned at her own cleverness. "And you have something juicy to tell me."

I looked down. I was going to *make* her force me to tell her. She'd be more likely to believe information she had to work for. That was how people were wired.

"Come *on*. You can't stop now."

"It was Lara. She was completely losing it. Mandy, I think she's the one who trashed your room." The look on her face would have been funny, if any part of the situation could have been funny. I thought about Miles and his definition of sanity—feeling many things at the same time.

"That's not possible." Blinking rapidly, she swallowed down half her wineglass. "Lara's my best friend."

I hesitated. "Remember that night we went to Troy's together? You went somewhere without her."

"I go all kinds of places without her. We're not *married*. Even if she'd like to be, she's such a dyke."

I let that statement speak for itself.

"I heard her talking about stealing things. From classmates. Little stuff. Kleptomania." I drank some wine, uneasy about the way I was squishing the truth so that Mandy would believe it was the truth.

"That's just . . . stupid." She threw back the rest of the glass and poured herself another. "Swiping pencil sharpeners and destroying all my worldly possessions are two different things."

"That's true. But it sounded like she was on the verge of copping to it. She sounded like she wanted to unburden herself about something else. Then her time was up." I shrugged. "I would have let her have my hour."

"Therapists," she grumped. "You could tell them you're suicidal and they'll ask you to make another appointment because they have a golf game." She topped off my glass. "Do you think she broke the head, too?"

I sat back in my chair and tipped my glass from side to side, watching the red liquid slosh. No, I didn't think Lara had.

"I saw your brother," I ventured.

"I know. He brought us the messenger bag." She bent sideways and grabbed something, then hefted it onto the table like a dead fish. It was the bag, moldy and smelly. I made a face and cradled my wineglass against my chest.

Did he happen to mention I bit him? I mentally asked her. I gazed down at the bag, remembering that night of screaming ghosts. How terrified he and I had been. *Our first kiss.*

She opened a tiny black leather shoulder clutch and got a tissue. Cupping the tissue, she opened the messenger bag and reached inside. "He found these in the road."

It was a pair of men's black leather gloves. They smelled like smoke, and I recoiled. Then I took the tissue from her and lifted one up, examining it.

"Lined with cashmere, very nice. There's a burn on the inside of the left wrist. Miles thinks it's from a cigarette."

"Was there any ID?"

"We have no clue who they belong to. But he found them at the side of the road, right where he saw the white thing that made him swerve on the Vespa. *And . . .* "

She pulled a wad of transparent fishing line from the bag as well.

"Check it out." She wadded a fresh tissue into a ball and covered it with another one. Then she wrapped the line around the newly formed "neck" below the covered ball and dangled it above her head.

"So someone stretches this line across the road. If you're on a motor scooter in the rain, and you see something in the road . . . "

"Oh, my God."

"Or, someone was going to do some beading and also dropped their gloves." She reached into the bag a third time. "While they were smoking."

She showed me the soggy remains of a white box with a red rectangle on the front. The writing was too damaged for me to read.

"Dunhill cigarettes. Pricey. Miles loves them. But these aren't his."

"If someone wanted to kill me, they could have done it while I was unconscious." I felt cold chills running through me. I should be used to almost getting killed, but I wasn't.

"They were probably after Miles." She said it like a joke.

"Your brother *is* scary. Did you find anything else?"

"Aside from all my papers ruined, no. Nice of you to tell him everything, by the way. About the possessions."

When I started to defend myself, she held up a hand. "It was the right call, Lindsay. I should have told him myself. It just seemed like it would be so . . . tedious to go through the persuasion part. 'Ghosts are real, spirits are real, I'm possessed . . . '"

"I skipped it," I told her. "I told him he could believe it on his own time."

She snorted. "Sweet. You know, you two skulking around . . . it could make *me* jealous."

So maybe you alienated my best friend by destroying her prized possession? I wondered. Or had she talked Miles into doing it? He'd just happened to be outside the storage room when I'd come blasting out. It was a short walk from my dorm to there. Maybe he'd snuck in, ripped up Julie's things, then waited to see what would happen next.

Maybe he hadn't found the gloves and other things. Maybe he just said he did. And he was waiting to see what would happen now.

I glanced through the leaves of the conservatory's lush garden, out the windows into the darkness. Above us, the moon hung fat and yellow.

"You don't seem too upset about Lara," I said.

"I'm just hiding it well. I'm upset about all of it." She nervously tapped the glass with her fingernails. "I look around at everyone, wondering who's doing these things. Who tried to kill me. And you."

It's different now that you're *in danger,* I thought. *Now that your evil little schemes have come back to haunt you.*

"They're isolating us, don't you see?" She kept drumming on the table. "Your best friend made you move out. By trashing my room, they're making me doubt all my friends. Maybe Lara wasn't even in that office with Dr. Morehouse. There might have been a tape playing. Like in my haunted house."

There was no easy way I could let her know I was sure Lara had been in there without tipping my hand. I was confused about how much to tell her.

"They who?" I asked, to redirect her attention.

"They who. Exactly." She shifted anxiously in her chair. "While Miles and I were going through the moldy, disgusting papers in this bag, I did remember that I originally performed the ritual on the full moon. It was a big deal. Like magic is more powerful because of the lunar pull or something. And we can use that to our advantage."

"We can? Why?"

She huffed at me as if I were a complete dolt.

"There's a full moon tomorrow night. It's a Friday night, too. So I thought I'd have one of my parties. We could invite all our suspects and see if anyone acts suspicious." Her nails clicked on the glass.

"Like . . . if they're moonstruck?" I said.

"*God.* How dense are you?" She tipped the wine into her glass, killing the bottle. "Maybe the moon has nothing to do with it. Maybe that's just a superstition. But if someone else knows about how this stuff works and holding it then helps make anyone nervous, that'd be a good sign."

I thought a moment. Mandy gathered up her pretty blond hair and let it cascade over her shoulders. The lack of hair emphasized her bruises, making it look as though her injuries were seeping out from inside her head.

"So we'll have a full-moon party. And tell people not to moon each other. But if the killer is plugged into any of what's going on, maybe it'll be an extra pebble in their shoe."

"Or maybe it'll make things go haywire."

"We can't hide. That isn't working," she countered.

Celia had chosen her host well. Like her, all I wanted to do was hide. But that was no longer an option for either one of us.

"Okay, what's *your* suggestion?" she demanded, drumming the table.

"Maybe Celia or Belle knows who it is."

"I got nothing," she bit off. "You?"

"No. I—I'm kind of afraid to deal with her."

"Good." She mouthed, *I'm done.* So we both wanted to stop being possessed. That was good.

"I'm not going to sit around and wait for another attack. Spread the word about the party." She reached down and picked up a second bottle of wine.

"At the lake house?" I hated that place.

"If we're going for shock value, we should have it at ground zero," Mandy argued. "The operating theater."

I hated that place even more. I hated it the most of all the bad places on campus. Mandy had tried to kill me there. She had set it on fire. Snow had drifted in through the gigantic hole in the roof. And still, it remained standing. And haunted. And evil.

"That was where it all happened," Mandy said. "The

lobotomies. The fire. And *that's* why we're having another bottle of wine."

"Bring it on." I held out my glass. We toasted each other.

"We shouldn't invite too many people," I said. "We won't be able to watch them all."

"I disagree. There's safety in numbers. Plus we don't know if it's someone in our inner circle. It might be some sad little loser stuck in one of the bad dorms, out to pay me back for failing to acknowledge her pathetic existence."

"You do have a practically infinite number of enemies."

She moved her shoulders. "I like to make an impression."

"I'd just like to make it to spring break."

"We'll say we're both throwing the party," Mandy said. "That way, all the have-nots and are-nots will feel emboldened to show. That'll mix it up even more."

"Why do you have to be so mean all the time?"

She picked up her wineglass and squinted at it. "There's sediment in this." She looked at me. "I'm not mean. I'm honest. And direct. You think these things too. You just don't say them."

"I don't," I insisted.

"That's why you're in therapy. To learn how to be honest with yourself."

I exhaled. "I'm not going to argue with you."

"Good. Because I really don't care if you're honest with yourself or not." She swirled the wine and frowned at it. "This is garbage. Now listen, since you're poor and have no resources, I'll provide all the refreshments. But we won't serve any of this crap."

"Thank you, your majesty. Do you want to decorate? Meet early?"

"*Decorate?* Gee, yeah, maybe we should get a piñata, too." She looked heavenward. "See, this is why you'll never command any respect."

"I'll help you carry the supplies over." She wasn't grasping that I was attempting to find out the time of her appointment with Dr. Morehouse without asking her. So that I could spy on her.

"I see the shrink right after dinner. Then we can get to work." *Bingo.* "Okay."

She pressed her teeth together in a rictus grin, indicating her unease. "I've been wondering something. Have you ever worried that Celia might make her presence known while you're talking to him?"

"Yes, I have," I answered frankly. "But he seems to soothe her."

"Soothe." She drummed her nails on the table again. "There is nothing soothing about any of this."

"I agree. And may I say, thanks for that." I looked at the bag. "How did you find out about all this? How did you learn how to call Belle?"

"I'll save that for another time," she said coyly. "Suffice to say, I couldn't find anything about uncalling. Believe me, I have looked."

"I want to see all of it. After the party."

"Okay," she said. "Sure."

ALONE. IN MY ROOM.

Dressed in sweats for bed, I kept the light on. I decided that tomorrow, I'd ask for more lamps. There were too many dark corners.

I dug out my knitting needles and my prized Casbah yarn

in shades of purple and plum. I could knit and stare at the same time. And stab an intruder, if it came to that. As I got to work, the knitting soothed me. I had missed the clack of the needles, the sensation of the rich wool, creating something out of nothing for someone I cared about.

"Memmy?" I called out. "Can you hear me? Can you come to me?"

No answer. No geraniums.

I started to doze. Shaking myself awake, I kept knitting, planning some socks for Heather. My back was stiff, my shoulder blades pinched together. Claire was right: I was crazy to stay in this room. The shadows moved, shifted; creaks made me jump.

"Memmy, come to me," I said again.

Come to me

Come to me

Come to me

Come to me

Come to me

Get her. Hold her down. Silence her.

I'm coming to you

I'm coming to you

I'm coming to you

I'm coming to you

Something was scratching against the other side of the wall. The floorboards in the corridor were creaking. Someone was opening my door. I couldn't move. I couldn't scream.

I couldn't wake up.

I'm here.

TWENTY-TWO

BREAKFAST WAS AWKWARD. Julie didn't show. I woke up with a neck ache and a headache, having fallen asleep knitting. Claire, Ida, Elvis, and Marica all had headaches too.

"We all have hangovers," Marica confessed, rubbing her forehead. "Please don't be hurt. Julie was so upset that we broke out a few bottles of Cristal. I went to your room to share with you, but you were out."

"Yeah, about hangovers," I said, feeling even more awkward. "There's going to be a party tonight. Everyone's invited. Including Julie."

Claire did a double take. I had never thrown a party before. In fact, given my somewhat anti-social stance, it was out of character for me to even attend a party. I figured I might as well get it all out and over with.

"I have a co-hostess. Mandy."

More consternation. Claire spread her palm on my forehead as if to check for a fever but quickly lifted it when I winced from pain.

"But you hate Mandy," Elvis said.

"We're both in therapy now."

I got up to fetch myself more coffee. As I was filling my cup, Mandy and her crew pushed through the entrance, faces all pinched and surly, yet everyone was dressed in the best. Mandy had on a stylish pastel-pink sweater and butt-clinging jeans, but they somehow didn't look right on her. Frizz stuck out from a massive bun updo of hair extensions that had to be one of those cool "anti-hair" looks that I didn't understand. The total effect was that Mandy looked as exhausted and disheveled as on the night of the Troy stunt.

She came straight for me. I held my mug in both hands, waiting. Heads turned. From a distance, Lara glared.

"Bad night," Mandy said under her breath. "Nightmares. Or whatever. And I kept waking up. I thought someone was in my room. I didn't find anyone."

"I had a similar night," I murmured.

We shared a look. Then she wrapped her hand over the crown of her head. Her bruises were changing from purple to sickly green. "And I've got the worst headache."

"Do you want to cancel the party?"

"No way."

"Okay." I drank my coffee. "Watch what you say to Dr. Morehouse. I'd skip telling him . . . everything."

She grabbed my coffee and took a sip. "I'm not an idiot."

"Yeah, you kind of are." I took my coffee back. "Because this is all your doing."

I turned on my heel and stomped over to my table. They'd been watching my every move.

"By the way, it's a full-moon party. Not like the book. Like the moon, moon."

They gaped at me. I grabbed a piece of toast and left. I didn't want to answer questions. I didn't want people to stare at me and dissect how I'd gotten so lucky as to become the new best friend of Mandy Winters.

I lurched through the day, trying hard to be friendly when the least cool among us cautiously approached me to confirm that yes, even they were invited to our party. I could see them cringing, bracing themselves for rejection or to be humiliated via some superprank that we'd punked them into signing up for. Mandy hadn't pulled any mean-girl shenanigans since we'd returned from break, so we were overdue for something massive. They didn't realize that she'd already pulled the cruelest prank in the short history of our school—allowing the dead to haunt us. And for some, to possess us.

"Wow, you're having the party in the operating theater," Charlotte Davidson said to me in PE as we sat on a bench in the gym. The rest of the class was getting ready for fitness tests. I was excused because of my pneumonia and my head injury. I didn't know what Charlotte's excuse was.

"Well, you know what they say. You have to get back on the horse," I told her. She didn't know what to make of that, so she smiled and nodded at me.

"You're invited," I added, and she relaxed. I realized then that the comment about the operating theater was merely her opening gambit, her way of making sure that she could come.

I was embarrassed that our stupid party meant so much. I

took it out on Charlotte by ignoring her for the rest of the class. As we watched the class do push-ups and sit-ups, looks were cast my way. I knew I had newly acquired social clout only because I was Mandy's co-conspirator, and it made me mad because the same girls who feared and respected Mandy were the ones who had given her the power over them in the first place. In a way, Mandy possessed each one of them.

My surly behavior was so evident that during free period, Mandy took me aside in the statue garden to lecture me. The stone-faced statues observed me like judge and jury as she gave me the evil eye.

"No one will want to come if you don't at least *act* like you want them to come."

"And miss a Mandy Winters production?" I scoffed.

"Yes. They'll be too scared. Of you."

I nodded and hung my head. She was right.

"Remember, we're doing this for a reason. An important reason."

"I know."

"I'm actually glad I'm going to see Dr. Morehouse," she said. "I need a break." She tapped her forehead carefully, checking her fingertips, maybe for makeup. "Someone's watching me. I can feel it."

"Mandy, people are always watching you. You're Mandy Winters. Maybe it's Miles."

"No, I'd know." She moved her shoulders. "We have a twin thing."

"WE HAVE A twin thing," she told Dr. Morehouse. "And I—I worry about him all the time." She was weeping. I knew what she was doing, using Miles as the cover story to explain why she was so upset.

"Family issues can be very trying," Dr. Morehouse said.

I had sat down to dinner with my dorm mates—including Julie, who was avoiding me—when I'd noticed that Mandy wasn't at her table. Since we were co-hosting the party, it wasn't considered odd when I'd asked the princesses of Jessel where she was. It turned out that Dr. Morehouse had rescheduled her appointment.

"They should be finishing up about now," Alis had informed me.

"Great. I'll go wait for her," I'd said, and flew up the hill as fast as I could.

Breathless, I snuck into the storage room and crawled into the dumbwaiter. I really, really wanted to know what Mandy had to say to Dr. Morehouse.

"So, we'll meet as agreed," Dr. Morehouse said. "I have exactly what you need to make all the pain go away."

"I won't have to wait too long?" she asked anxiously.

"No, I should have it by later tonight."

No way, I thought angrily. *She's getting the shortcut!*

Typical. Typical that the wealthy got what the poor did not. Waves of fury surged through me for all the shortcuts my mother had been denied and for the free ride that Mandy was getting again. I tried to calm down; it didn't matter. And I should be glad that one of us would have an easier path. I clenched my jaw and forced myself to be quiet. But my fists were clenched. It was always so easy for her.

Celia loved David Abernathy, the young doctor. And he said he loved her. But Belle had set her cap for him, and she tortured Celia, pushing her head under the ice water in the great tub, shrieking at her to give him up. Screaming, "He is mine!" And as Celia ran down the lane, every inch of her body burning, she knew that Belle had been right. He had loved the beautiful, wealthy Belle and used the poor one, Celia Reaves, used her and cast her aside.

Murdered her . . .

"God," I whispered aloud, wiping my forehead. I was shaking so hard the dumbwaiter jittered. If I didn't shut up, I would give myself away.

"I'll be there," Mandy promised.

There was silence. And then he said, "Good girl."

――――――

GOOD GIRL, I told myself as I got myself under control. I waited for Mandy to leave and lingered to see if Dr. Morehouse had another appointment. But he got up from the desk and went out the door. So I waited some more, to give him time to leave the admin building without running into me.

The sky was darkening with heavy clouds; the wind slapped at me and made the trees shake as I walked past them. The shadows shifted on the horse heads, and I jerked when I noticed that every fourth head was wearing a tiny Irish hat. Shiny, oversized shamrocks were fluttering from the trees of Academy Quad. In the midst of all the craziness, someone had started decorating the campus for St. Patrick's Day. Marlwood did things in a big way.

I went over to Jessel and knocked on the kitchen door. Lara grudgingly let me in. Her short red hair needed a trim—why *did* I even notice these things?—and her boyish prep clothes in tans and blues hung on her. She'd been losing weight. Without saying a single word to me, she loaded my arms with a heavy cardboard box—probably the heaviest one in the batch. Bottles clanked. Three things were forbidden on Marlwood soil—boys, booze, and cheating. Oh, well.

I had a thought. Setting down the box, I said, "Mandy wants me to go down into the basement. She's got another Ouija board down there. For the party."

"All her stuff is stored in the attic," Lara argued, but I just stood there. Lara had never liked me. I was sure that now she liked me even less. I had direct Mandy access without going through her.

"Whatever," she said. She unfolded the flaps of the box she had handed me and put in a stack of paper plates. Probably just to add to the weight.

I sauntered out of the kitchen and walked into the living room. The foyer of Jessel was stupendous, with a twenty-foot cathedral ceiling dominated by an oversized cut-crystal chandelier just dying to fall and crush me to death. Directly across the room, a varnished oak staircase ran along the brick wall, leading to the balcony that hung over the back half of the room. The bedrooms were upstairs. I was itching to go up and have a look at Mandy's. It was probably locked, and

I thought Lara might balk if I tried to go into the forbidden zone.

I made a point of not looking at the fireplace mantel to my right. A trio of photographs of Belle and two other girls sat behind votive candles. Mandy had been caught talking to them a couple of times, and it had freaked out the others, but not too much. After all, she held séances, too.

I walked down the hall to the laundry room, grabbed a flashlight from a basket of them next to a container of detergent, and opened the door that led to the basement. It was as dank and dark as I recalled it. I flicked on the light, scanning the walls for a light switch, and found a rusty chain connected to a bulb dangling above my head. That didn't seem up to Marlwood standards, but I pulled it anyway. Watery light pierced the gloom.

I started down a flight of worn stone steps. And then I paused. Going down here alone wasn't a good idea. There were other girls in the house, sure, but if something happened to me, they might not ever know. If I fell, or if someone put a hand over my mouth . . .

I felt the coldness of Celia wash across the back of my neck. She was urging me to keep going. Either my instincts had been right, or Celia had whispered the idea into my mind.

"Of course, you're evil," I said aloud.

I heard her laughter echoing around me as I walked down the stairs. Angry, sad laughter, more like wailing, and I remembered the horrible things the Marlwood Stalker had done. The things Celia might have done, while existing inside me.

Had she been crazy when she died, or had dying made her crazy? I waved the beam of the flashlight; it landed on boxes and pieces of furniture covered with drapes. It smelled muddy. It was cold. I glanced back to make sure the door was still open. I should have used something to keep it from shutting.

But I knew there was another door down there. It was the one I had burst through when I had been running from the . . .

No.

My blood turned to ice.

The same wheelchair that had chased me before sat squarely in the middle of the room, facing me. It was made of wood, with hinged slats for arms and feet. Upright, its wheels were rusted, but I knew it could move fast. My throat tightened and I took an involuntary step back, up one step. I didn't want to look at it, but I was afraid to take my eyes off it. If I let down my guard, it might . . .

Oh, my God.

I heard the wheels squeak. Noises from the living room startled me; Lara was yelling to someone. Maybe she would come to check on me.

Maybe she would shut me in.

Could all this be one huge meta-prank, pulled off by Mandy with the help of half the school? The bad dreams, the visions, something she'd arranged? Anyone who had seen her haunted house knew she was capable of truly amazing special effects. The Winterses had enough money to create a theme park on the Marlwood campus, or buy their own chemical labs and create their own designer hallucinogenic drugs.

The chair squeaked again. I heard myself whimpering. Frozen, I stared at it, caught in the beam of my flashlight. As my eyes adjusted to the light, I saw that something shiny and square lay on the wooden seat. My flashlight glinted off it.

The wheelchair inched toward me. I cried out, then covered my mouth. It had never hurt me before. Maybe someone . . . someone was standing behind it, making it move. Someone I couldn't see.

A ghost.

"Is someone there?" I whispered.

The wheelchair moved again.

I wanted to run. I thought of going to find Mandy. My heart was racing so fast that I wouldn't have been able to count the beats.

Before I could stop myself, I dashed forward, racing around the furniture, the boxes, a Diet Coke can. I hit the can as I passed it, sending it rolling with a rattle-rattle-rattle, and I cried out again.

I kept my light on the chair; I shined it against the back, to see if there was a figure there—maybe the shadow man who had been in Mandy's room, if anybody *had* been in Mandy's room.

"Don't move," I said aloud. "Don't, okay?" I stared down at the things on the seat: a cigarette lighter and three little squares.

"Are these for me? Did you bring them for me?" I said loudly, to prove I wasn't scared; I was in control.

There was no response. It was as if the chair was staring

at me. I could almost see a figure in it, sitting still. I could imagine empty eye sockets staring at me. A mouth, opening in a smile . . .

. . . or a scream.

I jumped forward, grabbed the lighter and the squares, and fled back up the stairs.

TWENTY-THREE

I PRACTICALLY THREW myself against the washing machine when I reached the top of the basement stairs. I slammed the door, panting, I stared at the objects in my hand. A cigarette lighter. There was some kind of crest or logo on it, but I didn't recognize it. A red shield with three white squares and letters, two across, one down: *VE RI TAS*. Truth.

Miles had found cigarettes when he'd retrieved the messenger bag. The squares looked like gum.

"Hey," Lara said, peering around the corner. "Time to go."

I stuffed the lighter and the squares into the pocket of my army jacket. I folded my arms and followed Lara back across the living room. I could hear Ms. Meyerson's TV. She played it loudly so she could pretend she didn't know what her charges were doing.

"Where's the Ouija board?" Lara asked me.

"Couldn't find it."

She smiled sourly. "I told you, all her stuff is in the attic."

Had Lara taken any of Mandy's things from the attic? I

followed her into the kitchen, finding Sangeeta and Alis there, loading their arms with cartons of tequila, scotch, and wine bottles. Sangeeta was dressed in purple, from a suede jacket to a short silk skirt and purple ballerina flats. Alis had on skinny jeans, a green cashmere sweater, and a belted cardigan in a darker green. Alis was munching a fancy appetizer— their freezer was always loaded with fancy boxes, and they overnighted appetizers and fancy chocolate truffles, expensive cheeses, and cans of caviar without a moment's consideration about how much it cost.

We moved from their yard with the privet hedges to the path leading into the woods. I looked to my right, where the lake pushed back the forested shore. Lara had been friendly to me the first time I'd gone down to the lake, to watch the terrible prank Mandy talked Kiyoko into doing. It had been Lara's job to entice me into becoming one of Mandy's robots. Now she'd probably just as soon push me in the lake.

Lara walked in front, and Sangeeta and Alis flanked me. It would be easy for them to overpower me if they got possessed and decided it was time to kill me. I pretended that the carton was too heavy and stopped to reposition it in my arms. The three kept walking. I stayed behind all three of them, watching the backs of their heads.

The path grew steeper, and the trees began to crowd us. The sun dipped low, and gray shadows crossed our path. Tendrils of fog spread along the ground. The temperature dropped.

We kept going. The three friends were chatting about a spa in Santa Barbara they'd all been to. Even though they went to amazing, expensive places on vacations, it seemed that they

all went to the same ones. They even complained about it—
"Maui *again*! Oh, *God*, we're going to Paris!"—and cheered
each other up by buying more things. Clothes, jewelry, purses,
high-tech gear.

Fishing line?

I followed the climbing vines of fog with my gaze, because I
knew that we were getting close to the operating theater. I was
beginning to lose my nerve. I didn't think I could go in there again.

Lara looked back at me and smiled. I shifted the box again
and forced one foot in front of the other. The wind blew right
through me; I looked up at the darkening sky and smelled the
promise of rain.

Then I made myself face the operating theater head-on.
The circular roof had fallen in, as if a giant had made a fist and
pounded against it. Windows had blasted out, and their iron
fittings had completely rusted away. Huge gaps in the walls
revealed bushes growing inside the structure, their spindly
branches like veins.

Where a door had been, there was only a gaping mouth,
and to the right, the burned-out top of the tunnel looked like a
mound in a graveyard. That was where it had happened, where
the girls had died. The tunnel was the death trap where Celia
had started the fire, and the rage of her six victims had burned
for over a hundred years.

I felt it in the ground beneath my feet; I heard it in the trees.
Fury. Wounds so deep that they bled black hatred. Too much
damage for this land, for this place. The unfinished business
of the dead infected us like an illness. It owned us. We were all
possessions of Marlwood.

"Come *on*," Lara said.

She was standing in the doorway. Sangeeta and Alis had already gone in. I smelled smoke. I always did. At first it had frightened me. I had looked for fires. I hadn't realized the flames were burning inside me.

I'll die in there. I always thought it.

I had to do this. I had tried to go home, tried to ignore everything, but neither had worked. I knew there was nothing else I could do. It was time to face it.

I walked toward Lara, and she disappeared inside. Steeling myself, I followed, ignoring the stench. Battery-operated lanterns had been placed along the floor of the narrow passageway. The operating theater itself was on the same floor. Beyond the ruined wall to my left, Troy had performed the fake lobotomy on Marica on Valentine's Day. And on December 16, barely two months before, these girls had tried to kill me by setting me on fire.

They had made me stare at the white head until I was mesmerized . . .

I did do it. I did break the head, I realized with a start. I could almost remember it, but not quite. But I *knew*.

Julie had been right to get rid of me.

Swallowing hard, I almost dropped the heavy box. The bottles clanked. My back ached. My forehead was throbbing.

"Yo," Lara shouted from below. "Let's *go*."

She had reached the lower level, down a flight of stairs, where the tunnel led into the building—where a hundred years ago, they would wheel the girls in and prep them for surgery.

A surgery that David Abernathy would perform on them.

I carried the box down the stairs to find Mandy's usual party arrangements intact from the last blowout—the little tables and chairs, lit by a votive candle. The votives were green, and scatters of glittery shamrocks had been sprinkled around them. So much for mocking my suggestion that we decorated. When on earth had anyone had time to order St. Patrick's Day party supplies?

The first party I'd gone to here, Mandy had assembled a wind ensemble. Judging by the weird Eurotrash trance music booming over a music system, tonight we were wired for sound.

"Oh, God, finally," Mandy said, rushing to me. She reached out her arms; I started to hand the box to her, but she made two fists and put them under her chin. I rolled my eyes and set my burden on the nearest table, knocking over the votive candle. I leapt forward to grab it.

"Careful," she chided me. "Jeez, Lindsay, I began to think you weren't coming."

"Wouldn't miss it," I replied.

"What did you bring?" She opened the box, peered inside, and gasped in horror. "*Paper* plates?"

"And plastic glasses. Sorry, the elephants have the night off. We had to trek all this in on pack mules."

"I guess that's not the point tonight." She showed me a bottle of tequila, unscrewed the cap, and chugalugged several healthy swallows. Pressing the back of her hand to her mouth, she held it out to me.

"We have to be careful," I warned her. "We have to keep our wits." I felt a pang; that was what Shayna had told me. Keep your wits, in case a dybbuk came after you—a spirit haunted by what had been done to it or what it had done to someone else.

"We have to stop from screaming," Mandy countered, giving the bottle a wag.

I took it from her and had a swallow. Frankly, most hard liquor tasted the same to me—horrible—and I didn't understand the allure. I mostly got weepy and tired when I drank the stuff.

"Okay, now, we need a strategy." Her eyes darted from side to side; she was jittery already, and the evening hadn't even started.

"Are you on anything?" I asked her suspiciously.

She scowled at me. "*Not* that that's any of your business."

"Are you insane? Of course it's my business." I hesitated, and then I made a decision. "Listen, I went in your basement and I found this. On the old wheelchair."

She jerked. "What old wheelchair?"

She knows about it. She knows it moves by itself.

I pulled the lighter and the candy from my pocket. She picked up the lighter and flicked it. A small yellow and blue flame appeared. Then she examined one of the squares.

"I think this is gum," she told me. She handed it back. "Save it."

I put it back in my pocket.

"Anyway, okay, we're all done here." She rubbed her hands along her arms. "What are you going to wear?"

"What I have on, I guess." Which was my baggy flares, Doc Martens, my black long underwear top, and my jacket.

She blanched. "You can't. You're my co-hostess. You look like you've been sleeping in a Dumpster."

"So what? Mandy, we're not having a party to have a party, remember?"

"But we can't just give up. I mean, then they've won." She was serious. Her blue, Miles-colored eyes were enormous. Her shiny lips were parted in distress. Mandy could not fathom going through this evening without looking good.

It was such a different way of thinking that I couldn't even go there. It wasn't so much that she was shallow as that she had a strange sort of integrity.

"Okay, that's it," Lara announced, walking up to us. "Everything's ready. We'll go get dressed."

They were all leaving. I couldn't stay here by myself.

"Come over to Jessel with us," Mandy said. "We'll fix you up." She grabbed a handful of my curls and scrunched them. "I'm sure we've got some products you can use." I remembered products. And measuring my eyebrows and caring about all that. I'd lost ground while my mom was sick, too distracted to worry about my fashion IQ and what my kind of scent I should be wearing. Despite that, I'd gotten sucked into the Jane machine and I had briefly turned into a hot chick. Once that had blown up, I'd chucked all my magazines and makeup and turned into a "crazy-haired lesbian," as my cousin Jason had called me, only without the lesbian part. Too bad for me: my first mad crush was Riley, and look how that had turned out.

The four girls headed for the exit. I forced myself back down the corridor, breathing more freely when we got outside.

We trooped back to Jessel, and Mandy took me into her

room. It was pristine. She had folded all her ruined clothes and put them in bins in the attic. She had ordered scads of new clothes, and at least half of the coats, sweaters, pants, shoes, and tops she showed me still had their price tags.

First there was an interminable fashion show, during which she decided to wear a sleeveless black and metallic handkerchief top over bronze leggings and black and bronze high heels that she told me had been handmade, using measurements of her feet that she had faxed the company. She applied bronze makeup with the skill of a professional, using sleek, natural-bristle brushes and a magnifying mirror. She added bronze earrings and a cool cuff with abstract designs of beaten metal.

I knew she was going to dress me up, and I just let it happen. In the house with the ghosts and the wheelchair that moved, the haunted turret room and secret tunnels, I was Mandy's dress-up doll. She swathed me in a short scarlet dress, sheer black leggings that came down to the middle of my calves, and black stilettos. She threaded black and gold bangles up my arms and twisted gold chains through my hair until it was pulled up and away from my face Jane Austen style.

Then on came the makeup, layer by layer. I remembered the smell of makeup, the excitement of girls putting it on together. Concealers, highlighters, blush. She decided to make me smoky, which I found bizarrely ironic, but I let her do it. Her hands were shaking and she cracked open a bottle of champagne to calm down. I was thinking tequila and bubbly were not the best combination, but I didn't say anything this time.

"Oh, you look so great," she said. But she was getting shakier. It was getting closer to go time.

Then she was glossing my lips and adding something sparkly to my cheeks. She sprayed my hair and misted me with perfume from Spain that had an unpronounceable name.

"Close your eyes," she said, grabbing one of my hands with both of hers and leading me toward her full-length mirror. She was excited for me, happy for me. This was the part of Mandy that sucked me in, and made me want to like and trust her. She had charisma to spare, when she felt like sharing it. Girls like Mandy were storms, then clouds, then sun. And the sun was so warm that you wanted to bask in its glow when it was out, daring the burn.

She tugged on my wrists. There were heaps of clothes everywhere, and because my eyes were closed, I was stepping on them in my ridiculously high heels, which were a bit tight. I was definitely wearing my Doc Martens on the walk back to the party.

"Ready?" she asked.

I wasn't. I was terrified that when I opened my eyes, I would see Celia in her tattered linen shift, staring at me with her white face and her black eye sockets. Or worse, wearing my face. I had a horrible image of Mandy putting makeup on over a bare skull, running lipstick over rotten teeth. That I wasn't going to be there in the mirror.

"Mandy," I said in a low voice. "I can't look."

There was silence.

"I know," she whispered finally. "I'm afraid to look too. Here." She pressed on my wrists and I made a half turn.

"Now," she said.

I opened my eyes. We were facing each other. We would be

each other's mirror. Mandy smiled at me and shook her head in amazement.

"Behold. You are transformed." She wrinkled her nose. "I think I did too good a job. No one is going to look twice at me."

"You look fantastic," I said honestly.

"Really?" I had never heard her sound so unsure. Dressed in thousands of dollars of designer clothes, wearing the best makeup money could buy —much of it hand-mixed to the specifications of her San Francisco "style team," she still wasn't certain that she looked good. It completely blew my mind.

"This is you, being nice," I said. "Being really nice."

"I have it in me," she confirmed, "to throw the occasional bone."

"No. You are part nice. You'll just have to accept it."

She smiled shyly. Mandy Winters, shy. Down beneath all the wounds, there was a sweet girl fighting to get out.

"This is you, rising from the misery," she said, almost as if she could read my mind. "To party again."

She started to reach out her arms, the way she had in the operating theater. Then she pulled back, again. And I was the one who initiated the hug, wrapping my arms loosely around her. She was bony.

"Don't mess me up," she said, holding back.

Hugs could mess people up.

Wise Mandy.

———

MANDY LENT ME a beautiful black wool maxicoat and a little purse. I put in lip gloss and then, on an impulse, the lighter and the gum. I wore my Doc Martens and carried the high heels.

We went back to the operating theater, broke out the bottles, and cranked up the music. The girls started arriving, gawking at the tables and chairs, asking how we got all this stuff into a condemned building. I really couldn't say. It had happened before my time in the Mandy brigade.

My dorm mates arrived in a group, and none of them recognized me. Rose told me she wanted to marry me. Julie still said nothing, but she couldn't stop staring. The music throbbed and the candles flickered, and no one but me could hear the echoing screams of dead girls pleading for their lives.

Our guests included dozens of girls and a few guys, including Julie's Spider, who made a point of coming over to me and giving me a hug. He told me how great I looked, then fixed Julie with a meaningful stare as she kept her distance. She finally smiled at me, but her heart wasn't in it.

You were right, I wanted to tell her. *I broke your head. I am crazy.*

Tension was building in the room—and in me, and in Mandy. As part of our detective work, she was playing a "game" where she would sit across from someone and hold their wrists with her fingers pressed against their pulse. Then she'd ask them questions. If their pulse sped up, they were lying. I watched carefully, taking mental notes.

"Have you ever done something really . . . evil?" she asked Charlotte Davidson.

Charlotte was silent for a few seconds. Then she said, "Yes."

"Was it here at Marlwood?"

Paling, Charlotte nodded. Then, without prompting, she blurted, "I peed in the pool."

Everyone who was looking on—a circle of at least twenty people—burst into groans and laughter. Charlotte looked down, humiliated.

"Oh, my God!" Lara shouted. "That's disgusting!"

Why did you tell her that? I wondered as Charlotte wobbled to her feet and shambled away. She was completely mortified. *What made you think you had to?*

Mandy made party guest after party guest answer her questions. There were no more confessions like Charlotte's. Susi didn't tell about her bed wetting. Gretchen's OCD stayed private. And there was no way in hell that Maeve would reveal her dreams of becoming a guy.

"Okay, enough of this," Mandy declared. "New game."

I had approved of this one in advance too. This time, you had to let Mandy look you in the eyes. Sitting practically nose to nose, staring, she would tell you if your pupils were dilating, which meant you were lying. Because excitement made pupils dilate, and lying was exciting.

Spider was her first victim. He made faces at her while she tried to embarrass him with her questions: *Do you lie awake at night thinking about Julie? Have you ever written Julie a love poem?*

Laughing, he played along. As Mandy and I had agreed, I watched the watchers. I kept track of who came and who went. I looked for suspicious activity.

The night wore on. Lots of drinking, dancing. More guys from Lakewood showed up. Troy was not among them, and his schoolmates had the decency not to mention his name.

"Okay, now, let's see, how about Marica?" Mandy said as she plowed through victim after victim.

Marica sat down in the hot seat. Mandy leaned forward to gaze into her eyes. Then Mandy jerked back her head and looked over at me.

She was completely white. Her lips moved, but no sound came out.

Marica made a face. "What is it? Do I have bad breath?"

People laughed. After another moment, Mandy threw back her head and joined them.

"No. I saw a zit," she replied, and looked at me again. I dipped my head. She had seen something in Marica's eyes.

A ghost?

There was more laughter. Mandy cleared her throat and leaned forward again. I zeroed in on Marica, watching her like a hawk.

"Have you ever kissed a girl and liked it?" she asked Marica.

"I sure have," said a voice behind me. A very familiar voice. A voice that had shattered my world.

I turned around.

TWENTY-FOUR

RILEY.

I almost fell off my high heels.

Riley, *here*.

Now.

He was tanned, light brown hair surfer sun-streaked. His brown, gold-flecked eyes wide with amazement. His Grossmont High blue and gold letter jacket bulked over his broad shoulders, and a white T-shirt was loosely bunched around his nonexistent hips. He had on a pair of faded jeans and scruffy cowboy boots. A look I had always loved. Loved. Yes, yes, yes.

Troy was a distant memory, if, oh, *if* . . .

There was no if. No one drove fourteen hours by accident.

He stared at me as if he had forgotten how to speak. I panicked, wondering if he was seeing someone else—Celia— until I remembered that I was glammed up as I had never been glammed before. He had seen me in the Jane days, but these were the Mandy days.

"Whoa," he rasped, and Mandy rose gracefully from her chair and threaded her arms through his.

"This must be Jason," she cooed. Riley blinked at her. "Oh, sorry. Lance? Tim? Estevan?"

She smiled at me. I understood that she was implying that I had a harem of guys—or at the very least, that I had never mentioned Riley around her. Hard-to-get-back tactics. She might not know who Riley was, but she did know how to push a guy's buttons.

She added quickly, "Possibility on Marica. Big pupils. Not sure. Got . . . spooked."

"*Yo comprendo,*" I replied. I understand.

"No need to panic," she said.

I looked at Riley again, who was clearly puzzled by our conversation. "What are you doing here?" I blurted.

"These kids need something to drink," Mandy announced. She looked around. "Lara?"

Lara, who was wearing a tux, rolled her eyes and started to fold her arms across her chest. She was not going to fetch me anything. Then she must have realized that Mandy would keep at her until she capitulated, so she stomped over to a table and grabbed an open bottle of champagne. She started to bring it over to us. Mandy raised an eyebrow. Lara clenched her teeth, wheeled around, and grabbed two plastic champagne glasses.

She stomped over to me and practically threw them at me. Mandy plucked the bottle out of my hand and poured the bubbly into the glasses, handing one to each of us.

Riley was gaping openly at me. I no longer felt like a circus clown; I was actually grateful to Mandy for giving me the works. Because I was working it, and it was working.

"Can we maybe . . . go outside?" Riley asked me.

"Gladly," I said, cool as cool.

I slid a glance Mandy's way, and I was taken aback by what I saw. Her cocky smile had slipped; her shoulders were hunching. She wasn't frightened; she looked wistful and sad, the princess of everything except for a prince.

She really loved Troy, I thought. *He broke her heart. All that stuff we did, trashing his things, that was just bravado.*

I felt so sorry for her, having to keep appearances up, to be solid and in control. Troy had complained about being paired for life with Mandy by their families. But she had liked it. Correction: loved it. And it was gone.

If she caught me pitying her, she would probably say something calculated to embarrass me. She was already pulling herself back together, plastering a smile on her face.

"Take a break," she said regally. "I'll do a recheck of you-know-who."

Of Marica, I translated, and nodded at her.

Riley looked surprised, unsure how to respond to this girl who was acting like my employer, but said nothing as I grabbed my little purse for the sake of the lip gloss inside it and led the way out of the room. We didn't talk as we walked back through the tunnel and out into the chilly night. I had forgotten to take the gorgeous wool maxicoat Mandy had lent me, and I shivered, hard. Riley took off his letter jacket and draped it around my shoulders. I inhaled the scent of him— leather, cinnamon, soap—and my throat tightened.

I knew exactly how Mandy felt, longing for some guy.

No one else was outside. Our breath condensed as we walked along without touching. I liked the sensation of the satin lining of Riley's jacket against my skin. The brittle stars overhead tracked us. I stepped on branches in my high-high heels. I held onto my little shoulder clutch as if for moral support.

We reached a large gray boulder, very much like the one that Troy and I had sat on when we'd run into each other—literally—the first day of Thanksgiving break. I smiled to myself. I was so done with Troy.

"What happened to your forehead?" he asked me.

"I fell off a scooter. But I'm okay now. Really."

"It looks painful."

"It isn't. Not right now."

I smiled at him. He flushed. It was a joy to behold.

"Sit?" Riley asked, and I nodded.

Hip to hip, we sat down. Our fingers brushed and Riley closed his hand around mine. Electricity jolted through me. I couldn't stop smiling.

"So there's hope," Riley said, wiggling my hand.

I didn't say anything. Like the rest of my life, the situation was unreal. But unlike the rest of my life, it was great.

"I meant everything I said in my voice mail," he began. "Lindsay, I don't even know why I—I went in there."

My parents' bedroom.

"I was so stupid." He unfolded his hand, as if anticipating that I was going to pull away. I didn't move. I held my breath. I wanted to hear it all. "I didn't even like Jane. But she was . . .

I . . . " He ran his hand through his hair. I remembered sand and salt, getting busted for kissing on the beach. In the arms of Riley Kinkaid.

After all the nightmares, this was such a beautiful dream. Joy surged through me in huge waves. After all the horrible, scary things that happened, Riley was too good to be true . . . just as he had been before. I was scared, but I knew he meant what he said. He'd driven fourteen hours to find me, in my haunted dungeon on the hill.

"I've missed you." He turned to me. "I thought after you left, I'd get over it, but I think about you all the time. I want . . . " He searched my face. "I want it to be how it started, between us. We were a couple. That's what I want."

He waited. I made him wait longer because I didn't trust myself to speak. And then I wondered why I thought I needed to say anything. I turned and looked up at him. I knew that was all I had to do.

He kissed me. His lips warmed mine and I thought my head would explode. He put his arms around me and held me, very tentative and gentle, as if he expected me to ask him to stop. I hadn't kissed Riley in over five months, and I wasn't going to miss a second of it.

I began to melt. I was so, so, so happy. And afraid, too, that if Riley knew what my world was really like, he'd dump me just as Troy had. But for now, there was this sweet, shy, getting-back-together kiss, just the nicest, slow—

An icy waterfall cascaded over me with a huge, rushing *"No!"* as Celia screamed inside me. Cold on cold on cold; terror, panic.

"No, no!"

I stiffened and fought against her as she pushed Riley away as hard as she could. He wasn't expecting it and he fell off the boulder, landing flat on his back. I stood frozen in horror, listening to Celia screaming inside me.

"Oh, unhh," Riley moaned, barely moving.

At the same moment, Miles crashed through the bracken, lurching toward us. He moved awkwardly, as if he'd been drinking. Before I realized what he was doing, he stepped over Riley, straddling him, grabbed his T-shirt, and raised his back off the ground. Then he made a fist and slammed it into Riley's face.

"Ow!" Miles shouted.

Riley sat up and made a double fist, ramming it upward between Miles's legs. Miles bellowed and collapsed on top of him. Grunting, gasping, Miles rained blows on Riley's head. Riley fought back, pushing Miles off him, leaping to his feet and taking a boxer's stance.

"Stop!" I shouted, but they didn't hear me. Miles landed a punch; Riley counterattacked. They were actually fighting each other; it was surreal, bizarre. Frightening.

"Get away!

"Get away!

"He's here!" Celia shouted.

"Both of you, stop!"

"He's here!" she screamed.

I heard myself whimpering. Celia was forcing me to leave. I staggered, trying to move toward Riley and Miles as they bloodied each other.

Miles looked over at me. Riley landed a punch on his face and Miles's head snapped back.

I heard voices, shouts. Partyers who heard me scream. People coming. People who would stop the fight.

Celia took possession, and I ran. Through the dark trees, with the full moon glinting in and out of the limbs, I raced as if my life depended on it.

Celia was in a blind panic, shrieking in my head, *"He's here; he's here!"*

I was partly myself and partly Celia, aware of the overhanging tree limbs as they slapped me, yet feeling her terror. I couldn't control my body. Fear swept through me, more violently than ever before, worse than when the six ghosts of the girls Celia had murdered charged after me, to kill me.

She was screaming *"He's here!"* and I didn't know who *he* was, but I was just as afraid as she was. More afraid than I had ever been in my life, even at the moment when Memmy died.

The wind screamed like a human being in agony. Sobbing, I clapped my hands over my ears. The ground tilted downhill; the incline was steep. I slipped and fell. Rolled. Rocks scraped; branches cut. My feet were cut and bruised. I had lost my shoes and Riley's jacket.

Every second counted. He was coming.

Then I burst free of the woods. I saw Searle Lake sprawled before me, and there was someone down there. In the darkness I couldn't see who, but it was . . .

. . . she was . . .

Screams shot up around me, geysers of sound. Screams,

exploding around my feet like land mines. Falling from the sky like bombs. Screams.

I ran toward the screams, away from them; they threw me to my knees and slammed my face in the wet earth of shoreline. I crawled through the screams to the person lying faceup, moaning.

It was Mandy. Who was not screaming. Who was making no sound at all. Who was silent.

From her nose up, her head had been crushed in by a large rock the size of a soccer ball, and blood was gushing out beneath it, out over the dirt. In the moonlight it looked black. Panting, I wrapped myself around the rock and tried to heave it off her. It was too heavy. Falling to my knees, I threw my weight against it, sobbing, pushing. Again. Again.

It rolled. And I screamed as I had never screamed before. Her face, her beautiful face.

"Mandy, Mandy!" I said, holding my hands inches from her wounds, shaking, with no idea what to do. "Help," I croaked, throwing back my head. "Help us!" But I couldn't make enough noise. Only the moon heard me, and the black water of Searle Lake, and the wind. I ripped off the lower part of my top and tried to staunch the blood. I didn't want to cause her pain, but I didn't want her to bleed to death either.

I tried to gather her up, to keep her warm. She was icy. It was so cold out. Cold as the grave.

"Get the evil one," she whispered, but her mouth didn't move. Blood streamed out of it. Her voice was not her own; it was Belle's.

"I want Mandy," I ordered her. "Let me talk to her *now*."

"*Can't,*" Belle replied.

"Why not?" My voice cracked. The world was spinning, blurring. I forced myself not to break down. Mandy needed me.

"*Dying, sweet bee.*" With that horrible, ruined face, Belle glared at me. I saw her fury, and her hatred. "*Because of you.*"

"No, she's not! Mandy, don't die!" I screamed. "Don't die!" I held her, rocked her. Tears spilled down my face, landing on Mandy's cheeks. "Help!"

"*Too late.*"

I was heaving and sobbing, looking around, trying to decide what to do to save her. Aware that the killer might be watching me, waiting to do the same thing to me. I opened my purse to get my cell phone, but it wasn't here. Just the lip gloss, the lighter, and the gum.

"Belle, tell me who did this!"

There was a long silence, cut by my weeping and my hoarse croaks. Then the answer echoed from a distant place, like a muffled cry, a bell that was tolling from another shore. Grief-stricken, shocked, broken.

"*Da . . . vid. Aber . . . nath . . . y.*"

The name came out so slowly, I had to force myself to listen to each tortured syllable.

I felt a horrible chill. Someone was possessed by the man who had betrayed Belle and Celia both. Someone who was here.

"*He is coming!*" Celia cried deep inside me.

Celia wanted me to run. Now.

"*Yesssssssssss,*" Belle hissed. "*Run, Celia.*"

"But where is he? Who is he *in*?" I leaned over her, pressing my ear against the unmoving lips. I thought I could hear whispering, as if of other voices speaking from wherever Belle now was. I could feel Celia scrabbling away from the brink of hysteria, like someone dangling from the edge of a cliff by her fingernails. Forcing me away. Making me run.

"Where is he?" I pleaded, taking Mandy's hand. "Oh, God, help us, please, someone! Mandy, I'm getting help. I'll save you. I will!"

There was no answer.

Mandy Winters was dead.

BOOK THREE: THE SCREAMING SEASON

I have never seen a greater monster or miracle in the world than myself.

—Michel de Montaigne

He that studieth revenge keepeth his own wounds green, which otherwise would heal and do well.

—John Milton

TWENTY-FIVE

March 23
possessions: me
    nothing. i have nothing left. it's all been taken. i am lost.

    haunted by: her death, their deaths; ours.
    listening to: the screams.
    mood: they've won; how can I feel anything? how can I do anything, stop them?

possessions: them
    nothing. they have sold it all for this horrible vengeance. they're bankrupt. they're adrift, with nothing to hold them down.

    haunted by: hatred that is immortal. it's what keeps them alive.
    listening to: my tears, with glee.
    mood: triumphant. they're winning, and they know it. they'll dance on our bones.

ARMS CAME AROUND me, dragging me away from
Mandy. A hand went across my mouth to stop my screams.
It was covered in blood. I panicked, flailing, struggling. I
was forced away, into the trees, into the darkness. Then I was
pushed against the trunk of the tree, and I saw my attacker.

It was Miles, sobbing. He was holding me, but staring back
toward Mandy. Going wild. We both were.

I realized how it must look. "I didn't kill her, I didn't!" I
shouted.

He clamped his hand over my mouth. Tears rolled; he was
shaking his head back and forth so hard I was afraid his neck
would snap.

Mandy was dead. No, it was a terrible dream. A nightmare.
I would wake up. Now.

"Miles," I said in agony. "I didn't kill her."

"I—I know." He clutched his head. "You have to help me.
We don't have much time."

"Don't . . . ?"

"Mandy will be found. Evidence will point to you or to me.
Once we're locked up . . . " He broke down sobbing. "Mandy."

I put my arms around him and held him. He wailed against
the crown of my head, completely lost. I cried too, trying to
keep him upright as his knees buckled. He sank to the ground,
covering his face. There was blood all over his hands.

"Lindsay, they'll take you away. Criminally insane. They'll
do that. We need to move fast. Find out who did this. Fast."

He kept crying. "He'll be after you too. He's probably

coming now." He whipped his head around and looked over his shoulder.

"Is it Miles?" I asked Celia. *"Do you know?"*

"Men, men!" she screamed. *"Run!"*

Miles looked back at me. His face went white. He took a step backward, his shoulders raising, his eyes widening.

"Are . . . are you Celia?" he said.

"Die," she said.

"Stop it!" I shouted. "It's me, Miles. I'm here."

He bit his lower lip. He was terrified. I reached out my hands to him.

"Please," I whispered. "Oh, God."

He ran for me and threw his arms around me. He kissed the top of my head, and then my forehead, and my right temple. Then with a deep, heavy sob, he kissed my lips. We stayed that way weeping and kissing, panting and gasping with fear and pain until he pulled away.

"Oh, God, we have to get you out of here." He took my hand. "Come on."

"We can't *leave* her there," I said.

"*You're* alive." His eyes were so swollen with tears I could barely see his eyes.

He ducked from out of the trees and looked around. "There must be somewhere to hide. I know there's a tunnel in Jessel . . . "

"No." I shook my head, fighting to focus. "The storage room in the admin building." My eyes widened. "There's a dumbwaiter."

"Okay, good. Does it work? Where does it go?"

"I don't know."

"And it's halfway across the campus." He ran his hand through his hair. "If we could get to the parking lot, I've got my car back."

"Too far. Too out in the open." I grabbed his hand. "Miles, someone is possessed by David Abernathy. Mandy told me that before she died." I gave my head a shake. "*Belle* told me that."

"Oh, God, God," he said. He was beginning to lose it again.

"*Run!*" Celia shrieked inside my head. Her screams ricocheted around my skull. I pressed my fingertips against the bridge of my nose, then winced at the pain. A dull, icy ache throbbed across my forehead, like a tooth when a filling falls out.

"Miles, someone is coming," I said.

"Come on."

He pulled on my hand and sprinted left. As we ran, I fought to understand who could have done that horrible thing. Murdered her like that. I shut my eyes against the memory of her face.

Girls were running down the hill to our right, running and screaming. The screams echoed off Searle Lake.

They had found Mandy.

Miles and I moved left again. The moon tracked us like a prison searchlight. He looked down and said, "Oh, God, your feet."

He picked me up and hefted me over his shoulder. Charging up the hill, we hid from more girls as they heard the screams and ran down the hill to see what was going on. The blood was rushing to my head.

We were going up the steepest part of the hill. I knew what that meant: the operating theater.

"No, not there," I whispered, but he didn't hear me. "Please, not there."

He was huffing and puffing, getting winded. I tried to pound on his back, but at that moment he stumbled, and I had to hold onto him instead.

He forked left, and as he stumbled on, I turned my head and saw the hulk of the building towering above the hill. The moon glowed on the hollows in the walls. I shook my head, eyes watering, trembling.

Then we reached the back, halfway around the giant circle of the foundation. A huge part of the wall had fallen away, and he ducked inside. I could feel Celia inside me, thrashing, so frightened she was incoherent. Still, I couldn't stop her as she flailed at Miles, totally losing it. Miles slammed against the wall, groaning, and slid to the floor.

"Miles," I said, crouching beside him. He didn't respond. I couldn't see him. My little purse still dangled from my shoulder. With shaking hands, I opened it and grabbed the lighter. I flicked it on. His head dipped forward onto his chest. I grabbed his head and my fingers came away wet. Blood. I gasped.

The lighter went out.

"Miles." I eased his chin up and flicked the lighter on again. His eyelids were flickering.

"I'm okay," he said thickly. "There's a flashlight in my coat." He reached into one of his pockets and pulled it out. After a couple of attempts, it came on.

"Where's Riley?" I asked.

"I think he went to the infirmary," he said.

"We can't stay here. This place is haunted. We have to go."

His eyes focused on my hand. He blinked and said, "Harvard."

I jerked. "What?" "That's the Harvard logo on that lighter." He tried to get up.

I stared at the lighter. "I think this was given to me. As a clue."

He shook his head. "Clue . . . ?" I opened my purse again and took out the squares. He plucked one from me and bit into it. "Nicotine gum. Cinnamon."

"Are you . . . *what*?"

"Been there. Tried that. To quit."

"Dr. Morehouse went to Harvard," I said.

"Maybe he smokes Dunhills, too," Miles said, his voice a little faint.

"And he told Mandy . . . he told her that he had something to give her that would make the pain go away."

I started to cry. "And he would give it to her tonight. Oh, my God, he's possessed by David Abernathy. Miles, he killed Mandy."

He didn't answer. The flashlight fell from his hand and rolled onto the floor.

"Miles?" I picked up the flashlight and peered at him. His eyes were half closed, his mouth slack. I touched his shoulder and then cupped his chin.

"Miles, can you hear me?" Nothing. I felt the walls close in, the night push down as I realized he needed help and I was the only person who could get it for him. I hadn't been able to help his sister. But he was still alive. Where could I go? What could I do?

My heart pounded. I looked wildly around, every muscle tensing, my senses on high alert. If I went to the infirmary, someone would come back for him, take care of him. Dr. Morehouse—Dr. Abernathy—should have no reason to harm him. The attack of the Vespa must have been aimed at me.

But what if Dr. Abernathy *did* want to hurt him? What if by leaving him here, I left him to die?

Celia was lying in the snow, more dead than alive, unaware of the cold or of any pain. She was completely numb. She was breathing shallowly, her chest fluttering, and the night sky above her gleamed like a burnished dome of ebony. She could hear the screaming through the snowy earth she lay on.

She drifted, and drowsed. She dreamed she was on a white horse, riding into a place of shadow. Then a shaft of white light flared in front of her, expanding; people in long white robes held out their arms, smiling in welcome. She would be warm there. She would be loved.

She began to ride toward it.

"Oh, God," someone said. It was David Abernathy.

She tried to shrink away. She was hideous; he had made her hideous. But perhaps he had come to save her, and to beg her forgiveness.

He crouched over her, with his handsome, strong features and his fine, short beard; he rubbed his fists into his eyes and his shoulders heaved. He was crying.

He said nothing to her. Maybe he didn't realize that she was awake. But he stood, and walked away. She tried to call out to him: I'm alive, I'm alive!

He came back with something long in his right fist. For a confusing moment she thought it was a sword. Then her vision sharpened.

It was a shovel.

He slammed it into the dirt and lifted it, then tossed it to the side. He built up a rhythm. Dig, lift, move. Dig, lift, move. She tried to grunt, to signal that she was alive. She watched him. His tears had dried up. His face was set with firm resolve.

She drifted.

Then suddenly she was hoisted up by one arm and one leg. David was wearing gloves. She felt featherlight; her head lolled. Then she turned toward the sky one time, upward . . .

. . . and then he tossed her like a bundle of oily, burned rags into the hole he had dug.

"No, for the love of God," she pleaded. "I'm alive!" But her words were unspoken and he didn't hear her.

As she lay shrieking in silence, he filled the shovel with dirt and snow and spilled it over her face.

I woke, weeping. That was how Celia had wound up in a shallow grave on the highway, why she haunted the road, why I had dreamed of lying in the frozen earth. She'd still been alive when he buried her. Did he know it? Had that haunted him? I was standing over Miles, gazing down on his lolling head. The flashlight was in my hand. I clicked it on and squatted down, scrutinizing his face. His eyes were closed. I didn't know how long I had lost awareness. I reached out and lifted his right lid. Flashed the light directly into it. I couldn't tell if there was a response.

Then he jerked, hard, as if he had suffered some kind of spasm. With a gasp, he flared open his eyes.

They were completely black.

He was possessed.

"He's got you now," he crowed in Belle's voice. *"He's got you now."*

TWENTY-SIX

A HAND GRABBED the back of my head and yanked it, hard. My scalp burned. A bright light shone in my eyes and I shut them trying to block it out.

Celia started shrieking. Her screams blocked out everything. I went somewhere black, and cold. I was lying in her grave, among the worms and bones, surrounded by screams.

"Look into the light. Now," Dr. Morehouse commanded me. Only, it wasn't his voice. It was the voice of my dreams and nightmares, soft, lilting, comforting. Dr. David Abernathy's voice.

Celia screamed.

He shook my head so hard my jaw ached. Again.

"No!" Celia screamed. *"No, don't!"*

Again.

I opened my eyes against the blazing yellow light. I flinched, but my head was held fast.

"Good. Now we start. I will count down from ten to one. And when I say your special secret word, the word you told me is your favorite, you will do everything I ask of you. Yes?"

"No!" Celia's scream rattled my eye sockets. My eyelids fluttered.

"Keep looking. Or I'll kill that boy."

I made myself look. My eyes burned.

"Ten," he said.

Celia thrashed. She struggled and screamed.

"Nine."

"Please, Lindsay, please, oh, God . . . "

"Eight."

I couldn't hear the numbers over her screaming. Maybe that didn't matter; I could feel myself sinking, dissolving, surrendering.

"Seven."

Deeper and deeper.

"Six."

Deeper still.

"Five." Light, blazing .

"Four."

Warmth.

"Three."

Heat.

"Two."

Safety.

"One."

Stillness. Utter silence.

"Memmy."

Love. I was loved, and I had always been loved.

"Memmy," he said, one more time. *"Good. Now stand up, darlin'."*

It was good to stand up. I liked doing as he asked. Slowly I rose, feeling languid and heavy, knowing it was all right.

"And come with me."

Come with me

Come with me

Come with me

Come with me

Come with—

Barefoot, I walked over dust and dirt. Something crept along my mind, like a ghost on all fours, a white blur. I stiffened.

"Memmy," he said again, and I relaxed.

He was my love; how could I not go with him? How could I deny him anything? *Whither thou goest, there will I go.* My second-favorite Bible passage, the one I had underscored in my copy of the Good Book, the only possession given me by Edwin Marlwood, my wretched, evil headmaster. I would take it with me when we left this place.

When I belonged to my David, and I was his.

My favorite Bible passage: *I am my beloved's, and my beloved is mine.*

What did it matter, if we had each other?

David began to sing my favorite song, our love song.

My love is like a red, red rose
That's newly sprung in June;
My love is like the melody
That's sweetly play'd in tune.

So fair art though, my bonnie lass,
So deep in love am I;

And I will love thee still my dear,
Till a' the seas gang dry.

Till a' the seas gang dry, my dear,
And the rocks melt wi' the sun;
And I will love thee still, my dear,
While the sands o' life shall run.

And fare thee weel, my only love,
And fare thee weel awhile!
And I will come again, my love,
Tho' it were ten thousand mile.

"*My red rose,*" David whispered, kissing the center of my forehead. "*Now come with me, sweet girl. I have exactly what you need to take the pain away.*"

TWENTY-SEVEN

WE WALKED HAND in hand into the operating theater. I saw the bed where I was to lie and the circles of gas lamps hanging above it, like a chandelier composed of suns. High above us, the three circular balconies were filled with men— young medical students, who had traveled far to witness the miracle of modern science. It would be quick, and then I would feel no pain, ever again. No anger, no sadness, no rebellion, nor moods. I would be sweet, biddable, a good girl.

A good girl.

The learned young men gazed down on us; I floated beside David, trusting him, loving him, sensing that this favor had been kept from me for a long time. That my struggle had been long and painful, but at last I was to have the sweet release that he had promised me.

He walked me to the bed. Then two nurses came forward, waiting to prepare me for the surgery.

They were beautiful. One had dark hair and flashing eyes. The other was a redhead, curls piled on her head. I knew them both.

"Marica," I said, pulling back slightly. "Rose."

They smiled at me.

"No, I'm Pearl," replied the one I had mistaken for Marica. She gestured to Rose. *"And of course you know Belle."*

"It'll all be over soon," Rose-Belle said silkily.

David gestured to the bed. *"Just lie down, my beautiful good girl."*

My vision was blurry. I looked at the bed, but it was hard to see. He wrapped his hand around my wrist to steady me, and then he led me to the little wooden block of three stairs. My foot came down on the first stair.

Something inside me . . . *shifted.*

"Please, no," I said. "I . . . this is not right."

"No, it's fine." He sounded impatient. He wiggled my hand. *"Memmy."*

I took the next step.

The third.

Pearl picked up a mallet from a metal tray beside my bed. Belle lifted a sharp, needle-like metal filament attached to a wooden handle. I squinted at it, willing it into focus through my blurry vision.

It was an ice pick. It caught the light of the gas lamps and threw prisms against the ceiling, each one like a bloom from a—

Flashlight.

I woke up. Flat, blue light from battery-operated camping lanterns revealed my surroundings. I was standing beside the hospital gurney Troy had snuck in on that Valentine's Day, beneath the shattered ceiling of the operating theater. Torrents of icy rain pelted me as I gasped.

I spun around. Marica and Rose faced me. Their eyes were completely black. *Possessed.*

Marica held a hammer and Rose an ice pick. I understood now that Mandy really had seen a ghost in Marica's eyes, when she had stared into them during her "game." If only Riley hadn't shown up, distracting us both. I had let down my guard, and now Mandy was dead. And I was going to die, too.

"No," I ground out. "You guys, wake up." I backed away from them, searching the triple tier of ruined balconies, where blurs shifted and moved. The iron railings were rusted and twisted, like water hoses flung into the ocean. Rain poured on the front seats, splattering as it fell, gushing back down to the floor of the theater.

A large hand came down on my shoulder. It clenched hard, and I jerked.

"You won't be able to feel it," said David Abernathy from behind me. Celia's enemy had hidden inside Dr. Morehouse, just as she had hidden inside me.

The shrill drone of a motor buffeted my ear. He turned me around, slowly, and showed me the cordless drill— silvery blue, with a spinning drill bit that would gouge a hole in me so enormous and so deep, my soul would come screaming out.

He looked from it to me and back again, and smiled. It was his face, and then it wasn't. It shifted, changed.

Then a skull floated over it, jaw open and grinning, eye sockets black.

"I'm here to finish what I started," he informed me, shouting over the noise.

"No," I ground out.

He blinked. *"No? You can't say no!"*

I understood now. Dr. Morehouse had hypnotized me into obeying his instructions. Whether he had done it as David Abernathy or as himself, he had assumed I wouldn't fight him. Had Mandy fought?

"No," I said again.

On my left, Rose and Marica took a step toward me. On my right, Dr. Morehouse-Abernathy approached as well.

"Dr. Morehouse, you've been taken over," I told him. "You're not yourself."

"I am David Abernathy," he said. *"And it is I, dear girl, who mesmerized you. While I slept inside him. And I soothed the raging bitch who lives inside you. The murderess, Celia Reaves. I have performed the mesmerizing. I have spoken the word that silences her."*

I bolted, whirling and running straight ahead, hoping that I would be quick enough to dodge the three of them. David Abernathy ran at me, the drill spinning in his hand. I fled into the darkness beyond the reach of the lanterns, out of the rain. My right foot came down hard on something on the floor. My ankle twisted. I grunted.

"Help me!" I screamed. "I need help!"

"Lindsay!" Miles shouted.

I looked in the direction of his voice. He braced himself inside the doorjamb, staring at the ghostly white figure now superimposing itself over Dr. Morchouse's body. Wisps of gray hair clung to Abernathy's skull, and ragged, moldly tatters of an old-fashioned suit clung to a bony chest and hung on hip bones.

"Holy shit," Miles said.

Marica and Rose headed toward me. Skulls rose over their faces too—the dead masks of Pearl Magnusen and Belle herself, here for the kill. Winding sheets floated around their skeletal bodies. Rose-Belle grabbed Marica's arm and pointed to the ceiling.

"Water puts us out," she said in her southern drawl.

They broke apart, each racing just outside the semicircle of rain, heading for me. I backed away, trying to remember where the gaping spot in the wall had been. I could see nothing behind me, only shadows. To either side, the dead flew at me, just a few feet away.

Miles propelled himself into the operating theater and ran toward Abernathy. He held out a cross.

"I abjure thee, demon!" Miles bellowed, arms shaking. He was half-covered in blood, and he staggered to the left.

Abernathy threw back his head and laughed.

Marica-Pearl grabbed my arm, and Rose-Belle showed me the ice pick. Pearl twisted my arm and pushed me to the floor, falling on top of me, grabbing my wrists and holding me down. She had dropped the hammer. I turned my head, staring at it. I struggled, but the ghost who held me was strong.

Belle approached, holding the ice pick in front of herself like a sacred object. Laughter bounced around the room.

She knelt beside me.

I couldn't stop looking at her. *Hammer,* I thought, *get it.* But I couldn't tear my gaze from the pick.

"Oh, God, Rose, listen. You're *possessed,*" I said. "You don't want to do this."

"You deserve it, sweet bee," Belle said. *"And we're not going to deny you any longer."*

She turned the pick point down and pressed it against my forehead. My heartbeat roared in my ears. I heard myself screaming. I fought, kicking my legs; for a confused instant, I thought I was back in the infirmary, in the grip of another nightmare. But this was real. This was happening.

"Lindsay!" Miles shouted.

"Miles!" I shrieked.

Belle raised up on her knees and placed her left hand over her right. She looked over at Pearl. I remembered Pearl. Pearl had possessed Julie, and she alone had felt remorse and horror over what they were planning to do to me. With her help, I had escaped to the lake.

"Pearl," I tried, "stop. I'm begging you."

My tears were sliding across my temples. I let out a violent wail as the ice pick pierced the skin on my bruised and battered forehead.

"Not this time, Celia," Pearl said, sneering at me.

"I'm not Celia, I'm not. I think she's gone," I babbled. "Oh, *please—*"

"Oh, she's here," Belle said.

The ice pick went in a little deeper. It was like the slice of a knife, stinging all my nerve endings, making me scream. It was going to happen to me; it was happening; and no one was going to stop it.

I thought of Riley, and my dad and CJ and my step-brothers, and I thought of my mom.

"Memmy," I whispered. My last goodbye, my last fare-well.

And something . . . shifted . . . in the air. I felt release of pressure inside the room. I looked at Belle as she gasped and dropped the ice pick. At Pearl, as she stared at something in front of her that I couldn't see.

A heavy bouquet of lemon and earth filled my nostrils. Geraniums. Light reflected off the skull faces of the two ghosts. I tried to tip my head back so that I could look too, but I couldn't bend it back far enough. Pearl still held me down, but her jaw had dropped open. It began to clack nervously, and she recoiled.

I still couldn't get free. I struggled, but Pearl's weight on my wrists kept me down.

The geranium scent washed over me. Images—words—flashed through my mind.

possessions:
full moon
mirror—Mandy's room
candle—on the tables
item belonging to dead person—me

part of dead person (hair, bone, etc.)—me

Memmy.

Memmy.

Memmy.

Memmy.

Memmy.

David Abernathy had summoned her five times. And I had collected the objects listed in Mandy's journal.

"Memmy," I whispered as electricity shot through me. I felt as if I were being jolted with a thousand watts. I felt it through the floor as the light grew brighter on Belle and Pearl's skull faces.

"We were never loved enough," Pearl wailed.

"We were betrayed by love," Belle shouted bitterly. *"Betrayed and murdered!"*

As I watched, the light grew more intense. No longer yellow, but bright white. Their skeletal faces shone, glowing; the gleam became so blinding that I had to look away.

"What are we doing?" Pearl cried.

And she released me and pushed Belle, hard. Belle landed on her side, the ice pick in her fist, staring at the glow. There was a soundless explosion of colors, flaring all over the room, beams of rainbows kaleidoscoping over the circles of ruined chairs in the balconies, the debris on the floor beneath me, the faces of the ghosts.

I whirled around.

And did something—*someone*—hover in the air for just one second? Did I feel a huge wash of sorrow rush through me, followed by a burst of happiness?

"Oh, God, what are we doing?" Rose bellowed, in her normal voice.

She and Marica ran to me and threw their arms around me. The skull masks had disappeared, and they were my two friends.

"What's happening?" Marica shouted.

Across the room, Miles was battling David Abernathy for possession of the drill. Already battered, Miles was losing. Abernathy caught him under the chin with the butt of the drill, then leapt on him and pushed him down as Miles lost his balance.

He aimed the drill at Miles's forehead.

We dashed toward him.

"No!" Abernathy shrieked. He lifted his head and stared at Miles and then at us. *"No! You all must die. All of you. You are filthy girls. You are wanton harlots. I hate all of you and I will see you dead before I rest."*

We made a semi-circle as we ran. The drill kept whirring, shrieking. Miles was panting, too weak to help himself. Abernathy narrowed his eyes, as if daring us to come closer.

"I did it for love!" Abernathy yelled.

"You did it for money, and to keep your job," I replied, holding up my hand. The other two girls stopped. I took a step toward him. "But you liked doing it. You liked the power. Is that why you came back here after you died? Because you *are* dead."

"I am not dead!" he shrieked. *"I am here!"*

"You didn't die here, but you are here," I said, forcing myself not to panic as the drill whirred closer toward Miles. "You're more alive here."

He sneered at me. "I walk, in the night fog. And I see all of you, parading your filth. Your wantonness enrages me . . . "

"*You* were the Marlwood Stalker," I said, swallowing hard, wondering if I was right, and if I should push him like this. "You did those things." I wasn't sure how. Did he move from person to person? "You killed Kiyoko. Pushed her . . . "

Then, as I stared at him, the skull ripped away from Dr. Morehouse's face. A white skeleton appeared beneath the skull, and shimmered with light. Old-fashioned clothing appeared—a black Victorian suit, and over that, a white butcher's apron, covered with blood. And then the gleaming skeleton became a dark figure made of shadow. Black on black on black, flat and heavy.

"Pushed her," the shadow said. "Yessssssssssss. Because she was unclean."

I realized it was the figure I had seen in Mandy's room.

"You were going to kill Mandy in her room that night," I said.

"She was Belle."

Which was why Mandy hadn't remembered it.

"I couldn't finish the job that night. But I just did," said the blackness. "Filthy."

"No. She was a *girl*," I said. "They all were girls. That's all they—*we* are. And deep down, you know it. *You know it.*"

The darkness clacked its jaws. "You're a liar."

"You're lying. To yourself. You knew those girls—and us— we're no better or worse than any other girls. Because no one is perfect. But something happened to *you*, didn't it? And it hurt you so deeply that you had to hurt back!"

The black eyes opened and stared right at me. I saw the whites. Ice shot down my spine.

"*No.*" David Abernathy's voice was ragged. "No, she was supposed to love me!"

In that moment, I felt my own anger, my outrage. It was like lightning coursing through me, making *me* alive. I understood its power. I had been so angry I'd wanted someone dead. Not because Riley had cheated, or Mandy had been rich and mean, but because no one had stopped my mom from dying.

But there was a difference between us—I had never killed anybody.

He had. Oh, he had.

I pointed at the hideous thing. "So you took your revenge. You became a monster because you hated *her*." I didn't know who she was. His own mother? A different beloved woman?

"No, no , because you . . . all of you . . . you need to be . . . to be *not* like her. Not!" The ghost threw back his head and screamed.

"But we are like her. We all are!" I yelled at him—at *it*. "We're human beings!"

"No!" it screamed again.

"And there's nothing you can do about it, *ever*!"

It screamed a third time, screamed so loudly the roof of the operating theater shook.

"Love me!" it screamed. "Love me, *please*!"

I wept, unable to respond in any other way .

"Love me!" it cried again, pathetic.

I wept, unable to respond in any other way.

The shadow crumbled, fading into fog. Screaming, *"Love me!"*

And then ... it vanished.

I blinked, stunned, aware only then that Rose and Marica were screaming, too. They held each other, sobbing.

"Oh, God," Dr. Morehouse cried, jerking. "Oh, dear God, what have I done?"

"It wasn't you," I said over the whine of the drill. "Dr. Morehouse ... it's all right."

Miles started to get up. Dr. Morehouse glanced down at him.

Then he reached back his foot and kicked Miles in the chest. Miles contracted, and the doctor ran toward the doorway.

Marica, Rose, and I began to run to Miles, through the rain, gathering around him and shielding him with our bodies. He grabbed my hand and squeezed it. Dr. Morehouse stood in the doorway, panting. He was holding the drill. It was still on.

"Dr. Morehouse," I said, "stop. Something bad has happened to you, but it's over. Let it be over."

I walked slowly toward him.

The drill whined as he lifted it toward his head. He was shaking, weeping.

"No," I said, as calmly as I could. "It wasn't you."

"Yes," he said. "Yes. I did it."

"No. You were possessed."

"Oh, my God," Rose said behind me. "What's happening?"

"I wasn't. Back there . . . Massachusetts . . . where I . . . " He sobbed. "I did . . . terrible things. *I* did them."

I knew at that moment that he had dark secrets of his own. From his own life. His self-hatred had been why David Abernathy had been able to control him so completely.

He lifted the drill. "I *should* be dead."

"Stop!" I screamed.

Then he aimed the drill straight at his forehead and pushed.

TWENTY-EIGHT

"LINDSAY, DON'T LOOK!" Miles shouted as Dr. Morehouse shoved the drill into his skull.

Reflexively I turned; Miles grabbed my chin and dragged me across the theater. I was staggering; we wove left and right, like drunks, sliding over the floor. He hit an aluminum pail with his left shoe and it tipped over, releasing an eye-watering stench.

Behind us, something crackled and made a zizzing, sparking hiss. Miles pushed me along into the narrow tunnel. I ran with him, screaming, and then I realized that *I* wasn't screaming. Celia was, inside my head.

"It was him, it was him, Lindsay, he did it to us, he did it," she wailed. *"He did it."*

I couldn't stop screaming as Miles grabbed me and whirled me around, shielding me with his body. My shrieks; Dr. Morehouse's horrible, garbled yell; Marica and Rose, screaming.

Miles picked me up again and barreled for the door. I saw

Dr. Morehouse's body facedown. The drill rattled and spun beside him.

We ran through the corridor, Marica and Rose too, then out the hole that had been the front door, into the rain as it poured from the sky like so much weeping, tears of agony for Marlwood.

Then we were outside, in the driving downpour. We outdistanced Marica and Rose as Miles flew through the trees. Lightning crashed and the trees shook. The ground shuddered beneath Miles's feet.

Horribly bruised, Riley burst from the trees with a flashlight in his hand, shouting when he saw me. He dove at Miles, pushing him backward, and I fell, hard. Then Riley raised the flashlight above his head, preparing to slam it across Miles's face.

"No!" I shrieked, hurling myself at him. "He didn't do anything!"

Riley pulled me out of Miles's reach, easing me beneath a thatch of overhanging pine branches. He peered hard at me. "Are you okay?"

"Dr. M-Morehouse," I said. I was stammering and quaking. My stomach clenched, hard, and I covered my mouth.

"He killed himself," Miles said. "I'm going for help."

Lightning jagged across the sky as he sprinted away into the darkness. In seconds he was swallowed up.

Another lightning bolt jittered. Thunder boomed. The entire heap of the operating theater groaned and shifted. Metal squealed, followed by a crash so loud it shook the ground where we stood. We both jumped. Then a series of clatters and clangs buffeted my ears. The horrible torture chamber was collapsing.

Celia shifted inside me with each sound, her icy presence grabbing hold of my bones, my lungs, my heart. My head throbbed.

"Come on," Riley said, taking my hand. "Mandy's been killed. I'm getting you out of here."

We ran among the trees, branches whipping in the wind. I was so numb from the cold that I couldn't feel them hitting my face. I was freezing, inside and out. Celia wanted something, needed something.

When we burst through the last stand of trees, I saw Searle Lake, in all its blackness, stretched out like a body in a coffin. I imagined the lake's black arms reaching up to grab me, and I took a step backward. A huge crowd had gathered where I had found Mandy. If they turned, they would see us.

"No, Lindsay, please," Celia murmured inside me. *"I need so badly to rest."*

Not by my own will, I lurched forward. One step, then two, toward the lake. At first Riley didn't realize I was going in a different direction. Then he said, "No, this way," and urged me toward Jessel.

"We go alone," Celia said. She wasn't asking; she was telling me. I remembered what had happened to Troy the night that Mandy and the other possessed girls—including Julie—had tried to kill me. He'd gotten "lost," and he had "fallen." Search parties scoured the forest for days, and when he was found, he had been taken to a hospital, half dead from hypothermia. Was she threatening me with that?

"No," I said under my breath. Riley didn't hear me.

"Alone," Celia repeated, and in that exact moment it stopped raining, as if someone had clicked it off with a switch. *"Please. You won't be hurt. I swear it. And neither will he."*

"No," I said more loudly. Riley looked at me, surprised.

"No, what?" he asked.

And then I felt her shifting inside me again, like ice cubes roaming through my body. Her killer was dead, but it wasn't over.

Not for me.

"We have to get out of here," Riley said, looking back in the direction we had come.

"He's dead," I said; then I began to shake all over. Tears rolled down my rain-drenched face. I couldn't stop seeing Dr. Morehouse with the drill, how he'd screamed. Dr. Abernathy had died in his sleep at a ripe old age. But how many times had the screams of his victims echoed in his memory? How often had he longed for the glory days when he could exorcise his hatred of some woman who had scarred him forever?

And I knew then that if I ignored Celia's command to go down to the lake, I, too, would hear screams for the rest of my life.

"Riley, I—I need a minute." I knew I sounded lame. But there was no way I could explain.

"We have to . . . " He looked at me. Really looked.

"What's going on? You look so strange."

I was sure there was makeup all over my face. I didn't know if Celia's white face blended with mine, but I couldn't stop to explain. This might be the last moment I had to be alone.

"Wait for me here." I took his hand. "Please."

Riley was soaking wet and shivering, and he probably thought I was more than a little crazy. But he nodded and crossed his arms over his chest. Then he unfolded his arms and handed me his flashlight. I flooded with gratitude. I wanted to tell him how afraid I was. But this had nothing to do with him.

Then alone with Celia—a contradiction in terms if there ever was one—I trudged down to behind some boulders to the lake. My boots sank into frigid mud, and the obsidian surface gleamed as if winter ice still crusted its surface.

Cautiously, I bent from the waist and gazed into the black water. She was there, the white oval, the eyes that were, once again, hollow sockets. Less human, more terrifying. Her mouth was open, a black *O*.

"You're safe now," I whispered. "It's safe to let go."

And across the sheen of the jet-black water, I heard a long, low wailing. Heartbreaking misery, longing; so much pain.

And it was coming out of me.

"Memmy," I said, gasping. I sank down onto my knees, hands pressing against the mud, and stared at Celia. Bubbles dotted the rippling circle of her face . . . were they her tears or mine? "Oh, God, Celia, I lost my mom. My mom *died*," I told her. "For a while, hardly anyone would talk to me, like I had a disease. And then, sometimes they would forget, and bitch about their mothers, and then they would stop, and act so bizarre and tell me how *sorry* they were."

"I know. I am so sorry. I'm so sorry for you, Lindsay," she said.

I was crying hard. My stomach was a knot. My throat clenched and I let the tears fall into the lake. "I miss her so much."

"I know. I know. I—I thought I was going to have a long life. But my daddy . . . I got sent here, and I wished they had just killed me."

She was weeping, hard. I held out my hand, as if to touch her face.

"It was horrible. And I was so angry . . . I went mad, I know I did. I did terrible things . . . and then . . . I died so young. Like your mama, Lindsay. She died so young."

"Yes, she did. And you did." I licked my lips. "Please, tell me, have you seen her? Can you talk to her for me? I think she was with me in the operating theater. I think she saved me."

"No. I'm sorry. I think she's moved on."

I felt as if she had punched me in the stomach. How could Memmy move on and leave me?

"You don't want that for her, honey, if you love her," Celia whispered. *"Lingering like this . . . it's worse than death. We have to move on, all of us. Or the pain is too much to bear. It drives us mad."*

"But what he did to you . . . "

"It's done. He knows what he did. Until tonight, he never faced it. The why of it."

"But why did Dr. Morehouse have to die?"

"Don't waste your tears on that one. The truth will come out. The truth of what he was. What he did, back in Massachusetts. It's a blessing for the living that he's gone."

She sobbed, and I heard the wail ricochet off the water. Night birds fluttered and cried on the water's edge. I held out my hand.

The coldness rose up into my chest and then out through my arm. As I watched, and we both cried, white light poured from my fingertips and covered the lake. It lit up like a beacon. Celia was leaving me.

"You've carried me with you, dear Lindsay," she whispered. *"You can lay me to rest."*

It was safe to let go.

"I'll find your grave," I promised her. "I'll tell your story."

"Bless you, sweet love. Bless you."

The light intensified, like back in the operating theater, until I had to shield my eyes. The other ghosts of Marlwood were coming back to where their ashes had been dumped to hide the terrible crimes that had been committed against them. White faces shone, then melted into the light. Echoes and crying and papery weeping shook me, and I gave in to it too. I was sorry for myself, and for them, that such horrible evil could twist them and make them crazy and mean.

I leaned farther over and dipped my hands into the water, teetering. A hand wrapped around mine, colder than the grave, and then it gave me a squeeze.

I squeezed back. "I actually think I'm going to miss you, just a little," I said.

"Live," she replied. *"Oh, Lindsay, live."*

The light in the water went out. I wiped my hands on my dress as I got back up to a stand position, turned, and saw Riley approaching from a distance.

"This is where your friend died, isn't it?" he said. "Kiyoko."

I didn't know he knew about that. It was as if everything that had happened up here had taken place in another dimension.

"Yes," I said steadily. "She died in this lake. And I found her."

"Damn." He reached out and pulled me against his chest. I let out a deep breath. "Damn, Lindsay, no wonder you're wacko."

Despite everything, I laughed through my tears and batted him. Then the wonder of what had happened with Celia, and the knowledge that I was no longer possessed, slammed into the nightmare of watching Dr. Morehouse kill himself.

And Mandy Winters was dead.

He let me cry while we shivered and trembled, and the sun finally began to rise.

TWENTY-NINE

JUST AS CELIA REAVES and I finished our goodbyes, the police pulled up at the edge of Searle Lake. In their headlights, birds skimmed the water, then landed. My nightmare was over.

With my frantic parents' permission, I spoke to the police. From the way they framed their questions, I was certain that they believed Dr. Morehouse had killed Mandy. They would never believe that a ghost had roamed Marlwood, and had killed Kiyoko. I remembered when Celia told me that Troy had been pushed, when he had been found unconscious in the woods. I shivered, realizing that the spirit of David Abernathy had nearly killed Troy, too.

It doesn't matter anymore, I reminded myself as Riley, Miles, and I drank coffee in the headmistress's office. *Marlwood is free. And so am I.*

We three were wrapped in blankets, shivering. All my dorm mates had surrounded me, hugging me, crying with me. Julie had brought me some clothes. Now they were all sitting in the reception area with Marica, who didn't remember anything but knew she had somehow been involved in the horror of that night. Miles and Riley were given a change of clothes as well. I wasn't sure where they came from, but I was grateful that the two guys were sitting quietly—in shock, but not taking swings at each other.

Riley was ragged, but Miles was in terrible shape. All the color had drained from his face; he had seen his sister dead and her murderer kill himself in a horrible, gruesome way. Did he truly believe that Dr. Morehouse had been possessed? If he did, he didn't tell the police that, and neither did I.

His father was on his way, with an army of lawyers and people to "take care of" Mandy's body. I couldn't help but bitterly wonder if all her so-called friends were speed-dialing their designers to get them dressed for her funeral. Poor little rich girl.

Dr. Ehrlenbach arrived at about three in the morning, and I was shocked at the change in her. Her mask-like, wrinkle-free face was sagging and lined, as if all the Botox had been drained from her body. Her black hair, usually slicked back, hung in unkempt lanks around her chin line. It was said that Dr. Ehrlenbach was at least sixty-eight. That morning, she looked it.

But I had never been gladder to see her. She took charge, ushering us all upstairs. We climbed creaking stairs into a spacious room dominated by a fireplace with a heavily carved wooden mantel. A staff member glided in quietly and laid a fire, which soon crackled and blazed. I didn't even flinch at the smell of smoke and the sight of the fire.

A border of two-foot-tall stained glass windows of nature

scenes rimmed a bay window that looked out onto the campus. I had no idea how much of the campus would be visible from the second story of the admin building. How much had we really gotten away with, thinking we were sneaking around unobserved? *How much did Dr. Ehrlenbach really know?*

Lights were on in all the dorms. Tonight the housemothers couldn't pretend that their charges were safely snuggled in their beds. No one was asleep. Mandy Winters was dead, and Dr. Morehouse had drilled into his own skull.

Riley and I sat next to each other on a burgundy leather couch, me in sweats and socks I had knit myself, wrapped in blankets. He put his arm around me and I shuddered hard and leaned my head on his shoulder. Miles stared out the window. We were the survivors. We had made it through.

Through this, and through my past. Riley had seen me at my worst—when I had completely lost it in the theater at Christmas; when I had dissed my best friend, Heather Martinez, to impress Jane. And I had seen him at *his* worst—when he had had sex with Jane in my parents' bedroom, during a party Jane had pressured me to throw.

He'd jumped in his car and driven fourteen hours to find me, and help me, without a real explanation as to why. All he'd known was that I needed someone. And he had come because he wanted that someone to be him, Riley Kincaid. For the crazy girl in the torn jeans and the army jacket and the ripped, oversized sweatshirt that she wore because it had belonged to her dead mother.

My mother who came back to me, and saved me.

"Oh, God," he whispered, in a voice so low only I could hear it. "If anything had happened to you, I would have died."

"Don't say that. Don't ever say that." For one sharp moment I was afraid that if I loved Riley . . . if I let myself *feel* the love I felt for him, that I would lose him. Maybe that was something to talk to a good therapist about.

Riley kissed me very gently, as if I were a fragile creature. Which I was. But ramrod strong, too. Bowed but not broken.

After I had finished my fourth or fifth statement for the police detectives, Dr. Ehrlenbach sat across from me in an uncomfortable chair, her back to the fire. Miles was on his phone to his father. Riley was watching me protectively.

"I'm leaving," I said, before she could speak. She opened her mouth, and then she nodded.

"I think . . . " She looked off as if in the distance and slipped a lank of her hair behind her ear. "I think we might all be leaving," she murmured. "But if for some reason . . . "

She took a breath. "You know that we consider you part of our Marlwood family, and we always will. Our resources are available to you as you continue your education, Lindsay. If you reconsider . . . "

Are you insane? I almost blurted, but I gave my head a little shake.

"I won't be back."

"Yes, of course. But we can still help you. And we will. Letters of recommendation from us will go a long way in your college applications."

Her voice broke. Her lips trembled; she slid a glance at

Miles, who had turned his back as he spoke quietly, grimly. Would there still be an "us"? The Winters Sports Complex was probably going to transform into the Winters lawsuit. I wondered if the scandal would shut down the school. Two student deaths, a horrendous suicide. The rich parents would be yanking their daughters out of here. For all I knew, the parking lot was already full of limousines and Mercedes-Benzes, chauffeurs, nannies, and the occasional actual parent.

I lost track after a while, and Dr. Ehrlenbach and Ms. Simonet discussed putting Riley, Miles, and me in the infirmary for the night. Finally it was decided that Riley and Miles would stay in one of the guest cottages reserved for visitors, and I would be permitted to sleep one last night in my dorm.

I was escorted to the dorm. Of course none of us slept. Mostly we cried, and hugged each other, and went over what had happened, obsessively. We couldn't stop talking about it, reliving it.

"It's going to haunt us forever," Julie whispered, sitting the closest to me. And the white faces of my friends floated in the darkness, like ghosts.

I PACKED THAT night; in the morning, Julie brought me breakfast so I wouldn't have to face everyone in the commons. Marica, Elvis, Claire, and Ida were crying, hard. No one tried to smile through their tears.

I walked down the hall and into the bathroom with the tubs where the insane had been tormented. Ms. Krige, my housemother, came over and gave me a hug. I remembered returning from Christmas break, when she shared her homemade gingerbread with us and we watched TV together. She had seemed like a regular person, like me. Would she have to find another job if the school closed? Would she be able to, if it was discovered that we snuck out on a routine basis, drinking and partying?

"I'll miss you," Julie told me, and it seemed that she wanted to say something more but thought the better of it.

"I'll miss all of you," I told my dormies. They didn't know that I had spied on them, addicted to learning their secrets. Which one would have been next, after Dr. Morehouse killed Mandy? Had any of them—or all of them—been taken over by a dead girl, as Marica had been, and marched all over campus like a puppet?

Did one of you push Kiyoko in the lake, possessed by the spirit of David Abernathy?

"It's not goodbye," Julie said as I took one last look around our room. "We'll see each other this summer, promise?"

We hugged tightly. I wasn't certain I would ever see her again. I didn't know if I could leave the nightmare parts behind, yet keep the gift of our friendship.

———

IN THE MORNING, there were more rounds of goodbyes and confused reactions from Mandy's clique—Lara, Sangeeta, and Alis. They were cast adrift. None of them could take over for Mandy to keep the group together.

Outside the admin building, Riley was waiting for me, alone. I walked steadily toward him as the sunshine glowed on his tanned but bruised face. His lower lip was swollen.

"Your parents are going to start the drive up the coast," he said, "and we'll meet them. And we'll start over." He ducked down and peered into my eyes. "Right?"

"Right," I replied. I was done, gratefully done. The ghosts of Marlwood had been laid to rest, once and for all. The hauntings were over.

I felt eyes on me and glanced over my shoulder as Riley led me to the parking lot. Miles slouched beneath a pine tree, face shrouded by the shadow of the admin building. My cheeks felt hot. His hands were stuffed in the pockets of a long black leather duster. He wore jeans and boots, and there was a cigarette dangling from his mouth.

When he saw that I was looking at him, half his mouth quirked in a sad smile that didn't reach his blackened eyes. He looked lonely, and sad, and . . . *unfinished*.

My heart tugged and a sharp thrill rattled my insides. I didn't understand him. He fascinated me, and I didn't even know if I liked him. But I owed him. I wasn't sure it was a debt I could ever pay. Whatever it would took to make things, if not better, then bearable for him—whatever it was that Miles needed—I wasn't sure I had it. Mandy was dead, and I was leaving, and he was still whoever he was.

Wrapped in the folds of the coat, he shrugged as he took the cigarette from his mouth and dropped it onto the cold dirt. He tamped it out beneath his boot, a cigarette in the dirt.

In my mind's eye, I saw other cigarettes on the ground. A sharp, icy fear seized hold of me, and doubts rushed in.

Could Miles have *ever* been possessed by Dr. Abernathy?

Had he played me all along? How could he have not known what Mandy was doing? He was her twin brother. And he loved her.

He loved her.

He was staring at me.

"Linz?" Riley asked softly, giving my hand a little wag.

And I was staring at Miles.

"Just a sec," I said. Then, tearing my gaze away from Miles to reassure Riley, I reached up on tiptoe and kissed his cheek. "Don't get weird."

I let go of his hand and walked over to Miles, aware that we weren't alone and probably never would be again. He blinked and pulled back slightly, as if bracing himself for a blow. I saw in him the same hurt I had seen in Mandy and my heart broke a little more for him.

"Hey," I said quietly, "you're going to be okay."

His brows began to rise; then he caught himself and brought out his lazy, mocking Miles Winters smile. I knew that smile well. I used to be so intimidated by it. Now I knew it was a mask, and I had seen what lay beneath it.

"You're going to be okay," I said again.

"Thank you, Dr. Cavanaugh." He didn't have it in him to force some snarkiness into his tone. Instead, he dropped the act entirely and searched my face, as if I had the answers and he didn't. I saw longing there, and not having. He wanted *me*.

I saw Miles Charles Winters coming up empty.

The wind ruffled his white-blond hair as he ticked his head in Riley's direction. A sunbeam caught the blue of his eyes.

"He's going to let you down."

"Maybe. But maybe *not*."

"Oh, my God. You drank the Kool-Aid."

You can't stop doing it, can you? I thought. Push away with sarcasm, blot out the truth of what someone else was saying with a joke. I wanted to touch him, give him some comfort, some contact, as we had last night, but I was Riley's girlfriend now. And I was just another ghost in Miles's past. Or would be, soon.

"Gotta go," I said, swallowing. I was suddenly unsure if it had been such a good idea to push this moment on both of us . . . and on Riley, who would have no idea what I was saying to a guy he'd tried to beat up on my behalf—a guy who had saved my life.

"Keep in touch," Miles said. Then he stepped away, pulled his pack of cigarettes from the pocket of his duster, and drew one out with his mouth. I heard the *click-sss* of his lighter. "I will," he added.

"Smoking is repulsive," I informed him.

"Run away, little moth. To your dim bulb."

I tried one more time. "We're not in a play, Miles," I said. "We're not here to be clever with each other. This is real life."

He drew in the cigarette smoke and held it, picking at a piece of tobacco on his lip. He was wearing a couple of leather thongs around his left wrist and his red thread. "You're the big Shakespeare buff. You figure it out." He gave me a wink. "Hamlet."

"'I must be cruel, only to be kind,'" I quoted. "You don't need to do me any favors. I'm fully capable of moving on when I need to."

"Okay." He turned and faced me. "Then someday, when you least expect it, I'm going to get you back." I wasn't sure how he meant that—to get me back, or get back at me?— but I knew I was beginning to lose my nerve. Most of the time I could give as good as I got, but Miles was in a class by himself.

I turned around. Riley was watching us, and the frown on his face melted as I smiled at him and quickened my pace. Things were simpler for Riley. With Riley. He put his arm around my shoulders and didn't so much as look in Miles's direction.

"We need to get going," he said. "I don't want to be on that road if it starts to rain again."

"Me neither." I settled myself against his side. "I never want to be on that road again, period."

Then we strolled along, short me and tall Riley, our gait matching perfectly, as if we had covered a lot of ground together and would walk down many more sun-dappled roads. San Diego in March was usually warm. Flip-flop weather.

Wherever Celia was, I hoped she was at peace.

Swinging my hand, Riley began singing under his breath, whispery and low. I didn't know he liked to sing.

"My love . . . "

It sounded like that horrible song that Dr. Abernathy had sung to Belle and Celia. The song I had overheard Troy singing on our Valentine's Day dinner date and had nearly killed him over. It went like this: *"My love is like a red, red rose . . . "*

"My love . . . " Riley sang again.

"Riley?" I blurted, stopping dead in my tracks. *"Riley?"*

There was a beat before he answered. "What?" He brought

my hand to his lips and kissed my knuckles, smiling down at me. Dimples, check. Warm brown eyes, check. Yummy breath, check. One hundred percent Riley. Just him, just me. *"My love is alive,"* he sang. "What, you don't like the song stylings of Chaka Khan?"

"I have no idea who that is. And you almost got weird," I accused him, trying to recover. Hearing him almost sing that horrible song was like making it through the aftershock of a bad earthquake.

"Naw. I leave weirdness to the pros." He wrinkled his nose at me, in the event that I didn't realize he was teasing me. Then he bent over and kissed me on the mouth. Little tingles blossomed at the base of my spine and shot along the tendrils of my nervous system. There was going to be more where that came from.

Yay.

And then . . . something else left me.

I hadn't really known until that very moment that you could really, truly just let go of something. Whatever it was— bad memories, wounds, tragedies—you didn't have to spend your whole life dealing with it and endlessly processing it. Until then, I'd always thought of myself as Lindsay Anne Cavanaugh, plus my baggage. Like I had to add some kind of explanation for why I wasn't . . . *more.*

I had pictured myself as a vine—maybe a geranium— pushing up through the dirt, searching for the sun. Then I had hit a rock and grown up and around it, needing light, forever changed. Then another rock fell from the sky, and another, and I'd bent myself like a pretzel to bathe in light.

I had thought the rocks would always be there. But they could just disappear. That could happen. And it had just happened to me. And you didn't stay bent. You stretched out, all the kinks gone. Because the light that made you grow wasn't out there; it was inside you. It was life.

My life.

"Let's get out of here," I said, and suddenly I couldn't get away fast enough. "Race you to the car. On your mark, get set . . . "

I broke into a run.

"Ten yards! Cavanaugh makes the first down!" Riley yelled, laughing as he caught up to me in three strides, threw his arms around me, and hoisted me skyward. Throwing back my head, I raised my face to the sunlight. It felt warm, and happy, and good.

It felt like home.

I was free. I was leaving. And I was never coming back.

"Riley, Riley, put me down," I said, laughing as he jogged effortlessly toward his beat-up old clown car. I pounded on his back, shrieking in protest.

"No kicking," he ordered me. "You'll ruin my future family."

Then he set me down and gave me another kiss. He fished in his pocket, aimed the key lock at my door, and opened it with a flourish.

I slid in like a princess, in my raggedy jeans and boots, making sure my jacket was tucked inside the car.

Then I saw the long-stemmed red rose tucked under the windshield wiper. Riley saw it too, and as he lifted up the wiper to retrieve it, the bloodred petals detached from the head of the rose and showered down in front of my eyes, like bloody rain. *One, two, three, four, five...*

Miles was gone.

... six, seven ...

My love is like a red, red rose.

Eight.

I didn't make a sound. Didn't cry out, didn't scream.

Nine.

At least, not then.

————

The secret waits for eyes unclouded by longing.

—Tao Te Ching

ACKNOWLEDGMENTS

Many thanks first and foremost to my wonderful editor, Brianne Mulligan. You make me want to be a better writer. Deepest thanks to my publisher, Ben Schrank, for supporting my work, and to the entire Razorbill team: Gillian Levinson, Will Prince, and Emily Osborne. Thanks to Caroline Sun, my publicist, and Anna Jarzab, in charge of online and consumer marketing. Lori Thorn, my cover designer, I am so grateful for my beautiful covers. I thank the stars every day that Howard Morhaim is my agent; Katie Menick is his assistant; and Erin Underwood is my assistant. Belle Holder, Leslie Ackel, Debbie Viguie, Pamela Escobedo, Beth Hogan, and Amy Schricker, thanks for being my home team. And thank you to the rest of my family.

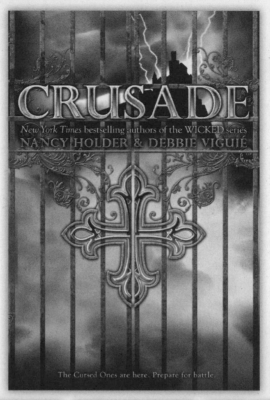